'...' Gabe said. In one swift move, he had captured both her wrists, pinning them down on the bed over her head.

A frisson of excitement skittered through her. She wasn't into hardcore S&M, but a little light, frisky bondage was a nice diversion from the usual. She hadn't had a chance to wonder whether Gabe felt the same way.

'You're staying here,' he said. 'In my bed. I'm far from being through with ravishing your naked body. The only reason you can leave is if we decide to go exploring while we regain our strength, or you've got pets to feed at home – and, if you do, I'm going with you, because I'm not letting you out of my sight.'

She insinuated a thigh between his, pressing against his crotch. 'Well, if you're going to be that insistent about it . . . And no, there are no pets.' She could check e-mail tonight.

As if reading her thoughts, he used his free hand to caress her breasts. 'All day,' he said. 'All night.'

Cat Scratch Fever
Sophie Mouette

XO XO,

Sophie Mouette

Black Lace books contain sexual fantasies.
In real life, always practise safe sex.

First published in 2006 by
Black Lace
Thames Wharf Studios
Rainville Road
London W6 9HA

Copyright © Sophie Mouette 2006

The right of Sophie Mouette to be identified as the Author of
the Work has been asserted in accordance with the Copyright,
Designs and Patents Act 1988.

Design by Smith & Gilmour, London
Printed and bound by Mackays of Chatham PLC

ISBN 0 352 34021 5
ISBN 9 780352 340214

For Jeff, Ken, and Random,
who know how to make me purr.

1

Felicia DuBois was at a critical moment when her cell phone started ringing – the critical moment when Bob (or was it Rob?) had finally extricated her from her skirt and silk knit T-shirt and tossed her, clad only in a blue satin bra and Brazilian-cut panties, on to the flowered hotel comforter.

She sent a mental message to her phone – *Go away* – and tried to keep her focus on the tall blond man exploring her body for the first time.

'You're not answering that, are you?' It might have been a question, but the way his big hand stroked at the damp satin crotch of her panties as he said it made it purely rhetorical. In response, she growled under her breath and raised her hips to encourage his touch.

Bob-or-Rob grinned smugly. 'So wet already. What a bad girl.' His fingers circled slowly, not moving under the thin fabric of the panties, teasing her engorged clit.

Desperate was more like it, but Felicia wasn't about to say that. Desperate not just for sex, although it had been far too long, but also for the momentary oblivion it offered, the distraction from work-related worries. Like the cell phone relentlessly ringing on the hotel nightstand. It had gone to voicemail once, but the caller, apparently as desperate to reach her as she was to avoid being reached, must have hit redial right away.

Yes, she was desperate all right, desperate enough that, when a broad-shouldered stranger with a Texas drawl had hit on her at Brennan's, she'd said yes. He hadn't talked to her much before making an offer; she figured he'd gotten as far as long legs, green eyes and wavy brown hair and decided that was enough. He hadn't even asked what she did for a living – and that complete lack of interest in her real life, in anything beyond a quick fuck, seemed to offer the temporary oblivion she craved in a more interesting way than overpriced Sauvignon Blanc would.

If only he (Bob – she was pretty sure the name was Bob, not Rob, but, to be on the safe side, she mumbled and ended up with 'Ob' when she felt the need to moan a name) would stop toying with her and get down to business.

'Lick me,' she begged, spreading her legs wider, raising one leg to allow him better access.

'Relax!' he said playfully, continuing to stroke her through her panties. 'We've got all night.'

Actually, they didn't. She had a hot date with an event press release and a grant proposal, because heaven forbid a day at the office should actually give her enough uninterrupted time to write anything.

But he didn't need to know that. Not now, not when the phone had finally stopped ringing and the movement of his fingers was driving her crazy.

He pushed aside the thin strip of fabric that covered her smoothly waxed sex. The touch of the air alone made her arch her back and mewl. That was a good thing, because for a second the air was the only thing that was touching her. She writhed on the bed, heard herself making incoherent pleading noises.

'Don't worry, honey – I'll take good care of you.'

'Then do it,' she hissed. A part of Felicia's brain that was still functional and detached realised that normally his smugness would have turned her off. Then again, she supposed that, if she hadn't been close to losing her mind, she wouldn't have picked up a smug stranger at Brennan's. She usually preferred playing with friends.

Alas, she was just clean out of fuck-buddies at the moment.

There were some interesting prospects amongst her co-workers at the Southern California Cat Sanctuary, but the fact that they also worked there meant they were as stressed as she was, and not everyone would consider wild no-strings-attached sex with a co-worker to be a good stress-management tactic.

No. No thinking about work. Must get back into the moment. Back to a place where all rational thought disappeared and there was nothing left but a throbbing sex, sensitive nipples, the spiral towards orgasm. She took his hand, guided it where she needed it to go.

The phone rang again.

She cursed and then said, 'Could you hand me that damn thing? I'm going to shut it off like I should have in the first place.'

When he did, though, she saw the number: the security office at SCCS.

'Shit!' She scrambled upright. 'I've got to take this.'

Felicia ran towards the ocelot enclosure, her high heels clicking on the pavement. After a warm day, the temperature had dropped abruptly. The cool desert night air felt good on her heated skin, but not so good on her sopping panties.

She'd expected Alan, the night security guy, to be there waiting to show her the damaged lock that had allowed several of the adventurous little cats to escape. She hadn't expected to see José Martinez, the zoo's vet – or the small, spotted form stretched out on the grass.

'No!' She stopped so abruptly she almost tottered over, not daring to move closer to what might be a dead or gravely injured animal.

'It's all right, Felicia.' José stood up, and stepped towards her. He reached out his hand as if to touch her reassuringly, then noticed the blood on his gloves and pulled back. 'Magnolia just has a cut paw, nothing serious. I'll be taking her inside to stitch her up in a minute.'

'But she's so still.' Seeing the usually alert Magnolia motionless, yet with her eyes open, made Felicia queasy.

'I had to trank her. She was panicking and wasn't going to let me near her otherwise.'

José's deep, gentle voice had a hypnotic effect on her, much the same as it would have on a nervous animal. As he spoke, she could feel some of the adrenalin draining from her body.

Of course, it didn't hurt that he was easy to look at: a dark-skinned, broad-shouldered man with salt-and-pepper hair and soft brown eyes. He was definitely older, but not old enough to be her father – maybe her naughty young uncle, the one she would have had a crush on when she was a girl. The uncle who wasn't really a blood uncle, so she could act on the attraction.

What *was* she thinking?

It wasn't the first time she'd noticed her colleague was handsome. Looking at him had allowed her to while away many a boring staff meeting, back when SCCS still had boring staff meetings instead of ones that were heart pounding in a 'Will we be able to stay open another month?' way. But what was racing through her mind now was several steps beyond her previous idle fancies. This was not the time to start speculating about what José was like in bed.

Even though her underwear needed to be wrung out after her earlier adventure and she was so on edge she'd consider jumping him – or just about any other attractive male – on the spot.

Breathe deeply and concentrate. 'Did any of the other ocelots get out?'

'Captain did,' Alan chimed in. Thank goodness for his

solid, middle-aged presence, and his homely face and slightly crossed eyes, which she made herself focus on. 'He was up a tree. I thought we were going to have to call Mel.'

'But you know Captain,' José added. 'A little bit of meat and a little wheedling and he'll go to anyone.'

Captain had been an illegal pet, rescued and brought to the sanctuary, and he still wanted to crawl into people's laps. Captain was one of her best fundraising tools.

José turned back to check on the cat. 'Magnolia's completely out now,' he said softly. 'I'll go take care of her.' He scooped the limp ocelot up in his arms, cradling her gently, and headed off to the medical centre.

Felicia felt an unworthy flash of envy for the creature about to receive close, loving attention from José. Even stitches might have something to recommend them if José was doing the stitching. OK, she'd draw the line at actual stitches, but playing doctor with José would be fun. She imagined herself spread-eagled on the big steel table in the medical centre while he 'examined' her in loving detail.

The image went straight to her clit, jolting her with a force that made her rock her hips forwards.

This needed to stop. She had work to do. Taking a deep breath to steady her voice, she asked Alan, 'So, what happened?'

Alan glanced away briefly, watching José fading into the darkness, then looked back at Felicia. 'I did my usual rounds after closing time to make sure all the visitors were gone. Everything was fine. All the enclosures were locked up and no one was on site except Mel and one of her volunteers finishing up the evening feeding. I walked with them on the last bit of that and locked the main gate behind them.'

'About what time was that?'

He shrugged. 'I didn't notice. It was twilight, so maybe seven.'

About the time she was starting to chat up Rob/Bob.

'Then I took a look at the Pallas' cat kittens. They were just waking up for the night and I must have lost track of time watching them. They're so cute, like an alien tried to re-create a house cat and didn't get it quite right.' Alan looked away, as if embarrassed to be caught in his fascination with the nocturnal Central Asian cats.

Despite her worry, Felicia smiled at that. Alan, a retired cop from a neighbouring town, had taken the job to supplement his retirement pay, but obviously cared for the animals now as much as any of them did.

'The next time I passed the ocelot enclosure again it was around eight-thirty. That was when I saw it was open.'

'Did you actually see Mel lock it after feeding? The ocelots are smart enough to push the door open if it was just closed over.'

Alan closed his eyes as if trying to reconstruct the earlier scene. After an interval that seemed longer than it actually was, he opened them again and shook his head. 'I didn't see her, but we're talking about Mel. She's always a hundred per cent where the cats are concerned. Even if security has had to let her into her own office more often than the rest of the staff put together.'

Felicia nodded slowly. She'd thought that herself, but Mel was a close friend and it was good to have confirmation from someone more neutral.

'I didn't want to bother you at first,' he added. 'But obviously I had to get José. He said I'd better contact you or the director, and the director . . .' He didn't finish his sentence, but Felicia could fill in: *The director needs the stress right now even less than you do*. The Sanctuary was Katherine's baby. The rest of them risked losing their jobs if it closed down; Katherine would lose her purpose in life. 'And then, when we were waiting for you, I noticed this.' He beckoned her closer and shined his flashlight on the lock.

It was badly scratched around the keyhole.

It took Felicia a few seconds to take it in. Her brain was still swimming, sex and stress hormones and the long-ago glass of wine she'd had at Brennan's conspiring together to make clear thought difficult. 'You think someone picked it?' she finally asked.

Alan nodded. 'It sure looks that way. The main gate was locked – José had to unlock it because he'd gone out to grab dinner – but that could have been someone covering tracks.'

At the idea of a police investigation and the inevitable publicity, Felicia's head cleared abruptly. 'Don't call the police,' she ordered.

'But . . .' Then Alan's eyes narrowed with understanding. 'It's the fundraiser, right? You don't want a ruckus this close to the fundraiser.'

'I want to talk to Katherine and the board chair before getting the police involved. Bad publicity would kill us right now. And this may be nothing. Maybe Mel thought the volunteer locked up and the volunteer thought she had. The scratches could just be from years of opening and closing the cage in the dark.'

'Could be.' Alan didn't sound convinced.

Felicia wasn't either. Even without the police background that made Alan notice the forced lock, she could smell something fishy. But the local media had already been having a field day over the Zoological Association investigating their financial problems. She didn't want to throw any more fuel on the fire.

'The Zoological Association! Shit!' she exclaimed and darted off towards the medical building, as Alan stared after her in bewilderment.

Despite her precipitous dash over, she entered the building quietly, not wanting to disturb José at a delicate moment. He didn't even look up as she entered, intent on his small patient. Stretched out to her full length on a table big enough to accommodate a tiger, absolutely limp, but with her eyes open and staring at nothing, Magnolia looked like road kill.

The surge of protective anger that went through Felicia astonished her. She might not be able to call the police right now, but she was going to get to the bottom of what happened. If it were deliberate vandalism ... Oh, payback would be sweet.

Finally, José finished with the ocelot, looked up and acknowledged her presence. 'Open the cage door please,' he asked. Felicia complied and held it as he settled the sedated cat comfortably on a pile of towels.

'She'll be fine,' he said as he stripped off his gloves and washed his hands. 'She only needed a few stitches. I'll just keep her here a day or two so she stays off the paw.'

'I knew she was in good hands, José.' Very good hands indeed. She found herself studying them as he washed them, wondering what those deft dark fingers could do to her.

The vet stifled a yawn. 'I'll do my reports in the morning. It's not that late, but I'm exhausted.'

'Could you hold off on the reports a while longer?'

He turned to stare at her. At first, he looked uncomprehending. Then he chuckled softly. 'You mean "lose" the copy that's supposed to go to the Zoological Association? I'd love to. I still don't understand where they're getting off, sending someone to check up on us. They say themselves that our animal care is first rate; who cares if the buildings are shabby?'

'If they want us to repair the facilities so badly, they should give us the fucking money. Nice shiny buildings won't do much good if we have to shut down.' And to her horror, Felicia felt tears coming to her eyes.

God, she really was overtired. There was no way she was going to do any work at home tonight. A hot bath and bed.

When he put his hand on her shoulder, though, she had to steel herself to keep her face impassive. The touch, merely friendly as it was, resonated right through her.

'It'll be OK,' he said in his soothing voice. 'You've got a great committee for the fundraiser. We're all behind you.'

'The Barbery Foundation isn't.' She sent a curse in the general direction of their former largest funder, who had cut them off without any warning. 'The Zoological Association isn't. Whoever let the ocelots out and hurt Magnolia isn't.'

'That's one thing we don't need to worry about. No one hurt Magnolia. She stepped on a sharp bit of gravel – it was still in the cut when I got here. And she's going to be fine.' José made a movement as if he wanted to hug her against his broad chest.

Out of the corner of her eye, Felicia could see the big steel operating table. Despite wanting very much to have hysterics, José's closeness, the heat of his body and the table that had been the setting of her earlier fantasy were affecting her. She could see herself stepping into his arms, rubbing herself against him, reaching for his cock.

'That's a relief!' she said, pretending not to notice his body language. Instead of leaning into the hug and anything else it might entail, she angled herself away from him so she could scratch Magnolia through the bars of the cage. 'This is sad; I'd almost rather have her trying to bite me like she usually would. But her fur's so soft. I can't resist stealing a chance to touch her.'

Felicia could still feel her clit pulsing and her nipples straining against her bra, but the critical seconds had come and gone. She'd maintained professionalism. Barely, anyway. And that, she told herself, was more important than a hot fling.

Her brain believed it, even though parts of her were chiming in with another opinion.

By the time she was partway home, she was wishing she'd taken the risk. Now that the immediate crisis had passed, horniness seemed to have taken over all the brain cells it had been occupying. Her whole body ached with frustrated desire. Fantasies were coming between her and the road – Bob-from-Texas, José, various ex-boyfriends, Antonio Banderas, Jude Law and that guy who'd played Spike on *Buffy: The Vampire Slayer* doing her in every possible way and some which might not be possible but were pretty hot to imagine.

Finally, on a lonely stretch of Desert Canyon Road, Felicia pulled over, turned off her lights and opened her moon roof to let in the cool, pinon-scented night air. Heart pounding, she raised her skirt over her hips and wriggled out of her soaked panties. She hiked up her shirt and unfastened the front hook on her bra, letting her oversensitised breasts pop free.

Exposing herself to the stars, she clasped both nipples and began to twist and knead. Sometimes, a slow, light build-up was good but, overheated as she was, she craved the kind of stimulation she liked when she was about to come, a little harsher and more direct; an edge of what might be called pain, except it felt too damn good.

The good feelings flowed down her body, pooling between her legs. Her hips began to rock as if she were fucking thin air, but she continued to concentrate on her nipples, first twisting them like taffy, then caressing them more gently. Her juices had been flowing before, but she could feel herself getting wetter.

Faces, bodies, cocks flashed through her mind. She couldn't settle on one so she conjured up an imaginary gang-bang: Antonio Banderas in her mouth, Bob-from-Texas caressing her clit with excruciating skill, José fucking her hard but tenderly and an ex-boyfriend who'd been particularly good at such things doing her up the ass. And, what the hell, Mel playing with her breasts. Felicia considered herself 'straight though not narrow,' but Mel, with her cool, pixie-Asian looks and short-cropped black hair, was cute enough to nudge her towards 'mostly straight', at least in her fantasy life.

Her posse of imaginary lovers in place, Felicia moved one hand between her legs. Two fingers plunged inside while her thumb worked on her clit. Oh yes, good, but not quite good enough. She relinquished her nipple, used the freed hand on her clit and adjusted the other so she could caress her ass as well. Her mouth worked as if she had a cock in it.

Picturing the scene with as much detail as she could – José's warm, spicy smell and deep voice; the noises her ex used to make when he was buried deep in her ass; Antonio Banderas's sexy accent; Mel's small cal-lused hands – she worked herself over. Her internal muscles milked at her fingers and she tried to imagine how José would move faster when he felt that, pound-ing into her to bring them both over the edge. That image was doing it. She was so close . . .

The gunning of a motor jerked her back from the edge of the abyss. Startled, she saw headlights in her rear-view mirror. The truck slowed as it got to her, probably wondering why she was at the side of a deserted road and whether she needed help. She motioned him by.

It was only after he'd passed that she realised she

hadn't pulled her skirt back down. Well, if he'd got an eyeful, more power to him.

Once her heart rate got back to normal, she cleaned herself up with some paper napkins she'd found in the glove box and rearranged her clothes into something resembling propriety. As tempting as it was to continue, that had been too close a call. Getting herself arrested for indecent exposure would most definitely not help SCCS's publicity.

Grinding her teeth, she slammed the car into gear. Now her only goal was to not get arrested for speeding on the way home.

2

'Yes, Mrs Turner.' Felicia doodled Mrs Turner's name in the margin of a yellow legal pad. The rest of the page was covered in notes, scribbles, circles and arrows, and a few exclamation points near things she absolutely had to remember. It echoed the organised chaos that was her tiny office at SCCS.

Her laptop sat on the only guest chair, drawn up next to her. Most of the time she typed with it on her lap, because her desk had been taken over by catering brochures, tent rental booklets, a pile of letters that needed to be reprinted because she'd spelt someone's name wrong, pens, Post-It Notes and a very dead aloe. She was still distraught over the plant. Who killed aloe?

'That's certainly a unique take on the idea, Mrs Turner.' On the yellow pad, she drew a circle around the name and a slash over it so hard that her pencil lead broke.

Valerie Turner was certifiable. Crazy as a skunk. She was a board member and the zoo's biggest donor, though, so Felicia had to listen to her. Even when she came up with the world's stupidest ideas.

'I'll see what I can do, Mrs Turner. Thanks for your always valuable input. Have a great day!'

Felicia dropped the phone and buried her face in her hands. Clowns. Now she wants f-ing clowns. The image of clowns fucking flashed into her head. That wasn't fair. Why should the clowns get all the fun? It should have been silly but, in her sexually charged state, it made her thighs tremble.

Unsurprisingly, Rob (Bob? No, Rob) was long gone by the time she checked back at the hotel. The aborted attempt to pleasure herself in the car had almost driven her insane. Desperate for relief, she'd crawled into bed with Mr Twitchy, her bunny-eared vibrator. Mr Twitchy never let her down – unless his batteries died. Thankfully, she'd recently fed him fresh ones.

She'd been horny enough that she didn't need to reach for a convenient magazine. Instead, she let her mind wander. Her sadly departed date, his long blond hair tickling her chest as he sucked on her nipples. José, his hands both strong and gentle – they would feel so good on her body, caressing, squeezing, lifting her up to impale her on his cock (which she imagined was dark and uncut). Mel joined in Felicia's fantasy, as she imagined the other woman's kittenish tongue lapping against her clit . . .

A knock at the door. Felicia jerked upright, realising she'd been squirming in her chair, her hand starting to slide up under her skirt as she relived the memory of the orgasm she'd given herself last night. An orgasm that hadn't quite curled her toes the way she'd wanted it to. It had taken the edge off, but only just.

She pulled her hand up and smoothed her skirt as the door opened.

'Off the phone?' Katherine, her boss, asked, poking her head in. Katherine had the ever-present pinched look on her face, a furrow between her eyes. Katherine lived on caffeine and tightly wound stress.

Felicia firmly believed that what Katherine needed was to be relieved of all control; ideally, to be tied up and spanked. She could picture her boss, her face as red as her curly hair, squirming helplessly, finally free to scream away all her tension. Not that Felicia wanted to be the one administering the spanking particularly – after all, Katherine *was* her boss – but she knew that the experience could be liberating.

Stop. Thinking. About. Sex.

'*Finally*,' she said in answer to Katherine's question. 'Mrs Turner thinks we should have clowns as entertainment.'

The furrow deepened. 'You're the expert, but I'm not sure how that will fit with our theme.' Poor Katherine. No sense of the absurd.

'Don't worry, there won't be clowns,' Felicia assured her. 'I'll figure out a way to let Mrs Turner down gently.'

'Well, good.' Katherine almost looked relieved for a moment. 'I'm glad you're free, because Gabriel Sullivan is here, and I need you to show him around.'

Who? Felicia scanned her desk, looking for a note to herself that might reveal who Gabriel Sullivan was and why she had to play tour guide.

'The representative from the Zoological Association,' Katherine said.

Oh. The Evil Suit who was coming to make sure that their budget issues weren't affecting the cats. The very thought made Felicia want to growl and unsheathe her claws. It was unthinkable that anyone on the staff here could bear to see anything happen to one of the cats. Hell, they'd all already taken voluntary pay cuts. OK, SCCS looked a little shabby around the edges, but it was all cosmetic. Their first priority was the cats: food, shelter and the breeding programme.

She didn't like him already.

Gabriel. The name conjured up the image of a nebbish little man, short and round and balding, with squinty eyes. Someone who hadn't been laid in far longer than she had. Felicia licked her lips and smiled. Fine. She'd blind him with her charms; he'd write a nice report and everybody would be happy.

'I'll be right out,' she told Katherine.

She felt around under her desk until she found the strappy sandals she'd kicked off, and stood, straightening her skirt. With the heat, she hadn't bothered to wear tights. Her legs were long, toned and tan. *All the better to entice you with, nebbish man.*

She slathered lip gloss on her lower lip and went to meet him.

There was no short, balding man in the gift shop. However, there was someone akin to Felicia's primary sexual fantasy: tall, broad shouldered and narrow hipped, with a fine ass evident even beneath the crisp khakis he wore. His light-brown hair was tipped with gold, like a Bengal cat's.

He turned from the rugby shirt display (the SCCS logo was appliquéd on them) and smiled. A dimple flashed.

Her mouth went dry. 'Mr Sullivan,' she managed.

His handshake was strong, his hand warm and dry with a hint of rough calluses that implied he worked with his hands.

Do not think about the work his hands could do on your body.

'Gabe, please,' he said.

Ah, now *that* name suited him. Short, masculine, easy to cry out in the height of passion.

No! She had to stop thinking like that. He was the interloper, the enemy. She plastered on her best marketing smile, took a deep breath and began her promotional spiel about SCCS. 'We're home to some of the world's most endangered species of cats, and are considered a foremost breeding centre.'

She held open the glass door for him. The dry desert heat slapped against her as they stepped outside, stealing the moisture from her mouth. They paused, letting their eyes become accustomed to the glittering sunlight. In the desert this far from Los Angeles, neither clouds nor smog filtered the sun's direct rays.

'I'm familiar with SCCS's work, Felicia,' he said. 'I've done my homework – I don't need the brochure.' Before she had time to huff out a breath of annoyance, he continued, 'How did you end up working here?'

'I was sick of working in the city,' she said simply. 'Sick of the backstabbing, the people who didn't care about where they were working, who just wanted to get ahead. It was all so ... pretentious.'

He didn't say anything as they walked, and something compelled her to add, 'I've always loved animals, especially the big cats – my parents used to have to bribe me with stuffed tigers to get me to leave the tiger enclosure at the LA Zoo – so this just seemed perfect.'

Good lord, she was talking about herself as a child. It was both unprofessional and unsexy. But he was smiling, and she totally lost her train of thought, staring in fascination at the dimple that flashed on his left cheek.

Then the smile was gone, and he was looking, not at her any more, but at the stark-looking cage before them. In the back, sprawled on a plywood box that served as a 'cave', a jaguar eyed them lazily.

Felicia hastened to explain. 'While we do have a few older cages left, we're working towards having natural habitat enclosures for all the cats.'

'Is that what your upcoming fundraiser is for?'

She debated what her answer should be. He probably already knew, and was testing her. 'Not exactly,' she admitted. 'Although that is our long-term goal, this fundraiser is for more basic needs. We've lost some key donors in recent years, and we need to build that support base back up.'

She didn't tell him about the wolves at the door. The local community of Addison had expanded closer to SCCS's land, and that land was now prime space for, say, a mall. If they couldn't build up their donor base, get some serious contributions and pay their bills, a buyer already lurked near by ready to snap up the land for his nefarious commercial purposes.

As if she wasn't under enough stress organising this fundraiser.

She was hyper-aware of Gabe's presence as they walked along the simple concrete path between the sets of enclosures. He smelt good, some sharp, spicy scent that was half aftershave, half healthy masculine sweat. He looked unfrazzled by the heat, though; his short-sleeved dark-blue shirt (which matched his eyes) was still crisp and dry.

None of it, not one bit of it, helped her libido. Or maybe it helped itself.

Her nipples tightened beneath her professional-looking, apricot silk shell, her lace bra suddenly erotically confining. In fact, all of her clothes seemed too constrictive. She wanted someone to peel them off her, slowly and deliberately. She wanted to sink into a cool pool of water with a very naked, very hard man.

She tried very hard, really she did, not to think about Gabe being that very naked man but, for crying out loud, she was only human!

His body hair would mirror the hair on his head, she guessed: gold tipped. There would be a dusting of it on his chest, just enough that she could run her fingers through it, gently tug on it. Pink nipples would peek shyly out from beneath the fur. She'd flick her tongue over them, and he'd respond with a gasp and a wordless plea. Many men didn't know how erogenous their nipples could be, and she amused herself by trying to decide if he was one of them, or if he knew, and would appreciate that she guessed the truth.

Either way, he'd like it – a lot. His cock, pressed against her belly, would twitch and throb. What would his cock look like? Pale at first, then blushing like a virgin bride as it fully hardened and begged for attention, a single sweet tear escaping, which she would lick away. Then she would pause, looking coyly up at him to see his reaction. Those blue eyes would darken further, to slate. Would he ask for more with just his eyes, or more? She guessed – hoped – he'd be verbal. It made her shiver with delight when a man pleaded. Told her what he wanted. Beseeched her for more.

But it went both ways. He'd want more, but he'd also want to give more. Oh, he'd be the type to not be satisfied unless he knew the woman he was with was satisfied, too. It would be a matter of pride.

Her thighs trembled, weakened by lust. The spike heel of her sandal caught on the edge of the walkway, and she stumbled. Gabe reached out a steadying hand and caught her arm. She swore her bare flesh sizzled where he touched her. Her already peaked nipples began to ache. His hand was strong, large, and then she was imagining that he was spanning her waist with those hands, lifting her up, pressing her against the bars of the cage and driving himself into her . . .

'Are you OK?'

She came out of the fantasy to see Gabe staring at her with concern.

She couldn't stop herself. She rested her hand on his and purred, 'I'm better than OK. I'm sensational.'

Later, she wasn't sure how they'd managed to finish the tour. After her unwise but unstoppable flirtation, he'd just stared at her – no longer in concern, but with an unreadable expression in those baby blues of his. He took a long slow deep breath in through his nose, and she realised he was struggling for control. It took every ounce of effort not to look down and check out his crotch.

Finally, she managed to smile. 'Anything else you'd like to see?' she asked, before she realised just how that sounded. The smile stuck on her face while, behind her eyes, the words 'I can't believe you just said that!' flashed neon in her brain.

His nostrils flared. 'Yes. Definitely, yes.'

This whole encounter was falling under the heading of 'the stupidest thing she'd ever done'.

But then he said, 'I'd like to talk to your vet, if he's not busy.'

Weak-thighed and wobbly-kneed, she led him to the gate that separated the public venue from the behind-the-scenes private area. She managed not to fumble the lock too badly, even though she could feel him standing very close, and the whole thought of locks and chains was suddenly more appealing than it ever had been.

She introduced him to José, then beat a hasty retreat back to her office. As much as she'd like to ogle the eye candy until her head exploded from unfulfilled desire, she had a mountain of work to do. If the fundraiser wasn't successful, it wouldn't make any difference what Gabe's report said, because there wouldn't be an SCCS any more.

The air-conditioned building felt blissful (it was one of the blue-moon days when it was working) but it couldn't entirely quell the heat inside her. Between returning the eight voicemails and thirteen emails that had gathered in her absence, she stood in front of the fan in her office and tried to think about anything except Gabe.

She succeeded. Mostly.

It certainly didn't help matters when she looked up to see Gabe standing in her office doorway, that incorrigible dimple flashing as he smiled hello.

Of course, with her sitting and him standing, she had a direct line of sight to his crotch. No erection (and, if he had one after visiting with José, she'd grossly misinterpreted Gabe's – and José's – proclivities), but she got the distinct sense of a nice package between those firm thighs before she dragged her gaze up his body, wishing it were her hands following that path.

'I just wanted to thank you for the tour, and say good-night,' he said.

Could he smell her arousal from across the room? She clenched her hands on her lap. 'No problem. Have a great evening.'

'I'll see you tomorrow.'

He was coming back? 'Tomorrow?'

He nodded. 'Didn't Katherine tell you? I'll probably be around until your fundraiser.'

She was left staring at his retreating back. Oh yes, she and Mr Twitchy would be spending some quality time together tonight, with some new fantasies to amplify the vibrations.

But why would Gabe be staying so long? Had he found them in violation of something? Her eyes narrowed as she realised if he had, if he shut them down, then her fantasies would convert to the murderous variety.

He'd seemed perfectly pleasant when he'd said good-bye. Then again, she'd dealt with enough Hollywood actors to know a pleasant goodbye could mask a stab in the back.

Well, he'd spent enough time with José – surely their vet would have an opinion to share with her. It was after hours already and, although she'd be taking paper-work home with her, she could lock up her office and pay José a visit before she left. One of the Amur leop-ards, Noelle, was very, very pregnant, and José was bunking down in the clinic until she gave birth.

As she approached the clinic building, a low utilitar-ian cement structure out of sight of the public area, she heard a long moan. The sound was almost eerie, but she'd been around long enough to know that some of the cats, when hurt, made very strange noises.

Her stomach twisted. After last night, she just didn't want to think about one of the cats in pain. It couldn't be Noelle, because the sound was coming from the clinic rather than the leopard's enclosure.

The noise filtered through the evening air again. The hair on the back of her neck prickled.

Not wanting to distract José, she looked through the window that comprised the upper half of the metal door to the clinic building. She gasped. It was neither a cat she was hearing, nor the sound of pain.

The moans of pleasure were coming from Mel. Felicia's cunt spasmed in empathy. She'd be making the same noises, too, if José's face was buried between *her* thighs.

Mel half-sat, half-lay on the very examining table Felicia had been thinking naughty thoughts about the day before, one foot propped on the table to give José maximum access. Her head lolled back, and she pinched her own nipple with her free hand. She had small firm breasts, with blushing nipples that made Felicia's mouth water.

And then, of course, there was José. Already prepared, he was naked on the metal examining stool, his slender, tanned legs braced to keep the chair from rolling away. Felicia's mouth watered more at the sight of his cock. Long and uncut, it looked like it had in her fantasies.

Her mind flashed to the night before. She'd used thoughts of both José and Mel to help her come. She hadn't known they were an item, and wondered how long they'd been acting out part of her daydreams.

She felt a fresh wave of moisture dampen her panties. Her clit ached. She wanted a mouth on it, a tongue flicking across it.

Annoyingly, it was Gabe's face that flitted across her mind. She had to get him out of her system. José and Mel were her friends ...

Before she had time to think the idea through and come up with reasons against it, she pushed the door open.

3

Mel heard her first, and froze, her almond eyes doing that deer-in-headlights thing. It took José longer to realise something had changed, probably because he was so intent on his task (definitely something to be commended), and because his hearing was somewhat muffled by Mel's luscious thighs.

Finally, he looked up (no doubt noticing that Mel had stopped responding), his face glistening with Mel's juices and his dark eyes just as wide.

Busted.

'Don't stop on my account,' Felicia said. 'I hope you don't mind me watching.'

Neither spoke, still lust fogged and surprised. Felicia bent over and flicked her tongue against José's chin, tasting Mel's sweetness.

'OK,' she amended. 'I hope you don't mind me joining in.'

By the time she'd kicked off her heels and peeled out of the silk shell, the other two had gotten the message. When she leant in and kissed Mel full on the mouth, José resumed his ministrations between the handler's thighs. Felicia felt Mel jolt as his tongue collided with her clit. Her own clit throbbed in sympathy.

Mel's lips were soft and pliant. It had been a long time since Felicia had kissed another woman. It took a special woman to spark her interest. Mel had done so from the first time Felicia had met her.

She was short and sturdy, her womanly curves hidden beneath jeans and work shirts. But her small breasts pressed against those shirts appealingly, and her lower lip pouted out in such an enticing way that Felicia longed to nibble on it while she ran her hands through Mel's short, flippy blue-black hair and pull the other woman closer, harder, into a kiss.

Felicia threaded her hands into Mel's hair and turned her fantasy into a reality. Mel moaned against her mouth, her tongue flicking out to meet Felicia's. A small, pointed tongue. Felicia's clit fluttered again. Now she wasn't sure if she wanted to feel José or Mel against her cunt.

Maybe one, then the other.

Sharing was good. She'd learnt that in kindergarten.

Then Mel's concentration faltered, randomly kissing rather than focusing on the action, and Felicia guessed she was close. She broke the kiss and bent her head, capturing one of Mel's plum-coloured nipples in her mouth and the other between her fingertips. She suckled and pinched, pinched and suckled, and then Mel was screaming and writhing and coming, crying out her thanks to God and whomever else might be listening.

Felicia whimpered, the same release denied to her so far.

But there was something about seeing another woman coming that fuelled her fire, enticed her to a higher state of arousal. She could almost feel the same orgasm rippling through her – not as intense, not nearly, but an echo, an empathetic understanding. Not to mention that there was a heady sense in knowing you were partly responsible.

Without another thought, she urged Mel back on the table, sliding her farther along it until she was lying back with both feet planted firmly on the chilly metal surface. Felicia ditched her skirt and now useless panties and, nudging José aside, clambered up between

Mel's bent knees, the metal table cold beneath her bare legs. She could smell the other woman's scent, spicier and stronger than her own.

She wanted to hear Mel scream again.

She toyed with the opening to Mel's cunt, her fingers dipping between the rough tangled curls to skid in the slick moisture.

Mel sobbed something incoherent that sounded like a plea.

'Tell me,' Felicia whispered, leaning over her so their faces were nearly touching. 'Tell me what you want.'

'F –' Mel almost couldn't get the words out. 'Fuck me.' Then, before Felicia had had time to fully slip her fingers inside Mel's demanding cunt, Mel looked over Felicia's shoulder and added, 'Fuck her.'

Intent on the delicious little Mel, Felicia didn't realise until just then that José had climbed up on the table behind her.

Sensation everywhere. His breath on her ass, as his hands, gentle yet firm and demanding, slid up her thighs, over her hips, around her waist. He reached beneath her and pinched both of her nipples at the same time, his fingers strong. Felicia felt the tug deep inside her, and she shivered, feeling as desperate as Mel.

Then she felt his cock at her entrance, nudging between her wet, swollen lips. She wriggled back, trying to suck him in, but he mirrored her movements, staying just out of reach.

He leant over her, his taut body pressing against hers, and said, close to her ear, 'You heard what she said. Don't keep the poor girl waiting.'

As Felicia sank her fingers into Mel's hot, wet pussy, José finally gave her what she craved, sinking his cock deep inside her.

For a moment, all three of them froze, a forbidden sexual tableau, hovering on the brink of passion.

'Please,' Mel said, and Felicia echoed, 'Please.'

She drew her fingers partway out, José doing the same, and then they were both plunging in. Two fingers, then three, fitting into Mel so snugly. Hands fisted, Mel pounded against the table as her hips rose to meet Felicia's hand.

Felicia was only dimly aware of that, just enough to keep her fingers plunging in and out of Mel. José's cock was slender, but the angle was just right, so perfect. He clutched her hips, pulling her back as he thrust forwards, and she arched her back, desperate to take more of him in. More, and more, and more.

She was lost in a frenzy of heat and wet and motion. She felt Mel's cunt clamp down on her fingers, and she crooked them, rocking deep within and drawing out the other woman's orgasm. Mel was screaming again, and Felicia added her own cries as Mel's pleasure triggered her own, tipping her off into her own waves of coming. She bucked back, pressing her ass against José's hips as his rhythm changed to a flurry of thrusts, signalling his orgasm.

They ended up in a tangle of limbs, and it was a long time before any of them had the energy to move.

With a phone meeting with a potential funder just finished and the new caterer due to arrive any minute, Felicia allowed herself yet another reverie about the night before. José and Mel, it turned out, were not exactly an item, but friends who fucked regularly when the opportunity arose. Once they'd regained enough strength to talk, they'd made it clear she was welcome to come play at any time. *Very* welcome. An invitation didn't get much clearer than what Mel had done to her using that luscious little mouth and her small strong hands before they'd gone their separate ways. José had been mostly content to watch at that point, but his touches and kisses had helped to slick her skin with heat.

So why did she keep imagining Gabe in José's place when she relived the scene? José certainly knew how to show a girl – or a couple of girls – a good time. But Gabe had got under her skin. She'd like to get him under *her*.

She'd like him all sorts of ways, but the first time she'd want to be on top, just so she could enjoy the view.

No no no. There was never going to be a first time, let alone other times. Flirting with him was one thing – it would keep him off balance and maybe make him feel friendlier towards SCCS. But getting involved with the Zoological Association's spy could only be trouble, no matter how sexy he was.

Nope. Time to force herself to review the menu the new caterer had sent – a sensual distraction of a different nature.

She hadn't met Debbie Landstrom yet, but they'd talked on the phone and exchanged many emails. Debbie's references from various Los Angeles establishments had been impeccable. And one of the board members, Richard Enoch, recommended her highly after using her for several of his corporate functions. Richard knew his food and wine, so that was almost good enough for Felicia.

Meeting Debbie would be the key. You could tell so much more about a person face-to-face – body language said so much.

Don't. Think. About. Gabe.

DonotthinkaboutGabe.

Felicia looked at the time, threw her disordered desk into only slightly less chaotic heaps and, as an afterthought, shoved the dead aloe into a filing cabinet. She did say a sad prayer over its brownish stalks as she relegated the plant to its ignominious grave.

She'd just got the drawer closed when Debbie arrived. Talk about body language! For a few seconds, that was Felicia's only thought. On the phone, Debbie had been bubbly but efficient, so she'd envisioned someone to match the voice. Short-haired, perky, wholesome and slightly plump, a soccer mom crossed with a gourmet chef.

The woman who walked in the door was a classic California bombshell – tall, tan and busty, with a wild mane of champagne-coloured hair. Her outfit was deceptively casual: jeans that accented her round bottom, a tight purple T-shirt with a deep V-neck that showed off both cleavage and a swirly D dangling from a gold chain, and tan sandals with staggeringly high heels. Lips, fingertips and toenails were all the same shiny red. Felicia was sure that neither the hair colour, nor the impressive cleavage, nor the tan was natural, but all three jobs looked to be top of the line. And that seemingly simple outfit was put together out of expensive components. The only off note was a rather awkward square shoulder bag but, for all Felicia knew, it was something trendy.

An outfit like that was hard to pull off without looking too relaxed or too slutty. But Debbie had got it just right, and Felicia doubted it was by anything other than sharp planning.

Impressive. Very impressive. A woman like that was one you'd expect to have a dead aloe in her filing cabinet, but wouldn't.

Debbie took her proffered hand and shook it enthusiastically. 'I am *so* glad to meet you in person! Richard has told me so much about you and SCCS.' The words practically ran together: 'Iam*so*gladtomeetyou!'

'He's told me a lot about you as well,' Felicia said. 'Or at least about your inventive takes on sushi, your godlike – his word – asparagus risotto and some amazing eggplant pockets stuffed with pork.'

Debbie leant forwards, beckoning Felicia closer. Felicia got as close as she could without getting her nose caught in ample cleavage.

'Don't tell anybody,' Debbie whispered conspiratorially, 'but I got that recipe right out of *Gourmet*. It's nothing that unusual. He hasn't tried the new version yet. Same technique, but I stuff them with morels and lamb. They just melt in your mouth. I do a vegetarian version as well, with three mushrooms and garlic, and they are just –' She blew a kiss, and then giggled like a schoolgirl on helium. 'Sorry. I get a little carried away talking about my work.'

Felicia's mouth watered. 'Sounds amazing.'

'Don't take my word for it.' Debbie opened the square shoulder bag and delicious aromas wafted out. Not an ugly purse after all, but an insulated container, full of tasty samples of Debbie's handiwork.

Felicia tasted, and swooned at what could only be described as food porn. Debbie might put on the Pamela Anderson act but, like Pam, there was a shrewd businesswoman underneath all that silicone and enough hairspray to have a hole in the ozone named after her. Even when Debbie was talking about food, she was all bounce and giggle, almost too cute to take seriously – but, at the same time, she waxed brilliant about food and food service. And the samples she had brought with her were sheer edible poetry. Erotica for the tongue. Stifling a moan, Felicia wondered if it was possible to come from just taste.

She pulled herself together and asked, 'Why come all the way out here for a job? With dishes like this, I'm amazed you're not booked for, oh, the next millennium.'

Debbie laughed and shrugged, but seemed about to give a real answer when the phone rang.

Valerie Turner, according to the caller ID.

'Sorry,' Felicia mouthed and picked up the receiver gingerly between two fingers as if it might bite.

Mrs Turner started right in without even bothering to say hello. 'I just got the best idea for the menu. You simply must serve wild game. I'd cover the costs, of course. Things the cats would eat themselves. Zebra, gazelle, like that. Raw, like steak tartare . . .'

Felicia rolled her eyes and made a throat-slashing motion with her finger. Debbie giggled behind her manicured hand.

'That is certainly creative, but I think there might be . . . supply problems,' Felicia said, improvising. An evil thought struck her. 'Fortunately, our caterer is right here. Let me put you on hold for a second and explain to her.'

Due to long practice, she managed to hit hold before she began laughing. Between bursts of hilarity made worse by her sleep deprivation, she filled Debbie in.

Debbie's perfectly lipsticked mouth curved into an O. 'Oh my God, you're kidding. You're *not* kidding. OK, I'll talk to her. I'm used to dealing with rich wackjobs.'

She straightened her shoulders – which made her breasts impressively torpedolike – and tossed her hair, then took the phone. 'Mrs Turner? Hi! Debbie Landstrom here, of Landstrom Catering. Ms DuBois was telling me about your *fascinating* idea! Totally unique! We'll have to modify it, though. Health codes and all that, you know.'

Partly because she talked so fast that Mrs Turner could barely get a word in edgewise, over the course of the conversation Debbie managed to convince Mrs Turner that serving ostrich tenderloin as one of the courses ('because, of course, lions eat ostriches') would carry off the theme well enough, without violating health codes or, worse, serving unpalatable food. 'Dear God, not zebra! I mean, have you ever had zebra? Oh my God! It's so tough!'

When the insane donor from hell hung up the phone, Debbie dropped back into her chair, looking as exhausted as Felicia usually did after a conversation with Mrs Turner. But only for a moment. She perked up faster than braless nipples in the frozen-food section of the grocery store. 'She's a wackjob even by LA standards, but I think I've got her pegged,' Debbie said. 'Control freak, right? Has to feel her ideas are being listened to?'

Felicia nodded numbly. Debbie was almost as overwhelming as Valerie Turner. But in a good, helium-sucking way.

Debbie had her Palm Pilot out and was making notes. 'It's all set. Ostrich is *fabulous* – everyone will love it. I know this great organic farm up north. They might even donate to get the publicity.'

'If I had any doubts, which I didn't after tasting the food, the way you dealt with her convinced me,' Felicia said. 'I could kiss you!'

Debbie grinned and leant forwards again. 'Go ahead.' She puckered up exaggeratedly and batted her lashes at the other woman.

She was joking, but for half a second Felicia considered it. Debbie wasn't her type, but anyone who could handle Mrs Turner deserved any reward she wanted.

Then Debbie leant back and giggled, then stood and held out her hand, seemingly all in once bouncy motion.

Felicia took her hand and said, 'I look forward to working with you,' and offered to walk Debbie out. She had a press release on Noelle's cubs for Mel and José to review in advance so she wouldn't have to bother them in the flurry after the birth – just add number and names and voila! While she could have emailed it and saved a few minutes, where was the fun in that? This way she could shoehorn a little flirtation into her mind-suckingly hectic day.

They were just heading past the visitors' centre when Gabe wheeled around the corner and almost ran into them.

Debbie's entire bearing changed as she got a good look at him. If she'd been joking about a kiss from Felicia, she wasn't now. The caterer was staring at Gabe like a starving woman might look at a chocolate buffet. That, Felicia could forgive as a sign of good taste, but Gabe didn't seem to be able to take his eyes off Debbie, either.

If she didn't do something fast, he'd start drooling and embarrass them all (well, except for Debbie, who'd probably love it). While Felicia had been ready to kiss the caterer herself for defusing the zebra tartare situation, handing over Gabe was another matter.

There were probably good, reasonable, professional solutions to the impasse. Instead, the first thing that came to mind was ashamedly high school. Felicia dropped the press release. And then turned away to bend down to pick it up. Carefully. Strategically. Straight-legged.

Her skirt wasn't *quite* short enough for Gabe to be able to tell what sort of underwear she was wearing, but it was short enough that she was sure he couldn't resist looking.

Upside down, she checked. He was looking, all right.

She could feel his blue eyes burning into her, as if he could see through her skirt and the even more dubious protection of her violet thong; as if he could see how blood was rushing to her clit just from being near him.

Damn, those yoga classes were really paying off.

Could he tell how much she'd like him to grab her hips and slide into her while she was upended like this? Sure, it could be an awkward position, but he looked strong enough to keep her balanced as he thrust into her. She could imagine the heat as their bodies joined.

Gabe moved his foot and caught the press release just before it blew away.

'Thanks,' she muttered. Great. Now he probably thought she was both a pushy flirt *and* a klutz. She grabbed the paper and straightened up, nonchalantly flipping her hair to distract from the fact that she might possibly be blushing.

But she'd accomplished her mission. While Debbie was still giving Gabe the sort of heated looks that men would kill for, Gabe was turning the power of his dimples at Felicia. OK, at *both* of them (and she grudgingly admitted he'd have to be gay or more likely dead to not enjoy Debbie's décolletage) but mostly at Felicia.

His expression looked familiar, but she couldn't say why until she realised it was what her own face must look like, the studied blankness of someone trying to hide inappropriate thoughts.

Must. Distract. Myself.

After taking a deep breath, she introduced Gabe to Debbie.

And was pleased to note that, while Gabe was charming in a professional way towards the caterer, he was nothing more.

They chatted for a few minutes, and then Debbie glanced down at her watch. 'Gotta dash – I've got a very nervous bride-to-be waiting in Pacoima.' She leant towards Felicia and stage-whispered, 'Potty?'

Felicia pointed her in the right direction and she headed off. Leaving Felicia and Gabe alone together.

'Looks pretty busy today,' Gabe said casually.

Or was it casual? This was one of the busier week-days they'd had recently. Did he know that? Would he want to hear her excitement that things were picking up, or would it be bad to acknowledge their poor attendance during the recent rainy season? Best, she figured, to be non-committal.

'We have a few big groups. Some school tours this morning, as you can probably tell from all the kids. It's about noon, so there should be two busloads of Japanese tourists, a senior citizens' group from Pasadena and the local YMCA day-care centre arriving any time now.'

'Day-care centre?' He flailed in mock-terror. 'Not in my job description. Anyway, I'm supposed to be meeting with Katherine and your bookkeeper for lunch and I think I'm already late.'

Felicia said goodbye and headed in search of Mel, still walking in a cloud of hormones.

She was nearly at the puma enclosure, where Mel probably was at this time of day, when a fire alarm went off. She froze, trying to place the source.

The visitors' centre.

Her first thought was relief that there were no animals to rescue in the visitors' centre in case this was a real fire and not a prank. Just four busloads of visitors checking in and the school group getting a conservation programme in one of the classrooms. Small children, old people and, just to add to the chaos, people who might not speak English. Easier than dealing with panicked animals – or maybe not. At least the animals wouldn't tell their friends, or the local TV station, if they felt things had been handled badly.

The press release could wait. This situation called for all hands on deck.

She arrived to find panic, milling about, shrieking children, sprinklers going off at random and a lot of very annoyed Japanese tourists demanding a refund – one English word they all seemed to know.

The one thing she didn't find was any sign of an actual fire. Which was a relief until she heard fire alarms going off from other areas.

By the time the Addison Fire Department had come out, reset the alarms and pronounced the incident a prank probably committed by one of the visiting children, most of the afternoon had gone, along with most of the visitors. Those from the area had passes to come back another day; the tourists had mostly demanded refunds. And got them, even though it had hurt to see the precious dollars, just arrived, flying out again.

'So much for the good day,' Felicia muttered to no one in particular, collapsing on to one of the visitors' centre's tiger-shaped benches.

'Would it help if I offered dinner to make up for the lunch you probably missed?' Gabe stood in front of her, looking cool, unruffled and absolutely edible.

4

Dinner. Felicia considered the proposition. A proper dinner that was served to her, with courses and napkins and maybe a glass of wine. It would be a radical change from her evenings of hasty frozen dinners, fast food and pasta-from-a-jar.

But dinner with Gabe not only meant that she wouldn't get any work done at home tonight, but also meant a few hours of frustration and temptation.

She pulled herself up from the tiger bench, smoothing her slate-blue skirt across her thighs, and flashed him a smile. 'I'd love to. Let me shut down my computer and tell Katherine I'm leaving.'

'Great. I'll meet you out front.'

She tossed her Palm Pilot, two file folders stuffed with paperwork, and a sheaf of correspondence into the russet leather bag that served as her purse, and powered down her office. She grabbed the linen blazer that matched her skirt from the coat rack and shut the door firmly behind her, then turned and leant into the office directly across the short hallway.

Her boss's normally neat, curly red hair was mussed, evidence that Katherine had been running her hand through it. Repeatedly. That wasn't a good sign; Katherine did that when she was particularly stressed. Felicia noticed the half-eaten Carl's Jr. bacon-Swiss chicken sandwich in a crumpled wrapper on Katherine's desk. Another bad sign: Felicia had brought her that sandwich at lunchtime, hours ago.

'Go home,' she said.

Katherine looked up, fingers poised over the calculator, eyes refocusing on the development co-ordinator standing in front of her.

'Go home,' Felicia repeated. 'You look wiped. Take a hot bath with one of those Lush bath bombs I gave you for Christmas, have a glass of wine and go to bed early. If you don't relax, you're going to have a melt-down.'

To her surprise, a smile played at the corners of Katherine's lips. 'Actually, I do have some serious stress relief planned for tonight.' She glanced at the clock on her wall, the one they sold in the gift shop with a different big cat in place of each number, and a monkey hanging upside down in the middle, its arms acting as clock hands. 'In fact, I can promise that I'll be out of here in half an hour, because otherwise I'll be late.' Her smile grew. 'I'm glad you're getting out of here at a decent hour for once, too.'

'I'm still kind of on the clock: I'm going out to dinner with Gabe,' Felicia said. 'See if I can't butter him up a little, away from here. Maybe I can get a hint of what might be in his report; whether he thinks there's a serious problem.' She lowered her voice and leant in conspiratorially. 'And, if that doesn't work, I can always drive far out into the desert and ditch his body where nobody'll find it.'

Katherine laughed, a sound that gladdened Felicia. She hadn't heard her boss laugh in a while.

'You're awful,' Katherine said. 'Have a great dinner. Don't do anything above and beyond the call of duty.'

Felicia only *wished* that jumping the bones of the extremely hot Zoological Association representative could be for the good of the Sanctuary, as part of her job description. But somehow, she had a gut feeling that, no matter how much Mr Gabriel 'Call-Me-Gabe' Sullivan might enjoy the experience, it wouldn't affect one iota of his final report. He was, she suspected, too honourable for that.

And she was probably too honourable to screw him just to change his mind, anyway.

Pity on both counts.

She said goodbye to Katherine and headed out.

Gabe stood on the wide path that led from the visitor's centre entrance to the parking lot, looking down at the bricks that paved the walkway. Many of them were etched with the name of a beloved family pet. They were one of the Sanctuary's most popular fundraising efforts, in part because the requested donation was reasonable.

The late-afternoon sun broke through the shading palm trees that lined the walk, dappling him with golden light that highlighted his hair. He'd loosened his tie, revealing a tempting V of hair-sprinkled flesh, and his hands were casually tucked in his slacks pockets.

Oh yes, *quite* a pity.

Since they had two cars, they decided to drive to his hotel and then share a car to the restaurant. Felicia had an idea for an interesting place to go, off the beaten path.

At the Radisson, he simply threw his briefcase in the backseat of her car, rather than going up to his room.

'Ah, the California cliché of the convertible,' he said of her Volkswagen Cabriolet when she offered him a ball cap, which he declined.

She shrugged. 'I suppose.' She already had a scarf tied over her hair. 'But the weather really is nice here most of the time, and it seems a pity to waste it being cooped up in a car.' She put the car in gear and pulled away from the hotel. 'I hope you're not too hungry and don't mind a bit of a drive. I was hoping to show you a different part of southern California – a less clichéd part.'

'I'm at your tender mercies,' he said. 'All I ask is that you be gentle with me.'

Felicia stifled a moan. Oh, no, she wouldn't be gentle with him at all. While she didn't like it rough, necessarily, she liked it hard and fast and deep, and she wasn't past a little scratching and biting and tossing around when the situation required it. If she had the opportunity to get her hands on Gabe, his shirt buttons would be history – and that was just for starters.

As her body responded to her own lascivious thoughts, it was all she could do to concentrate on merging into freeway traffic. She felt her nipples harden beneath the midnight-blue silk shell she wore – and she suspected that her reaction was obvious, because she hadn't bothered to wear a bra today, and the soft silk caressed her curves.

A sideways glance at Gabe confirmed her suspicions, and she hoped his own physical reaction was as positive.

They headed out of the city as the sun began its descent behind the ocean. She was aware of Gabe next to her, his firm thigh inches from her hand when she shifted gears.

Must. Think. About. Something. Else.

Thankfully, he provided the distraction (in a different way, thank goodness), asking her how she'd got involved with the SCCS.

'My liberal arts education didn't leave me with tons of options that didn't involve the words "Do you want fries with that?"' she said, and he chuckled. 'I got a job with the local chapter of an AIDS foundation and worked my way up to office manager and then development co-ordinator for the California chapter. But it was all so ... impersonal. I know that sounds horrible, but it was. It was all about money, all about sucking up to donors and begging for money. I'm not saying that it wasn't for a good cause – it was just ... too big. I wanted someplace where I could see the good I was doing, the effects of my hard work.'

'That's an understandable desire,' Gabe said.

Dammit. He said 'desire', sending her mind in directions she'd rather avoid.

The road narrowed, the landscape changing around them from barren hills to the steeper slopes of the mountain approach. Scrubby grass was replaced first by short deciduous trees and then by stately pines.

'It feels great when you've organised a thousand-person cocktail fundraiser that brings in close to a million dollars,' she continued. 'But it's nothing compared to how I'm going to feel when Noelle – she's one of the Amur leopards – gives birth, which will be any day now. I'm going to see those cubs and know that I was partly responsible for their being in the world. That's four more Amur leopards than there were before and, when the world population is less than three hundred, four is a significant number.'

'I can hear the passion in your voice – you really care about the Sanctuary, don't you?'

Dammit. He said 'passion'. Was he trying to drive her insane?

Distracted, she mumbled, 'You could say that,' then forced herself to focus again. 'What about you?' she asked. 'When you were a kid, did you say, "I don't want to be a fireman or an astronaut: I want to work for the Zoological Association"?'

He laughed again, the sound sending shivers of delight down her spine. His head tilted back, and he closed his eyes for a moment, obviously enjoying the cooling breeze that ruffled his hair.

Would he look like that during sex, his head thrown back, unable to keep his eyes open as pleasure overwhelmed him? Felicia felt a flutter between her legs at the thought of being responsible for that reaction in him.

'I was less the kid with ambition and more the kid voted most likely to see the inside of a jail cell before the age of eighteen,' he admitted. 'I was graduating from ditching school and joyriding to vandalism and theft when a counsellor gave me the choice between juvie and working on a community farm. It raised chickens and dairy cows, and grew vegetables for the local homeless shelter and welfare project.

'That and a beagle named Lancelot turned me around. I learnt about charity work and caring for animals, and it finally got knocked into my thick skull that there were more important things in the world than my own immediate gratification.'

Dammit. He said 'gratification'. Thank goodness they were almost to Big Bear.

'We've got a kid working for us who was in a similar situation,' Felicia said in a desperate attempt to get her mind out of the gutter. 'Lance Boudreaux. Maybe you should talk to him.'

'Maybe I will,' he said. His voice held little expression and, when she glanced at him, he was looking at the Swiss chalet-type hotel they'd just passed.

Katherine had been wary when Lance had showed up unannounced at the Sanctuary and offered his help. But Alan had championed him, having been the one to put the idea in Lance's head, and the young man had spent his first weeks working under the security guard's supervision, proving his reliability. Now he cleaned cages and handled minor repairs and grunt work without complaint.

They drove past log vacation cabins and hit the main drag, with cute shops that rented out skis and sold teddy bears, overpriced ski (and lounging) outfits, and locally made jerky and fudge.

As she pulled up in front of The Beethoven restaurant, a chalet-style building with a steeply pitched roof, her cell phone buzzed. She grabbed it out of her bag and groaned when she saw the number. How had Valerie, crazy donor extraordinaire, got her personal number?

She was tempted to ignore it, let Valerie leave a message, but her professional instincts – never, ever pass up the chance to talk to someone who might give you money – overrode the temptation. (Dammit. She mentally said 'temptation'. Now *she* was doing it!)

'Felicia, darling! So glad I caught you.'

'Mrs Turner, how are you?' Curving her hand over the microphone, Felicia whispered the situation to Gabe.

'I had another idea: instead of making it just a silent auction, let's make it a silent dinner! Nobody is allowed to talk. I mean, most of these people are just so boring anyway.'

Felicia clapped a hand over her mouth in time not to point out that Valerie Turner would be the first to break the silent rule.

'I'll go in and get us a table,' Gabe offered quietly, and she nodded her thanks, admiring the way his butt flexed as he walked up the stairs to the wide wooden porch that spread across the front of the restaurant.

'No, no, wait, that wouldn't work,' Valerie contradicted herself before Felicia could reply. 'How else would we give speeches? Or ask for money? Well, that wasn't the only thought I had. Let me cross that one off.'

Felicia heard paper rattle.

If she threw her cell phone in the woods, would any trees fall on it?

'Ah, here we go!' Valerie continued. 'We'll release

butterflies with very, very tiny homing devices, and people can bet on how far they'll fly.'

'Well,' said Felicia, 'that's certainly something to think about.' She pretended to smash the phone repeatedly against one of the porch columns, then put it back to her ear. 'Since I'm not at work right now, I don't have any of my files handy – do you want to send me an email that I can read tomor –'

'Whoops, I must dash, my dear,' Valerie said. 'Company's coming. Give me a call tomorrow morning, won't you?'

And with that, she was gone.

Felicia stared at the phone, shaking her head, then tossed it in her bag and went inside.

The Beethoven's chalet theme continued inside. White walls set off the dark beams that met in the peaked centre of the ceiling. The lights were low; the tables illuminated by flickering candles that made prisms dance off the cut-crystal wineglasses. Beethoven's music played low and unobtrusively from hidden speakers.

The smell of roasting meats, onions and spices made Felicia's stomach rumble. Thankfully, the sound muted before she reached Gabe where he stood with the white-jacketed maître d'. The maître d' led them to a small, intimate table in a quiet corner. 'Will this do?' he murmured to Gabe.

'Perfect,' Gabe said, and the man slipped away.

Felicia pursed her lips. So Gabe had requested they be seated away from the other diners, had he? What nefarious plans did he have?

The crisp white linen tablecloth was long, hiding their legs. Oh, the games they could play! She could easily slip off her shoe and slide her foot between his thighs, coaxing him to hardness with her toes. He could entice her to remove her panties and pass them to him

– or would he dare her to hand them to him over the table, rather than hidden underneath?

She let out a long breath and thanked him as he held her chair out for her. If she had to flirt with him to help the Sanctuary, she would. But she'd have to be damn careful to stay professional and not screw things up.

But, oh, why did he have to be so luscious? She watched him over the top of her embossed leather menu. He had a late-day stubble, the dark-blond hairs just visible against his skin, and she wanted to feel the roughness against her flesh. On her cheeks. Between her thighs. She shifted in her seat as her lower lips swelled and her panties dampened.

Desperate to get her mind off sex, she asked him what meal he was considering. He was leaning towards the house speciality of pork crown roast rack, although, he admitted, the wild game looked tempting. The Beethoven was known for its elk, boar and other unusual game cuts.

That made her think of Valerie Turner's suggestion for the fundraiser dinner. After the waiter came with their drinks – she was allowing herself just one glass of red wine because she was driving – she regaled Gabe with the tale. She delighted in making him laugh again, enjoying the sound.

It wasn't until after their meals arrived (Gabe did go with the pork roast, and she'd chosen the wild mushroom linguine) that she remembered their conversation in the car had been interrupted.

'You told me how you got interested in charity work, but not how you came to work at the Zoological Association,' she prompted.

'I don't remember any one thing being the impetus,' he said. 'But what I've learnt is that there are two types of people in this field that we have to police. The obvious ones are those for whom the bottom line is more important than the animals themselves – circuses that mistreat the performing animals, for instance.

'And then there are the groups that just can't get it together. There are so many ways to cut corners at a zoo that end up doing permanent harm to the animals. I'm talking about people who have their hearts in the right place, but they just can't provide the right home. When money gets tight, they do their best, but there's a point when the negative starts outweighing the positive. No matter if you've got the animals' best interests in mind, if you can't give them adequate shelter and food and space, you have no right keeping them.'

Felicia almost took the 'you' personally but, realising he was speaking in generalities, she bit back a sharp retort.

'I agree,' she said carefully. 'Sometimes it's just too late, but it's hard to see that it's best to give up. I've ... known people who keep searching for a solution, coming up with crazier, more desperate plans. Hell, one of our board members suggested we sell the land – we're on prime real estate for another damn strip mall – and use the money to relocate elsewhere. But Katherine won't hear of it.'

'I know about the crazy plans,' he said. 'I've seen places right on the cusp of falling apart, but there's nothing I can put in my report. No solid evidence that will let me recommend they be shut down. But I know in my gut that, sometime soon after I leave, things will go bad. It's times like that I'm half-tempted to create a problem so I have something concrete to pin on them.'

He put his hand over hers, and she nearly jumped out of her skin, startled by the feel of his warm flesh and aroused by the simple fact that he was touching her.

'I'm sorry,' he said.

For startling her? For touching her? She didn't want him to be sorry about that. She wanted him to be sorry about waiting so long to touch her. About not touching her ... elsewhere.

'I asked you to dinner to give you a chance to relax, to get away from work,' he said. 'I didn't mean to bring all that up.'

'That's OK,' she said. 'It's nice to talk about it with someone who understands. But, yes, let's talk about something else. New York ... do you ever go to shows?'

They lingered for a while over coffee, sharing a piece of caramelised pecan apple pie, then headed out.

'Top down?' she asked.

'Absolutely.'

The mountain night air was cool, but the breeze would warm up as they descended back to the desert. Up here, away from the light and smog pollution, the stars looked so big and hung so low, you felt as if you could reach up and pluck one like fruit.

Felicia loved driving the twisty mountain roads, letting her car hug the curves. They didn't talk much on the way back, just enjoying the silence and the contentment of a good meal.

At the hotel, he grabbed his briefcase from the back seat. 'Thanks for showing me another part of southern California.'

'My pleasure. See you tomorrow.'

She watched him walk past the burbling mosaic fountain and up the two shallow steps to the front door. Her pleasure, indeed. She suspected it would be another night with Mr Twitchy for comfort.

It was curious, really. Her adventure with José and Mel had temporarily sated her, but it hadn't been quite enough. Oh, she'd had lovely orgasms, to be sure. But somehow, there was just the tiniest upper echelon of satisfaction that she hadn't quite achieved. Like an itch in the very middle of her back, or a piece of chocolate melting on her tongue that wasn't quite dark enough.

The romp had been a nice diversion, but in the long run it hadn't satisfied her. Strange, yes, but she'd put it down to the continued stress.

Now, she started to worry that it was something else.

Her grandmother had warned her against pining for things she couldn't have, in the way that grandmothers make everything sound like an Irish legend or a Jewish curse (depending on your grandmother). The kind that rank right up there with the warnings about putting your own eye out. It seemed silly, but there was a grain of truth, deep down, that your gut couldn't deny.

Oh, Grandmum. This is exactly what you were warning me about, wasn't it?

With a sigh, she put the car in gear and pulled away from the parking lot. A strange buzzing noise caught her attention before she even got to the street.

What the hell? She backed the car up to the entranceway again, where there was light, and twisted around in her seat to peer in the back. She stretched and her questing fingers found the noisy object. It was one of those phone/email combo jobbers. It must have fallen out of Gabe's briefcase.

The text message had a New York prefix. Someone was contacting Gabe awfully late. Girlfriend? Wife? She'd never even wondered if he was already taken.

She didn't mean to look at the screen. She didn't intend to snoop. But the initials SCCS caught her eye, and how could she look away then?

Re: SCCS. Where RU on problem?

What the hell did that mean? Felicia stared at the device cradled in her palm. Well, she couldn't exactly ask him. She'd been snooping. But it was just ... weird.

She pondered it as she rode up the elevator and found his room and knocked.

When he opened the door, all questions vanished. He wore nothing but a towel wrapped around his waist. She drank in the sight of his finely muscled chest, dusted with that gold-tipped hair. The hair narrowed along his taut abs to a point between the sharp creases at his hips where his towel hung threateningly low ...

Oh, she was in trouble now.

5

Valerie hung up the phone.

Silly of her to have called Felicia about the benefit now, when she still had to make sure everything at the house was ready for this evening. But the 'silent dinner' had seemed like such a fabulous idea – until she started talking to Felicia about it and saw the glaring hole in the plan. Katherine and Felicia couldn't very well ask anyone for money if they couldn't talk!

Felicia was so good about taking the time to listen and help her work through her ideas. Sure, part of her job was catering to board members and donors, but Felicia was particularly good at it, never showing impatience even when Valerie realised afterwards she'd caught her at a bad time. Not everyone had that kind of grace.

She just wished she could help Felicia come up with the perfect idea, one that would take this benefit from a nice party to something really inspired. (There were so many charity dinners, and so many of them were so very dull!) Fine, there were health-code issues with the 'prey species' dinner, but that would have been unique – and so educational! But what was wrong with setting the whole thing up like an illegal rave, out in the desert, and giving everyone glow sticks and neon body paint when they arrived? Or having clowns, cotton candy and balloon animals? Clowns were great. Clowns guaranteed it wouldn't be just another stiff stuffy fundraiser. She loved clowns. She couldn't be the only person who did.

Oh well. Maybe for some other benefit. Or she'd have

an adult 'kids' party' herself. That might be even more fun. Some of her friends would be shocked at a party that served absolutely nothing healthy or Atkins friendly. They'd think she was crazy. But she bet they'd never say it.

Money couldn't buy happiness, perhaps, but it could buy you freedom if you wanted it, and room to play.

'The poor are crazy,' she misquoted to no one in particular. 'The rich get to be eccentric.'

A conversational meow let her know she wasn't actually alone in the office, which was decorated in dark wood and leather to simulate some idealised Edwardian library, right down to the decanters of port. (The fact the windows looked out over her xeriscaped garden of cactus, eucalyptus and other desert-adapted plants might have spoilt the effect for some, but she liked the incongruity.)

'Oh, hello, Cocoa,' Valerie said conversationally to one of her three Burmese cats, who flowed over and wrapped herself around Valerie's ankle.

She bent down and scritched the thick soft brown fur. 'We're having company tonight, sweetie. Want to help me get ready?'

The cat didn't seem particularly interested in the prospect of company, but she followed when Valerie left the office, clearly hoping for more attention.

Time to go and make sure everything was ready for her guest. Danny the houseboy had done his usual impeccable job on most of the house. But, for her special guests, there were certain areas she had to check on for herself.

Like the dungeon. Danny did a good job there too, but he had no way of knowing what toys and props might be needed tonight. Besides, some of her friends were quite open about their proclivities, but in this case there were reasons for discretion.

The cat at her heels, Valerie headed towards the gleaming kitchen. While Cocoa was distracted by her food dish, Valerie checked the fridge. Conchita had left a cold gourmet supper and the appropriate wine was already chilling thanks to Danny, so they wouldn't need to worry about that. Good. All was in order here. Time to check on the dungeon.

The dungeon, naturally, was on the lower level of the house. While she liked the resonances of the word *dungeon*, she'd eschewed the old-world faux-stone and black leather look in favour of something more Old West bordello – lots of burgundy velvet, with a big bed buried in pillows and a very comfortable, somewhat Victorian chair that she liked to sit in while someone knelt nervously at her feet. The whipping post and spanking benches were padded in burgundy leather – no point in distracting your subject from the fun and games with unintentional discomfort.

She took down a braided flogger from the wall rack, then hung it up again. No. She'd leave it handy, but she had something else in mind for tonight, a more intimate mood, but just as intense.

The doorbell rang, a distant echo down here, really only discernible because Valerie had been waiting for it.

Before she entered the living room, she put on the stern but loving face that her guest needed to see in order to relax into surrender. Then she strode into the room.

A figure was kneeling in the centre of the Turcoman rug, kneeling up with her spine very erect, but with her head bowed forwards so all that Valerie could see at first was a sweep of red curls and a crescent of fair skin.

'Katherine,' she said. Just a name, but she could feel its weight on her tongue, the intention giving it the force of some ritual greeting.

'My lady.' Katherine, so confident at SCCS, perfectly

capable of telling her an idea was too outlandish or if her teasing of Felicia had gone too far, in this setting became almost inaudible.

The shy whisper sent a thrill through Valerie. She'd had some delightful boys who'd been her play-partners. But, oh, nothing had ever compared to the pleasure of seeing Katherine kneeling before her.

And it was strange because Valerie wasn't normally that interested in women (men had always seemed more entertaining to hurt and then comfort afterwards) or in people who turned their submission on and off like a faucet. Katherine was unquestionably female, and in most contexts you'd think she didn't have a yielding bone in her body. But that made it all the more exciting when she did give up control.

Valerie crossed the room to her in a few brisk strides. She circled the kneeling woman slowly, once and then again. She never took her eyes off Katherine and maintained eye contact as much as was physically possible.

At first, Katherine seemed far away, lost in thought rather than lost in lust, the corners of her mouth tight. As Valerie started a third pass, though, she saw that Katherine was trembling slightly. Her eyes were wide, the pupils hiding so much of the grey iris that she looked like some frightened nocturnal creature.

Prey.

It was one thing to see that look on the face of someone you'd always known as a sub, someone you'd met through the scene. That was sweet in its own right, especially when you could get him to go just a little deeper than he ever had before. But seeing it on the face of someone who knew as much about big-cat genetics as anyone on the planet, someone who'd built a remarkable organisation starting from nothing but a vision, someone usually described by words such as tough, driven and fearless . . .

It was hard to say if the thrill started in her mind and worked its way to her groin or vice versa, but it seemed to hit every key point in between. Her nipples, suddenly sensitive, which didn't usually happen until a scene was well under way. Her skin, tingling with excitement. Her hands, aching to touch, stroke, slap.

And maybe her heart, too, because she found herself noting the circles under Katherine's eyes and feeling a surge of anger. Annoyance about the Sanctuary's financial problems was normal; it continually floored her that people couldn't see the value of the work SCCS was doing. But this was different. This wasn't about SCCS. It was about Katherine, and the tightwads in the community and the foundations who weren't coming through to help *her*, and the rule-bound idiots at the Zoological Association who were plaguing *her* and the damnable reporters who were making *her* life more difficult.

If Katherine were losing sleep, it should be because she was desperate with lust, not desperate for funding. Maybe it was time to do something more to help out. She had a few ideas. But, meanwhile, she could take both their minds off mundane matters for a while.

She was behind Katherine now, out of her easy line of sight. Quick as a hunting cat, Valerie reached out, buried her fingers in the disordered mop of red curls at the nape of Katherine's neck and pulled her head back.

Katherine leant with the motion, creating a lovely backwards arch to her body. Holding her in position, Valerie bent and gave her a hard, claiming kiss, biting at her lower lip. It was awkward, not a position either could sustain for long, but it made the point.

If Katherine's expression was to be believed when Valerie relaxed her grip slightly, it made the point very well indeed.

'Get up,' she ordered, giving a tug on Katherine's hair to emphasise the point. She did, although with a certain hesitation that probably came from trying to figure out how best to stand without looking too awkward. Something to work on in future. Valerie did like her toys to move elegantly and Katherine was athletic enough that it should be relatively easy to teach her. But meanwhile . . .

Smack!

Her hand felt better for having connected with Katherine's bottom. 'When I tell you to do something, do it immediately,' she barked, sounding far more harsh than she felt. She wasn't annoyed. She wouldn't have touched Katherine if she had been. She played at punishment with Katherine, but the redhead, though a masochist, was definitely not slavish, and she hadn't given Valerie the right to punish her for real.

And this wouldn't have merited real punishment even if punishment had been part of the rules; her awkwardness was far too cute. If anything, Valerie was delighted to have the excuse to give them both a taste of the pleasures to come later in the evening.

Katherine caught on to that immediately. She nodded and mouthed, 'I'm sorry, my lady,' but her eyes were sparkling. She still had a bit of that prey-animal look, but the kind of fear she showed was the kind only humans seemed to feel, the enjoyable kind induced by horror movies or amusement-park rides. Katherine carried her own Stephen King and Disneyland with her. And Valerie had the key.

'You don't seem very contrite.'

Katherine seemed unsure what to do. On the one hand, she knew how the game was played. On the other hand, after the sort of day she'd probably had, she must desperately need the release that only pain seemed to offer her. Valerie could almost see Katherine's mind weighing the options, trying to figure out whether she'd get what she needed faster by behaving or misbehaving.

Valerie would never let on that she'd get it equally fast either way. Oh, there were plans for later, delicious plans for pain and pleasure that built slowly and sensually to a crescendo. But Katherine wasn't the only one who was itching for some stress release. It had been a long day at her end too. She'd been working on some of her local contacts, trying to get them to donate auction items, and each 'no' made her want to spit nails – or spank someone.

While Katherine still hesitated, she grabbed her and pushed her towards a low leather chair. 'Take off your clothes and bend over.'

'What? We're in the living room!' Now there was a hint of real rebellion in Katherine's voice. Katherine was rather modest for a lady with her inclinations.

Valerie lowered her voice to a deep, menacing purr. 'Yes, we are, my dear. And I just told you to take your clothes off. I'm waiting. And you know how impatient I am.'

'But –'

'Do it!'

Valerie wouldn't have believed Katherine's eyes could get any wider, but they did. She seemed to have trouble with her buttons and the buckle of her belt.

Valerie didn't bother to hide her smile when Katherine stood naked before her. Clothes were purely functional for Katherine; she wore jeans or khaki shorts and T-shirts when she could get away with being casual and basic trouser suits when something more formal was required. And she tended to buy everything a little large. The result was that seeing her naked was always astonishing.

She had a body like a 50s pinup – generous soft breasts, a tiny waist flaring to rather wide hips, and a round spankable bottom. Her legs were a little short in proportion and a little full in the thigh, but well muscled. Skin of warm ivory was sprinkled liberally with golden-brown freckles. Not a fashionable look right now, but that just confirmed Valerie's opinion that most people weren't too bright.

Valerie noted that the red curls on her mons had been trimmed to a neat strip, the lips apparently shaved. Good – that had been phrased as a request and Katherine had been perceptive enough (or eager enough for a possible reward) to follow it as if it were an order. It was hard to tell, but it looked as though she was getting pouty from excitement, despite her protests.

For a moment longer than she should have, Katherine stood as if frozen under Valerie's gaze. Her eyes never left Valerie's, but they seemed unfocused. Her breathing was fast and shallow.

Again, prey.

Then she seemed to remember what her orders were, and she turned and bent over the chair.

Valerie decided not to complain about *that* bit of hesitation. She'd feel like a hypocrite, as she'd been enjoying the view far too much.

This view, though, was even better, accenting the ample heart-shaped ass, the curve of the spine that showed Katherine's submission. Her legs were slightly parted, allowing Valerie to see how slick she was starting to get.

Excellent. This worked nicely into Valerie's continuing quest to see just how many times, and how many ways, she could make Katherine come without direct genital contact.

Spanking usually worked. And that beautiful ass was looking much too pale.

Smack! Keeping the appearance of punishment for Katherine's earlier rebellion, she started in without any warm-up, giving a good hard slap right off.

Katherine let out a shriek, but the way she rolled her

hips told Valerie that she'd enjoyed it despite, or maybe because of, the initial shock. She let her hand linger a bit on the warm resilient skin, however, gauging the reaction a little longer before continuing, breathing in Katherine's smell. Sunscreen, a light perfume of green apples and vanilla, the musk of an aroused woman. And something warm and wild, like sun-warmed fur – even if Katherine had spent most of her day trapped at her desk, she always seemed to carry a hint of the cats with her.

Katherine's breath was already a bit more ragged, a combination of excitement and working through the sudden, sharp pain. But she didn't appear to be in any distress, judging from her Mona Lisa smile.

The next blows fell in a flurry, not giving Katherine time to process them or to catch her breath. Valerie wasn't holding back. Her own palm was pink and stinging, but she didn't care. Katherine's reddened ass, her noises that blended ecstasy and pain, the way she'd flinch away and then arch back, all conspired to arouse her as well. She'd meant to give ten and stop, a tease to both of them, but the reactions were just too exquisite. She kept going, sometimes staccato, sometimes with slow deliberateness. Her own sex seemed to pulse with the blows, or maybe with Katherine's reactions to them. She wondered if they were throbbing in rhythm.

Moisture was trickling down Katherine's thighs now. Her pussy lips were swollen, visibly twitching. Clearly, she was ready to come from just a little more attention. She must have needed this session even more than Valerie had suspected, as she didn't usually react so fast.

Valerie stopped. She stroked her hands along Katherine's trembling body. Although the room was air-conditioned to a pleasant temperature, the redhead was lightly glazed in sweat, releasing more of that delicious combination of civilised cologne and wild feline. Her eyes, too, looked glazed.

'Still with me?' Valerie whispered.

A nod showed that Katherine still understood simple English sentences.

'Good. I'm going to give you five more and on the fifth I want you to come. Do you understand?'

Another small nod.

Katherine made it to three.

Then she threw her head up and howled. No pain in there now, just ecstasy. Her hips twitched and bucked. Then she slumped bonelessly forwards, sprawling over the arm of the chair in a position only particularly relaxed cats could normally achieve.

'Good girl,' Valerie murmured, kneeling down beside the chair and gathering Katherine into her arms as best she could. 'That's my good little pain slut. Is that better now?'

Katherine looked up. Her grey eyes weren't very focused, but it was post-orgasmic haze now. Pain always relaxed her. 'Better? It's so much better I don't even remember what was wrong before!' she exclaimed. Then she began to giggle.

Another job well done. Now they'd have dinner, a little wine, and then they'd start again.

She wondered how Katherine would react when she learnt she'd be eating dinner naked on the deck.

It was late when Katherine left, so late it could equally well be called early. Valerie saw her to her car, a courteous hostess, then stood and watched as she headed down the long driveway and on to the winding back road. With all the road's twists and turns, the car's lights were soon lost to sight, but still Valerie lingered in the cool night air. The moon was high over the desert, just past half-full, and she was too charged to sit still, let alone sleep.

The rest of the night had continued as beautifully as

it started. The naked dinner under the evening sky had put Katherine into a strange frame of mind, receptive and malleable, perfect for an experiment with blind-folding, restraints, velvet scraps and leather 'vampire gloves' ornamented with small pointed metal studs. Valerie had finished off with the elk-hide flogger, leaving Katherine drained but happy.

Now it was closer to dawn than dusk and Valerie's blood was still racing. In the whole time they'd been together, she'd remained fully clothed, fully in control – excited but untouched.

Now, under the cool light of the moon, she reached down and touched herself through the fabric of her red silk jersey slip dress. She was wet, as wet as Katherine had got, yet curiously detached. It happened that way sometimes when she was playing the untouchable-goddess style of domme. To put herself into the right frame of mind, she cast her mind back to images from the night: Katherine's plump ass with her hand prints on it; Katherine shuddering to climax; Katherine shyly sitting at the dining table on the deck, nude and blushing and trying so hard to resist the urge to cover herself.

That was better. The self-control was starting to loosen. She stroked herself, not raising her skirt, but circling her clit through the soft fabric, letting the texture be another stimulation. Her pelvis felt heavy, weighted with blood.

She imagined pushing Katherine further, using the braided cat to slice at that fair fine skin, letting the little knots at the end of the falls leave bites like bee stings. Caning her. Oh yeah, she'd probably love that stinging, cutting sensation, the fiery line of pain it left behind.

Caning her across the breasts.

It was building.

She let her mind stray to Danny. He was staying with an understanding friend tonight, someone who knew enough about his lifestyle not to ask too many questions. She wondered if he was sleeping well in the chastity belt; she didn't have him wear it often.

Thinking of that – not so much the image of his imprisoned cock and balls but the look on his face, both stricken and blissful, when she'd given the instructions for their night apart – pushed her to release. She came silently, clutching the front-deck railing with her free hand until her knuckles were sore.

Once her breathing calmed, she went inside. In her office, she sat down at her writing desk and set heavy pale-green monogrammed notepaper and a Mont Blanc fountain pen before her. A glance through her address book unearthed Richard Enoch's address, not the business one he'd given to all the trustees, but a private one she'd had for several years now and had never used.

'Richard,' she wrote, 'several times in the past you've let me know that you would like to explore certain mutual interests with me. It was never the right time in the past, but if you're still interested, it seems the time may be right for me.

'There will, of course, be conditions. I always establish conditions. And you will be expected to obey them without question.

'But that's what you want, isn't it?'

Richard wasn't exactly her type – she liked them younger, prettier and more artsy. But, ever since they'd run into each other at a high-end fetish event in LA a few years back, he'd been saying he'd do anything for a chance to play with her.

She'd see if 'anything' included getting off his designer-clad ass and doing something concrete to help Katherine and SCCS – like writing a cheque.

A very large cheque.

6

Felicia's mouth went dry at the sight of Gabe standing there nearly naked and absolutely edible.

He grinned, the dimple flashing in his cheek. 'Just couldn't stay away from me, could you?'

He stepped back and gestured for her to enter, and she came through the doorway before she even thought about what she was doing.

The air conditioning in the hotel, as well as her proximity to his nearly naked, terribly enticing body, had brought her nipples to an almost painful peak. They pressed insistently against the silk of her top, and his gaze was drawn to them.

If she wasn't mistaken, she spotted a stirring beneath his towel. His own nipples peeked from his chest hair, and she imagined sucking on them, finding how sensitive they were, hearing him growl with pleasure.

Beyond him was his hotel room. She could hear the low murmur of the TV. From the entrance alcove, she really couldn't see much of the room itself – the only thing that her brain processed was that there was a bed, and she wanted to push him down on it, rip the towel away, climb on top of him and rub the wetness of her cleft along his hard cock, professionalism be damned.

Then the phone in her hand vibrated and hummed, reminding her why she'd come upstairs to his room. Reminding her of the message she'd seen, and the fact that Gabriel Sullivan was still, potentially, the enemy.

'You dropped this in my car,' she said, thrusting the phone at him.

He glanced briefly at the display, and regret flitted across his chiselled features. 'I have to take this.'

The spell was broken. She knew damn well when she was being dismissed. 'I'll see you tomorrow,' she said, and fled.

'Hey, Tom,' Gabe said into the phone. 'Hold on a sec.'

He peered out the door. Felicia stood at the elevator, one leg jiggling. She pressed the down button three times in rapid succession.

Damn, but he felt the same way. Restless, like he wanted to jump out of his own skin. It wasn't travelling that did it; one hotel room was the same as any other, and he was used to that.

No, it was Felicia DuBois who'd messed him up. He could still smell the spicy floral scent that she wore. He could still see in his mind's eye the way her nipples distended the soft fabric of her blouse, and he could still feel the urge to run the silk over her bare skin, to gather it between his fingers and pinch her nipples through it, causing her to arch her back like a cat.

'Gabe? You still there?'

He stuck the hands-free plug into the phone and tucked the earbud in his ear. 'I'm still here.'

'Did I catch you at a bad time?'

'I was about to take a shower.'

'Hmm.' Tom, his boss, was also a friend, and could usually read him pretty well, which meant he knew from Gabe's tone not to ask if the shower plans had been solo ones. 'Sorry about that. I waited to catch you after dinner.'

'It's fine,' Gabe insisted. He flopped into the easy chair in the lounge area of the suite. The chair was covered in that weird, semi-annoying hotel furniture fabric, but it was better than the bedspread. 'We agreed to talk when I'd be away from the office.' There were some things that shouldn't be overheard.

'How are the problems at the Sanctuary?' Tom asked.

Gabe blew out a breath and ran a hand through his hair. The problem was a sexy brunette with an admirable passion for her work and legs that went up to there – and possibly beyond there. *Wuf.* 'I only got here yesterday, Tom. There's not a whole lot to report yet.'

'But time is of the essence,' Tom said, stating the obvious. 'The fundraiser is next Saturday.'

'Well, how does a false fire alarm strike you?'

'As something that could easily be construed as an accident.'

'Precisely.' Gabe said. 'Give me a couple of days, OK? Oh, but I do have one possible lead; apparently, there's a kid volunteering who's had some brushes with the law. I'll see how easily he can be turned to the Dark Side.'

'Excellent.' Tom said. Gabe could imagine his boss giving the thumbs-up signal. 'How's the Sanctuary otherwise?'

'Efficiently run, with a smart, dedicated staff. It's a bit run-down at the edges, but the animals are in fine shape so far as I've seen.'

'Hmm,' Tom said again. 'Well, we'll just wait and see how it holds up to your scrutiny.'

'Roger that.' Gabe hit the disconnect button, tossed the phone on the desk and headed for that much-needed shower.

He'd never been much of a one for cold showers, but after the heat of the desert day he settled for lukewarm. His soapy hands brushed against his cock, still semi-hard, and he groaned. Damn Felicia DuBois and her floral perfume and killer legs and perky nipples that begged to be nibbled like ripe raspberries.

It made no sense. Oh, she was gorgeous, sure, but so were many women, and they didn't affect him the same way. The stacked blonde he'd seen coming out of Felicia's office yesterday had made him look twice, but that was it. A glance, a second glance of added appreciation, and then he was done.

But Felicia showed up at his door and all he could think about is what she would taste like and how her hot wet sex would feel as she posted up and down on him. He'd play with her nipples, twisting them between his fingers, and she'd throw her head back and scream, clenching against him and sending him over the edge with her.

He'd stroked his cock to full hardness now, the soap allowing him to squeeze as he ran his hand from root to tip. A flick of the wrist at the top, his fingers skidding against the sensitive base of the crown. God, it felt so good. It would feel better if it were Felicia's hand coaxing him to explode.

Random images flashed through his mind.

Felicia on her knees before him, masturbating him, licking her lips, eyes bright as she anticipated his come.

Felicia on her hands and knees as he ploughed into her from behind, her bottom reddened from a brief sharp spanking that had aroused both of them.

Felicia in lingerie: lace, satin, leather; scarlet, snowy white, dangerous black; high, high heels to accentuate those legs.

Felicia beneath him, legs wrapped around his neck as he drove into her, writhing and crying out his name as she shuddered through another orgasm.

His balls tightened, prepared to release their load. His cock swelled in his hand, purple and taut.

The mental pictures looped around to the beginning, with Felicia in front of him. He groaned as strands of slippery semen shot out and decorated her eager face.

His hand flashed up and down as he coaxed every last bit out, until he was gasping from too much sensation and had to pull away.

Then he'd gather her up and gently wash her face clean with the shower nozzle and kiss her ...

Gabe's legs wobbled and he leant against the cool tiles, his hand cupping his spent balls.

What the hell had she done to him?

Boneless from sleepiness and heat (the office air conditioning needed an upgrade, but office repairs were on the absolute bottom of the list), Katherine leant away from her desk and stretched.

Partway through the stretch, she froze in position, arms above her head. Then she settled back into a slightly different position, a sly grin taking over her face. Stretching had meant shifting in her chair. And, even though the desk chair was padded, she felt a sweet ache in her butt.

She rocked her hips back and forth, encouraging the sensation to resonate through her. It wasn't much, just a quiet reminder of her adventures with Valerie, but, during this brief lull in another hectic day, she wanted to enjoy what she could.

A little sting marked where Valerie had grabbed at her with the vampire gloves, leaving fine scratches behind. A duller, deeper ache radiated from bruises from the hard spanking and flogging. The sensations spread, slipping her back towards that soft languid state into which a session with Valerie could put her.

She'd been staring at the fundraising and event income projections that Felicia had sent her for an hour now, and no amount of rosy afterglow could make them look anything but discouraging. At least the new caterer was less pricy than the one who'd backed out.

Faced with this mess, it was tempting to lose herself

in erotic reveries, to try to get deeper into that blissful state of mind Valerie could give her. Val-vana. Bound, helpless, unable to make decisions, nervous – and utterly safe. Utterly cared for and loved, for those moments. Not that she and Valerie were in love in the usual sense, but to be the focus of so much care, so much fierce attention, felt a lot like love when it was happening.

And then there was the beautiful pain.

No, not exactly pain. Pain was having your life's work on the brink of collapse around your ears.

What she felt when Valerie was working her over was alive and aroused – just like she felt now. Her body was heavy and heated, as if she were moving through warm water. She could almost feel the sharp impact of Valerie's hands on her ass again, and the memory sent thrills through her body.

Katherine sank down in her chair. Without consciously willing it, her hand strayed between her legs, stroking at the crotch of her khaki pants. She could feel the heat surging. It wouldn't do to unzip or to slip her hand inside her waistband, but if she imagined vividly enough, rubbed persistently enough, maybe she could . . .

The jangling telephone made her jump, stifling a shriek. She let it ring four times before picking up – two more than she'd normally let it go – to make sure her breathing was more or less back to normal.

'SCCS. Katherine O'Dare speaking. May I help you?' she blurted out automatically.

A muffled laugh prompted her to take a belated look at the caller ID: Felicia. 'Guess I caught you in the middle of something?' Felicia asked.

You might say that. 'Just reviewing the fundraising report you gave me.'

Another chuckle from Felicia, but a different flavour,

one that two years of working together let Katherine identify as a sympathetic noise. 'I wish I were interrupting you with great news ...'

'But you're not.' The fire that had been building inside her suddenly felt more like boiling lead.

'Relax. I've just got Valerie Turner on the other line and she insists she needs to talk to you right now. And she's not going to be happy. She offered to donate some fur coats for us to auction off and I flat out said no. Thank goodness they were vintage furs, so I managed not to actually scold her, but still ... I wasn't as tactful as I should have been.'

Katherine smiled to herself, feeling the warmth rekindling in her blood. 'Put her through. You've got enough to deal with right now without managing an angry board member. If she's upset, I'll let her get it out of her system on me instead.'

At least if I'm lucky ...

The day had dawned bakingly, unseasonably hot, and now, at almost noon, it was worse. As Felicia dragged herself towards the clinic building in another attempt to deliver the press release, she found herself wishing for a big beach hat, or maybe a portable bubble of cool air that travelled with her. (Perhaps Valerie, with her fondness for wacky ideas, would finance the research to develop such a thing.) She'd headed out in hope of getting in a little flirting time with José and/or Mel. Maybe the vet's big brown eyes (and the parts of him less visible in his scrubs) and Mel's anime-character cuteness would exorcise the images of a towel-draped Gabe. That image kept popping up at the most inopportune times and causing the kind of hot, wet, sticky thoughts you didn't need when the temperature was hovering near a hundred degrees and your air conditioning wasn't working well.

Whether José and Mel would help with the hot and sticky problem was another question, but an increasingly irrelevant one with every step. The sun was baking all the juices out of her.

It seemed to take forever to make the relatively short walk between buildings. The only reason she wasn't dripping with sweat when she arrived was that, in the dry heat, perspiration evaporated too quickly for that.

She staggered into the back entrance of the clinic, where José's office was, gasping with relief at the blast of cooler air that greeted her. Due to SCCS's philosophy of putting the animals' needs first, this building's air conditioning worked.

'Guys, I –'

Mel burst out of the actual medical room, her face flushed, as if she'd been running in the heat. The door shut behind her before Felicia could get a look inside.

'What?' Felicia said, shaking her head in mock-disgust. 'Did I catch you two fooling around *again*?'

'Noelle's in labour! We've got to tell Katherine!' Mel was bouncing up and down in her excitement, and obviously she planned to run and deliver the good news in person.

'Whoa!' Felicia put her hands on Mel's shoulders. 'Katherine's in town, having lunch with the board chair and Richard Enoch. And Gabe. Something about finances.'

She tried to sound nonchalant, tried to *feel* nonchalant. As she said Gabe's name, though, her body filled up with knife-edged butterflies. Parts of her were focusing entirely on Gabe's utter sexiness. The thinking parts were pondering once again what Gabe might pick up from Donovan Martinez and Richard, and what he might then go and report to someone in New York City who was interested enough to send him text messages about SCCS at midnight Eastern Standard Time.

And anyway why did that Zoological Association interloper get to eat at a good restaurant when she'd be eating a microwaved burrito at her desk?

Fortunately, Mel's nervous energy distracted her before she could get too far down the slippery slope of resentment. 'Should I call?' Mel asked, an edge of anxiety in her voice. This birth was a critical one, not just for SCCS but for the species, and, even with someone as skilled as José in attendance, there was no guarantee everything would go perfectly.

Felicia thought for about two seconds. On the one hand, it wasn't good form to interrupt a meeting with the board chair. On the other hand, Katherine was Katherine. She'd want to rush back to be on hand for good or ill, not that she could do anything to assist José. And, knowing Katherine, she'd probably get Donovan and Richard to give 'birthday gifts for the cubs' before she left.

Gifts. That settled it. They needed all the gifts that they could get. 'You know her cell number?'

Mel nodded.

Yup, she thought as Mel made the call, once the cubs had arrived safely, she'd start calling some of their lapsed donors, and the corporations who'd said no to Richard when he'd asked them to support the benefit. Some companies just didn't like to sponsor events, but who could say no to the opportunity to 'adopt' a baby Amur leopard? Or maybe name one, for say $10,000?

She was so busy plotting her strategy that she didn't hear Mel's conversation. The rattle of Mel attempting to open the door back to the medical room distracted her.

Mel started pacing like a caged tiger. 'He locked me out,' she muttered. 'The bastard locked me out! *That* was why he told me to let Katherine know right away. Well,' she conceded, 'that and she'd want to know. I should be in there!'

Forget the frozen burrito. Someone needed to be distracted. 'Come on, sweetie,' she said, taking Mel's arm. 'We're going out to lunch. José'll page you if anything happens.'

'I shouldn't ... Oh, you're right. He's got a vet tech to help him, and there's nothing I can do except jitter. But can we forget lunch and go straight to dessert? At times like this, a woman needs ice cream.'

Sure, Felicia thought as they headed towards the parking lot, there was work she should be doing while she ate – but sometimes friends took priority.

Several places in town served ice cream, but The Acropolis Diner, with its gleaming chrome fixtures, cosy booths and waitresses who could tell when you needed a refill on your iced coffee and when you needed to be left alone, was where they ended up. After a lunch consisting mostly of hot fudge sundae, Mel seemed a little calmer, until her phone rang while they were finishing the last gooey bites. Then she literally jumped out of her chair. She pulled out her cell with trembling hands, glanced at the number – and sank back into her seat with a sigh of relief. 'Hi, Grandma.' She switched immediately into Vietnamese, but Felicia could recognise the tone: apologetic, but annoyed. After an obviously frustrating conversation, she hung up, shaking her head.

'My grandpa's birthday party is tomorrow night in San Francisco. Grandma expects me to be there. It's never sunk in for her that I'm six hours away, no matter how many times I tell her. She got off the plane from Saigon and hasn't left San Francisco since. And she's right that I really should be there, but I can't. No one else here has my experience in dealing with newborns and José needs someone to relieve him.'

She sat, chewing her lower lip and staring at the melting remains of her sundae, just as twitchy as she had been before they'd run away from work.

Felicia knew that any time Mel had to deal with her beloved, but not very Westernised grandparents, she needed to blow off steam. A long hike or a trip to the beach usually served, but there was no time for that now. And more ice cream, usually a cure-all, would be a bad idea, seeing their sundaes had been roughly the size of ocean liners.

Well, there was one form of stress relief that Felicia could provide on short notice. And the way Mel was biting her lower lip was adorable, even if it was from guilt and anxiety.

Felicia left cash on the table to cover the bill and herded Mel back to the women's room. As she'd hoped, it was a single-seater. Glancing around quickly to make sure no one was paying attention, she led Mel inside and locked the door behind them.

There was about a second's hesitation. Washroom quickies with other girls weren't part of her normal repertoire, and she wasn't sure how to proceed. Then she pulled Mel in for a kiss and realised the details were going to take care of themselves.

Having to bend to kiss her made Felicia feel strong, powerful. Never mind that Mel could probably bench-press her; logic had very little to do with this sort of thing.

Soft lips and a probing tongue. A sharp, citrusy scent from Mel's hair and the animal smell of the cats that always clung a little when she'd been working with them – dusty, sunwarmed fur and a hint of something musky and wild. And those delightful breasts that Felicia remembered so fondly, pressing against her. It combined to dizzying effect, reviving the Gabe-related stirrings that had been troubling her ever since the night before. But this wasn't about her – it was about Mel.

She could have happily kissed Mel until sunset, but in a public bathroom she couldn't afford to be so leisurely. She worked up Mel's uniform polo shirt ('veldt tan' with the SCCS logo over the right breast), unclasped the front hook of her purple lace bra and lightly caressed the dark prominent nipples. Mel shuddered.

'More?' Felicia mouthed.

Mel nodded.

She cupped the lovely breasts, one in each hand – they were just the perfect size to make a nice handful – and circled the nipples with her thumb until Mel was squirming and biting her lip from something other than anxiety.

So pretty. Could Mel be one of the lucky women who could come from nipple-play alone? She couldn't herself, or at least she never had, but Mel certainly seemed sensitive enough. But this wasn't the best place to conduct that experiment. Some games deserved a comfortable bed and all the time in the world.

If her own level of arousal was any gauge, the fact they didn't have all the time in the world right now wouldn't be a problem.

She stroked her hands down Mel's torso to the waistband of her khaki shorts. Not wanting to neglect the delicious nipples, Felicia captured one in her mouth as she worked on the zipper and struggled the jeans down just enough to slip one hand into Mel's panties. Slick, swollen, eager – no surprise there. Felicia felt that way herself. OK, she'd been roiled up on and off since the night before, and this encounter just kicked it up a notch.

Someone knocked on the door. No time for subtleties. She found the spot and, began to circle it. Mel pressed one bare thigh between Felicia's legs, pushing up her skirt. Pressing against her drenched panties with that heated skin.

Oh God. She'd *meant* it to be all about Mel, but there was only so much a woman could take. It was going to be about both of them – and quickly, if the way she'd just clenched and released was any clue.

On edge as she'd been, it built quickly as she rubbed herself against Mel's thigh. Mel was whimpering, biting at her own hand as Felicia's fingers worked. The happily stricken look on her face, the flush extending down over her breasts, added to Felicia's own excitement. Mel's legs began to shake. This was a happy thing for Felicia.

Then Mel began to buck under her hands. She didn't make a sound, but her face contorted and she mouthed something that looked like it wanted to be 'Oh God yes' or maybe just a wordless scream.

Felicia couldn't say if it was the added stimulation from Mel's thrashing or the beautiful visual that ultimately kicked her over, but the waves began at the soles of her feet and her scalp, rolled along her body and met in the middle with overwhelming force.

She kissed Mel violently to stifle the noises she wanted to make. And, for just a second, with Mel's juices all over her hand and Mel's firm little body pressed against her, Felicia flashed to Gabe.

They cleaned up quickly and left the bathroom trying to simulate the innocent faces of a couple of women who had been sharing makeup or helping each other with some clothing crisis.

It was a wasted effort. The young woman waiting outside – who screamed *baby butch* from the flat-top haircut to the Doc Martens – took one look at their expressions and flashed them a big grin and a discreet thumbs-up.

7

The call had come at 7.30 the previous night, while Felicia was at home, laptop on her lap in front of the TV on mute, putting the final touches to a grant proposal.

'Four healthy cubs, Felicia!' José sounded both tired enough and triumphant enough to have given birth to them himself. 'Three females, one male. The male's on the small side, but he should be fine.'

After that news, Felicia managed to get a good night's sleep for once, without resorting to Mr Twitchy or fantasies of Gabe.

As a result, Felicia faced the next morning armed with a merely large, as opposed to gigantic, iced coffee and more optimism than she'd felt in a while. She swept her desk clutter into neat piles: logistical details such as tent rental, grant files and, front and centre, the list of donors she needed to call. She even remembered to pour some water on the desiccated aloe and swore it perked up a bit.

One cub had already been named – she'd spoken to Valerie Turner after José's call, knowing she would want to know immediately of the birth. Valerie had offered a naming gift even before Felicia had to ask.

She faced a long list of phone calls to possible donors, but it didn't look as daunting as it would have on another day.

The first call was to the owner of a local luxury-car dealership. Mr Alfredi had always been supportive in the past, but had said no to Richard about sponsoring the benefit, according to her notes. Maybe the high gas prices were cutting in to Hummer sales.

When he got on the phone, she expected to have to do a hard sell. Instead, he all but greeted her with cries of joy. 'Felicia! I was meaning to call you. I got my invitation to the Sanctuary benefit last week. Is it too late to get in as a sponsor this year? We got your letter a few months ago, but no one ever called to follow up with us and it just fell between the cracks.'

Sure no one called to follow up! She had it right here in her notes. No doubt Richard caught you on a bad day and now your wife wants to know why your name's not on there.

She didn't say that, in part because she felt bad that she hadn't called herself as she'd done in other years. But, when the Barbery Foundation grant hadn't come through, she'd been scrambling to get other grant proposals done to fill in the huge gap that left and she'd had to put more in the hands of her committee chair than usual.

Instead, she said, 'I'm so sorry! And of course it's not too late. It's perfect timing, in fact – you can be the first company to take part in something very exciting honouring our latest arrivals. Noelle, one of our Amur leopards, had four cubs yesterday.'

She could practically hear his ears perk up. 'Baby leopards? My kids would never forgive me if I didn't do something.'

By the end of the conversation, she had a pledge for $2,500 from the dealership, the firm's usual donation – and an additional $500, straight on to Mr Alfredi's personal credit card, for the cub-care fund.

Maybe he really had been missed in the shuffle and Richard had written the wrong thing down. Mistakes happened.

Smiling, Felicia went on to the next company on her

list. And again got the 'No one called me this year' story. Odd. The company, an LA law firm, wasn't being especially receptive, so she figured the marketing guy might just be telling a little white lie.

Felicia was persistent, however, and the words 'naming opportunity' piqued his interest. Sanchez, Ackerman, and Leventhal LLC abbreviated nicely; he thought Sal the Amur leopard had a ring to it that the partners might like.

The call ended as a definite maybe. Felicia made a note to call back on Monday and moved on.

She took a few minutes to do a Google search on the next company, an unfamiliar biotech firm. Their areas of research included developing medicines from rainforest plants – so they took an interest in the environment – and genome research. She got on the phone prepared to talk about the scientific aspects of the captive breeding programme and managed to reach someone who had a few minutes to listen. They really had said no to the benefit; the local office was small and didn't have the budget for that sort of thing. Once the scientist-type on the phone heard about the breeding programme, though, she directed Felicia towards their parent company in Massachusetts, which sometimes made grants to support environmental projects. It wouldn't help the benefit bottom line, but any money that could go directly to the breeding programme would free up money for other things.

Couldn't Richard have done that? She shrugged. Maybe not. Fundraising wasn't his area of expertise. She couldn't expect him to have the instincts she'd honed over years of work in the area.

Still, by the end of the day, Felicia was scratching her head. She hadn't managed to reach every corporate contact on the list but, of those she had reached, most claimed not to have been called before, or said Richard had blown off a meeting with them. Most had still said no – more people always said no than yes – but she'd got a few decent-sized pledges and a fair number of warm maybes. And two other companies and one wealthy individual were considering the $10,000 naming opportunity.

Even odder, the people who admitted they'd talked to Richard seemed surprised to hear about the cubs or other good news from the Sanctuary. They didn't know about the Pallas' cat kittens that had been born in late April, the Siberian tiger cubs at the National Zoo that had been fathered by their Khan, or the summer education programme for local kids, with fees from those who could pay subsidising places for poorer children.

'It sounded like this benefit was a desperation measure,' one company president said. 'Like you were on your last legs. We don't like our investment going to stave off creditors, but we're glad to support such good work if we can.' And he'd ended buying a table so he could bring visiting Japanese colleagues to view the cubs.

What had Richard been thinking? She'd given him a script and they'd rehearsed how to deal with questions about the Sanctuary's financial challenges by talking about the new life they were giving to endangered species. He'd not only bollixed the script, but also he seemed to have gone out of his way to do so.

Time to have a little talk with him. Or maybe a big talk. It must have been a misunderstanding, but she was having trouble seeing how such a smart man could be so stupid.

He didn't answer when she called. It was after 5 p.m., so that wasn't unexpected, but she had this wonderful mental image of her anger blasting through the phone and blistering his fingers when he tried to pick up the receiver.

That said, the message she left, although painstakingly polite, *would* probably blister his ears if he was at all perceptive.

Felicia was still thinking about the oddity of it all at home that evening over a dinner of takeout Thai drunken noodles and a follow-up letter to people who'd pledged that day. She realised she was brooding too much when it occurred to her she was neither writing nor tasting the bold flavours of chillies and basil.

Very well. She shut down her laptop, picked up her dinner and walked resolutely out of the kitchen that served as an improvised office into her small, rather bare living room. Maybe she could find something cute and mindless to distract her on TV.

Instead, she found herself curled up on the shabby dark-green couch contemplating the fact that, after two years in Addison, she still hadn't got around to hanging pictures in the living room or getting a real couch instead of this dorm-room special. And, at this point, it hardly seemed worth the effort. If the benefit failed, she'd just be moving again.

When the phone rang, she thought it might be Richard calling to explain until she realised it was her cell and she'd never given Richard her cell number. Instead, it was José's familiar voice. His first words, even before hello, were 'Everything's fine.'

Once she started breathing again, he continued, 'One of the vets from town and Mel's assistant are keeping an eye on things so Mel and I can take a breather. So, Mel and I were wondering ... We have this bottle of champagne to celebrate and were wondering if you'd like to share it with us.' He sounded oddly hesitant.

While Felicia was still getting out 'Sure!' there was a tussle on the other end of the phone. Mel, apparently, won.

'What José means,' Mel put in, sounding more confident than José, 'is that we spent an awful lot of time on cub-watch talking about how much fun we had the other night and we were wondering . . .' And suddenly she got shy as well.

It was left for Felicia to say, 'Sure. Bring that champagne on by and we'll see what happens!'

She had a pretty good idea what would happen, but it was always best to leave these things open-ended in case they didn't go according to plan.

And then she scurried off, grinning and blushing, to change the sheets, sweep empty take-out containers into the trash and see if she could find three champagne glasses. She already knew that finding ones that matched was a lost cause.

By the time her friends arrived, the place looked almost decent.

She hadn't seen José since Noelle went into labour, and it looked like he hadn't managed to catch up on sleep. But he was still on a high a day later, clutching a bottle of Iron Horse Cuvée from Sonoma and grinning from ear to ear. Like a proud grandpa, Felicia thought.

Then he set the bottle down on a bookcase by the door and delivered a thermonuclear kiss, actually lifting her from her feet.

OK, not grandpa, unless grandpa had a prescription for Viagra.

Toes barely on the floor, she put her arms around his neck and melted into him. He was kissing like a starving creature eats. Felicia briefly worried that Mel might be upset by his enthusiasm, but then the other woman's arms slipped around her from behind and insinuated themselves between the two tightly pressed bodies. One reached up, cupping one of Felicia's breasts. The other headed down. Felicia felt its teasing pressure against her own crotch, but she surmised the main action was going to José.

Sandwiched between two very attractive bodies, Felicia lost all desire to think. Given the angle, Mel couldn't really do much, but simply feeling her there made Felicia all fluttery.

She could definitely get used to this threesome thing. She'd always have a bias in favour of the male anatomy, but the more she experienced them, the more she realised tender breasts and soft female lips (both sets) had a lot of appeal. Especially when there was also a hard male body to enjoy at the same time.

She cupped her hands around José's butt. She hadn't really had a chance to do that the other night, although she'd enjoyed the view.

Yup. His cheeks felt as nice as they looked, even through denim. They'd feel even better without the denim in the way, but that would mean letting go.

Mel snaked around to Felicia's side. José moved his arms, pulling the zookeeper into his embrace and turning his kissing attentions to her.

Felicia shouldn't have worried about Mel feeling threatened or excluded. Although each of them had an arm around Felicia, their focus changed as soon as their lips touched. They weren't deliberately shutting her out – Mel still caressed her breast, José still stroked her – but she was clearly secondary to their pleasure in each other.

She was aroused, but not so much so that she couldn't think. So ... was she upset to be an afterthought?

The answer surprised her a little. She wasn't. This was all about having a good time, as far as she was concerned, and she was honoured that two people she liked so much, and who could have celebrated privately, wanted to share their good time with her. If they were a little more into each other than they were into her, well, lucky them.

Although the rest of Felicia's condo was decorated straight from big-box stores in a style she'd once described as 'early overworked and underpaid', she'd put more effort into the bedroom. A queen-size brass bed in a clean modern design – a simple arched head-board and footboard filled in with two bold curves – dominated it. The linens, high-count Egyptian cotton in a striking shade of peacock blue, had cost her more than her second-hand couch and had been worth every penny. Several Orientalist prints adorned the walls, colourful, sensual scenes of a Middle East that never existed outside of artists' fantasies, where all the men were hot-eyed and handsome, all the women were curvy and seductive, and everyone was wearing more jewellery than clothing. On the dresser, a large, Victorian-looking bouquet – something she'd picked up at a farm stand on the way home one evening – added a subtle scent of roses and mimosa to the room. (The bouquet was a little ragged around the edges, but she'd figured no one would notice.) She'd tossed all the dirty laundry into the closet just before they'd arrived and pushed the door shut.

'Nice!' Mel said, rewarding her efforts at decorating the room that her mother had suggested leaving for last.

José didn't say anything, although he looked around and nodded approvingly. Then he started unbuttoning his shirt.

'Let us help with that,' Mel purred. 'Come on, Felicia.' And the mood, already charged, shifted into overdrive.

Felicia set the champagne down and closed in for the kill. She went for the shirt buttons. Tempting as it was to pull the shirt open quickly, get it off him, go right for the nipples, she didn't. She worked slowly, playing with the buttons like a burlesque dancer might. As she opened each one, she pulled the shirt open a couple of inches, stroking and kissing the newly exposed skin.

Mel, meanwhile, had knelt down to work on the belt and zipper. She apparently had a little trouble with the belt buckle at first; Felicia didn't take her eyes from what she was doing, but she heard a bit of giggling and a 'Damn' before the belt slipped open.

The sound of the zipper was magical, or maybe the magic was the noise that José and Mel both made as she came closer to exposing him. Felicia did look down for that. Mel had pressed her cheek against him, letting José feel her warm breath tease him through the thin fabric of his briefs. The long slender cock was mostly erect, forming a lovely line. Mel ran two fingers down it, then planted a delicate kiss on the head.

José drew in a sharp breath.

Felicia had two buttons on the bottom of the shirt left to go, but she figured her teasing had gone on long enough. She opened them quickly and, with a little help from José, wriggled the shirt off.

Getting the jeans off took a bit more effort, but that allowed both women to get in on the unwrapping. When he stood before them wearing only his blue bikini briefs and the smug smile that a man who'd just been undressed by two attractive women deserved to sport, Felicia and Mel looked at each other. 'You take the right side?' Mel said.

A matter of seconds and he was wearing nothing but the smile. Fully naked, he seemed a little nervous under their scrutiny, glancing at the artwork on the walls instead of meeting their eyes. But he still looked smug – and aroused. His whole body looked filled with the same delightful tension that animated the impressive erection that jutted in front of him.

So tasty. José had some streaks of white in his black hair and she knew he was older than she and Mel were, maybe in his early forties, but his body didn't show it. He was slim all over, his muscles sleek rather than bulky, his skin a delicious dark-honey colour, only slightly lighter where it was normally covered by clothes. She hadn't noticed the other night that he didn't have tan lines; she wondered if that was just his darker complexion or if he sunbathed naked when he had a chance. Now that was a lovely thought.

He wasn't as broad shouldered as Gabe, though, she noticed. And a bit of chest hair would make him all that much yummier.

She shook herself mentally. It wasn't polite, somehow, to compare the man she was actually with to someone else. Not to mention the fact that she'd never had a chest-hair fixation until she'd met Gabe. Somehow that tantalising glimpse of golden fur had got under her skin – and then the full view had finished her off. She was fixated on that body, that leonine gold-tipped pelt, that more sharply defined set of muscles. Even two days without really seeing him hadn't minimised the impact.

Before, she'd always liked smooth chests and slim catlike bodies. Hadn't she?

To prove to herself she still did, she stroked her hands down José's torso, not concentrating on the nipples yet, just on the feel of his skin under her hands. Heated silk over ... not steel, but something resilient, warm, yet just as solid. She wanted to think of a good word to go with the 'heated silk' image, but the sensation flowing from her fingertips seemed to short-circuit something in her brain. Forget metaphors: this was the male body in a particularly fine form, and her female body appreciated it. Appreciated it as in wanted to lick, kiss, nibble and otherwise taste every available inch of it. That lovely uncut cock, for instance – but all in good time.

All right, then. Just because she was a *little* fixated on Gabe didn't mean she was broken.

She let her hands roam back up, brushing the taut nipples, feeling her own tighten in empathy. Mel moved to join the action.

'Hey,' José said, laughing. 'Someone's overdressed for the party. Or should I say two someones?'

If José's unveiling had been slow and teasing, the women, by some unspoken agreement, undressed in a flurry of flying garments. Not that Felicia had much to striptease with anyway; she'd changed into a little Indian gauze sundress when she'd gotten home, trying to beat the heat, and that and minuscule panties were all she had to contend with.

Mel grabbed the bottle of champagne. 'Anyone for a drink?'

Felicia started to say no. Then she met her friend's eyes. Mel glanced from the bottle to José's body and back again, and that was enough to communicate the idea to Felicia. 'Sounds good!' she said.

Then she helped Mel tip José back on to the bed. Not that it was a lot of work; he was more than willing to be tipped.

Mel proved as competent at opening a champagne bottle as she was at dealing with leopards and margays. This didn't mean she didn't allow some of the bubbly to foam forth in dramatic (but not sommelier-approved) fashion – it meant that she aimed the alcoholic explosion carefully, getting most of it on José. She then poured some more on his flat belly. Most of it puddled in his navel, but some headed for the thicket of dark hair and the tree trunk of his cock.

'Don't move,' Felicia said. 'It's harder to lick off the sheets!'

The sheets were a lost cause anyway but, since the women seemed to have taken control, it might add to his sensations if he tried to keep still. Sort of like bondage without the trouble of actually tying him up.

They started on laving off the spilt rivulets of crisp gold wine from the expanse of José's chest. Felicia supposed a sommelier also might not approve of the flavour combination of brut champagne and aroused male. But she did. José's skin tasted good, very clean, but salty and a little musky, with an undertone of spice, and, leaving aside the way it made her own skin heat in empathy, it actually went well with the champagne.

They worked in towards the nipples, lapping there for much longer than the amount of champagne there warranted. At first, José was still and mostly quiet, trying to keep the puddle on his belly where it belonged.

That was no fun!

Felicia began to apply a little more suction, working with her tongue as she worked with lips and light pressure of her teeth. With a strangled noise, José put his hand on the back of her head. She thought for a second that he was trying to move her, but the pressure of his hand told the opposite: he wanted her harder.

Her peripheral vision told her that he'd done the same to Mel.

Oh. My. God.

Grabbing her hair like that made her clench and catch her breath – not the sensation in itself, but the unexpectedness of it. Rough directness from someone normally so gentle was exciting because it showed how much they were affecting him. And that, in turn, jacked up her arousal to a higher level.

Mel was the first to break off and begin kissing down his torso. This didn't seem to help José's level of coherence, especially when she began licking. Her pose was catlike, crouched on all fours like a lion at the watering hole, and Felicia found herself distracted from what she was doing by the visual feast. Mel's pink tongue moved over the quivering muscles of José's taut belly. She brushed her lovely little breasts against him, getting them champagne basted in the process. Mel was much paler than José, almost as fair as Felicia on her torso (no nude sunbathing for *her* evidently, or even bikinis) but her skin had the same golden undertones as José's and her hair was a similar blue-black. It made for a gorgeous effect, stylised as some kind of tony erotic photography, but brought to earth by scents: sweet flowers, sharp, yeasty champagne and warm, aroused flesh.

For a bit, Felicia was mesmerised by the beautiful sight. She continued to suck and play with his nipples, feeling herself getting slicker and hotter in response to the sensory feast, but unwilling to risk breaking the spell by taking a more active role. But she could only resist for so long and soon a second lioness joined the first at the waterhole.

Unfortunately, another tongue lapping at his belly was too much for José's self-control. He began to twitch, then to jerk around, laughing. 'That tickles,' he choked out.

They persisted until he threw them off. Flipping Mel over, he grabbed the bottle of champagne. She tried to squirm away, but José's greater strength, and his weight on her legs, kept her pinned down. She was doing a good job of resisting for someone who clearly wanted to lose.

'Help me out here!' He handed the bottle to Felicia, then grabbed Mel's wrists and pinned her to the bed.

Mel's lovely skin looked even prettier with a champagne glaze. And, as Felicia quickly discovered, girl-skin and champagne tasted just as lovely together as boy-skin and champagne, though subtly different, and tasting it sent similar waves of arousal crashing over her.

Mel stopped fighting as soon as their lips touched her. The giggling, though, went on for a while. Apparently, they'd got her to a point where she couldn't stop, even as they suckled at her breasts and she arched against them, silently begging for more.

The giggling stopped when José opened her legs and poured champagne so it ran from her blue-black pubic curls and down, its sheen mingling with the slickness on her dark lips. (He'd put her own shirt under her bottom beforehand, not that the sheets could be saved.)

He licked. 'Champagne and oysters!' he said happily, then buried his face between Mel's thighs and settled down, reaching up to play with her nipples at the same time.

Not wanting to distract from what looked like a damn fine situation for both of them, Felicia settled back to watch, tucking her hand between her legs and lazily stroking her clit, not ready to come, but enjoying the spirals of sensation that spread through her.

Mel went still, as if the feel of José's tongue had shocked the giggle-fit out of her. Her body began to tremble. Her belly moved like a Middle Eastern dancer's Felicia had seen once, a sea of ripples. It wasn't until he slipped two fingers inside her, though, that she cried out.

She was still trembling from the orgasm when José changed position to lie over her, teasing her slit with the head of his cock. 'Please,' Felicia heard her beg, her voice husky and urgent.

If she'd been José, Felicia didn't think she could have done what he did: seemingly ignoring that plea and continuing to rub himself against Mel's slickness without entering her.

Listening to her become more and more incoherent, watching her writhe against him, trying to slip his cock inside her, must have been gratifying. Felicia appreciated that kind of torment herself, both giving it and getting it. But Mel looked so hot – flushed, damp from the champagne bath, her midnight hair sticking up all around her – that, if Felicia had a penis, she was pretty sure it would have been doing all the thinking.

Then again, the way Mel shuddered and clutched at him when he finally did enter her probably made it all worthwhile.

They moved together, kissing each other, Mel's legs around his hips. Not a wild-animal fuck, but slow and sensual and affectionate.

And really lovely to watch, too.

Watching the show, Felicia realised – quite to her astonishment – that, while her body ached with arousal, she wasn't burning to be in Mel's position. Maybe she was more of a voyeur than she'd ever realised, but watching her friends' pleasure in each other was satisfying in its own right. Not the same as actually being the one doing the screaming, but damn hot anyway.

She stroked at herself, trying to match her rhythm to the leisurely one of the lovers she watched. At that moment José seemed to remember she was there. He whispered something in Mel's ear, nuzzling as he did, and she replied, though Felicia could not hear her.

With practised grace, the pair rolled over, only scrambling a little to stay joined. Mel remained pressed against José for a little while, her hips working against him, her mouth pressed to his. Then she sat up, arching back and reaching behind herself to support her weight on José's thighs. 'Join us?' she asked Felicia. Her tone was as calm and polite as if she'd asked Felicia to sit at their table in a café, but her face was red, her eyes glazed; the detachment was probably from the effort to talk at all.

Felicia scooted forwards, not quite sure of the best way to join in. She could lick where they were joined, play with José's balls ...

'Kneel over me,' he murmured. 'Sit on my face. I want to make you both come for me.'

Now *that* was an offer a woman couldn't refuse. (Well, she supposed *some* women could, but those women weren't likely to find themselves in a position to get such an offer anyway.) She climbed aboard.

José's tongue and lips seared. Little stabs of heavenly fire, radiating from her clit to fill her whole body. She was so sensitive she could feel his beard stubble against her. It was just on the right side of the pleasure/pain line, almost sandpaper, but not quite.

And still his tongue worked, his lips applied gentle pressure. After the long arousal, it was almost too much to bear. Felicia's head spun. She slumped forwards, suddenly lacking the co-ordination to hold herself up. Falling, but Mel caught her, and she toppled into a kiss. Once again, she felt a sense of astonishment at how soft Mel's lips were, even when her kiss was mindlessly fierce.

She wanted to touch them both, to stroke and caress, but she couldn't bear to let go of the sweet armful she held. Mel was breathing raggedly as she rode José. Her kiss grew more and more urgent.

Felicia understood completely. Her own body was tightening, contracting around its centre. It was all about José's tongue working on her and Mel's tongue in her mouth, about the triangle of bodies and lust they formed. She managed to slip one hand to Mel's breast, capturing a bobbing nipple.

Then her world exploded and it was all she could do not to disengage from Mel's mouth and scream, let alone do anything useful. José didn't stop, though. He slowed down long enough for her to catch her breath, then kept going.

She thought the first orgasm had been powerful, but the second dwarfed it. This time she really did slump forwards, done. When José attempted to pull her back to his mouth, she laughed, choked out, 'Too sensitive,' and squirmed away to watch.

Now he put his hands on Mel's hips and began to guide her movements as if she weighed no more than a doll. She seemed to like that. She leant forwards, grinding herself against him. He urged her up and down faster, bending his knees for leverage and thrusting into her from below.

They didn't quite come together, from what Felicia could tell. But, when Mel threw her head back and opened her mouth in a silent roar, José was not far behind her.

Afterwards, they made a puppy pile in the ruined bed – José in the middle, a woman snuggled on either side – and passed the remains of the bubbly back and forth. Most of it ended up in the women, since José was technically on call.

It was about 1 a.m. when they finally bid her a sleepy good night. 'You could stay,' she said, not sure if she really meant it, or if it would be comfortable to have three in her bed even if she did.

'We need to get home,' Mel said. 'My dog . . .'

Felicia nodded. 'Phu Dog will be going crazy by now.' Phu Dog, half golden retriever and half corgi, was a smart if oddly proportioned beast who loved everyone. Felicia was far more of a cat person, but she approved of him.

After they headed out, Felicia slumped down on the disaster of a bed, suddenly exhausted and a little melancholy. Physically, she was sated. Her limbs felt soft and languid, and she had a pleasant champagne buzz. Absolutely no complaints on that end. It had been a lovely evening.

But she was jealous of José and Mel heading out hand in hand, obviously planning on spending the rest of the night curled up together. Not because she wanted José – or Mel, for that matter – for herself. But because she was alone now. And lonely.

8

'It's so handy that you have a walk-in fridge!' Debbie enthused in Felicia's general direction as they exited the Sanctuary's little on-site café. It was hard to imagine Debbie saying anything non-enthusiastically, or at least non-bouncily and non-breathily. Fascinating.

'We'll have to rearrange some of the meat a little to give you more space,' Felicia said. 'But I think it'll work.'

'Absolutely!' Debbie said. 'And don't put the poor kitties out for me – make sure their dinners are still easily available, too.'

Felicia thought fondly of Pancho Villa the panther and how he expressed his concern about dinner (a nice bloody hunk of raw meat) not arriving expediently enough: with a roar that rattled your back teeth. 'Poor kitty' indeed.

The Sanctuary had no banquet facilities, but they did have a snack café on site. The kitchen was tiny, mostly used for making coffee and tea; sandwiches, salads, cakes and cookies were delivered each morning and kept in the immense refrigerator on the side away from the cats' meals. However, Debbie assured her that she could set up a temporary cook station with portable stoves and chafing dishes in the café. Since the weather would be warm, an assortment of cold dishes would work perfectly. Nothing like fresh shrimp with a spicy vodka-laced cocktail sauce to make people want to give money, and give it generously.

'So we'll be putting the tents over here?' Debbie had wandered into the grassy area between the main part of the Sanctuary and the lion house. 'Seems flat enough. Don't want anybody twisting an ankle.'

Well, if Debbie could totter around the area in those spike heels and not break her leg, everyone else would be fine. The area was bordered by a cemented area dotted with tables and benches, so if they had any guests in wheelchairs, they could be seated at a table on that side and still be part of the fundraiser.

Thank goodness the grass was doing as well as it was. For weeks now, Alan and his security staff had had an added duty: making sure the sprinklers were on. They were supposed to come on at dusk after the Sanctuary closed and then again at dawn, but they'd intermittently stopped working, and nobody could figure out why. They'd even had the sprinkler company out three times, but the technician swore up and down that there was nothing wrong with the timers or the lines.

And here in the desert, watering was crucial if they were going to have anything more than a barren patch of crunchy brown weeds.

At least they didn't have to worry about rain!

'Two pavilions,' Felicia confirmed. 'One for mingling and the silent auction display. And the bar – people always bid more when the bar's handy. The other one'll be for the tables and chairs for dinner.'

The board of directors had debated long and hard about whether to hold the fundraiser at a ritzy hotel or at the Sanctuary itself. A ritzy hotel had many advantages, but in the end Noelle the Amur leopard had made the decision for them with her pregnancy. Making a private viewing of the new cubs part of the fundraiser would ramp up the interest in attendance. Baby cats did that to people. They also warmed even the hardest of hearts, which in turn loosened even the tightest grips on wallets.

But, even with the cubs sparking interest, attendance was still looking low. Far better than it had been – for a while she'd been wondering if they'd make any money at all – but they were still about 75 guests short of sold out. Felicia made a mental note to call the board members *again* about pushing tickets and seeing if she could get the local TV station to run footage of the cubs.

'Wait staff,' Debbie said, and Felicia poised the stylus over her Palm Pilot. 'Is there a local temp agency we can work with? I'm used to hiring folks in LA, but we'd have to pay extra for them to drive all the way out here.'

'I'll look into that.' Felicia made a note.

'Awesome!' The caterer paused and gazed through fashionably large sunglasses across the lawn at a buff young man carrying a rake and green plastic trash bin. His T-shirt stretched to the maximum across his muscled chest and impressive biceps, all managing to enhance a lower half that was encased in tight jeans. His hair, spikily short and dark beneath with a frosting of bleach, was like a beacon in the sun.

'You know,' Debbie said thoughtfully, 'he would look so right in a little white jacket and black bow tie. Do you suppose he has any friends?'

Felicia laughed. 'I can't imagine you could convince Lance to wear a monkey suit, but you could always try.' The nineteen-year-old volunteer came from the proverbial wrong side of the tracks, and his idea of dressing up was wearing freshly laundered jeans and a black T-shirt as opposed to a white one.

'Hmm,' Debbie said, for a moment sounding vague. Then she snapped back into her usual fast-forward self. 'You're dealing with the tables and chairs, right?'

'Tents, tables, chairs, decorations and any display features,' Felicia confirmed.

'I'll handle dishes and silverware, but we need to

find a catering supply company for table linens, serving dishes, chafing dishes, that sort of thing,' Debbie added. 'I'll send you a list of exactly what I'll need.'

Felicia made another note. Debbie's bubbly efficiency was like a shot in the arm. She wished she could bottle the caterer's energy; goodness knows she needed some extra vigour this morning.

She'd tossed and turned last night, her mind filled with the memory of Gabe in a towel ... and fantasies of him out of it. A 3 a.m. session with Mr Twitchy hadn't been ideal, but it had at least allowed her to get some sleep.

Gabe was working with José today, reviewing the vet's files. Felicia knew the Sanctuary had a fantastic record in that respect – few illnesses, rare injuries. The information about Magnolia's injured paw would be in the log, but it was one of very few, and thankfully it was also relatively minor.

Still, she couldn't help but worry.

Not only that, but she was constantly aware that he was on site, that he was near by. The knowledge hovered at the back of her brain, had her body on edge, kept her thinking she saw him out of the corner of her eye and then feeling disappointed when she was wrong.

He'd said 'Good morning' to her as he'd passed by her office that morning, but that had been it. She hadn't been able to read the expression in his eyes. Was he uncomfortable about their encounter the other night? Or, now that the moment had passed, had he lost interest?

She didn't want his interest. She wanted him to give the Sanctuary a glowing report and then get the hell out of there. At the same time, she craved his interest ... and more.

'I need a cold drink, how about you?' she asked Debbie.

'Omigod yes! I'm just *wilting*.' Debbie fanned herself.

Felicia didn't see a hint of wilting, but she refrained from saying so. Debbie offered to grab the sodas, and Felicia took the opportunity to duck back into her office and check email and phone messages.

Ten minutes later, they stood outside in the shade of the building, chatting easily about plans for the fundraiser. Felicia dipped her hand in her cup and pressed bits of ice against the back of her neck, shivering at the contrast of hot and cold.

As Lance came out from the back side of the cheetah enclosure and headed across the edge of the lawn towards the fishing cats' habitat, Debbie dropped a piece of ice down her ample cleavage and squealed. Lance did a perfect double-take. His steps slowed and his head swivelled as he walked, never taking his eyes off Debbie. He was so blatantly smitten that Felicia giggled.

Debbie flipped her blonde mane back and waggled her fingers at Lance. He stopped dead in his tracks. Across the green, his single utterance was loud and clear. 'Shit!'

'Language, Lance,' Felicia called.

'Crap!'

'We've talked about appropriate language –' Felicia tried again, amazed at his sudden descent into crudeness after weeks of being successfully polite. Cleaning up his language, both grammar and colourful euphemisms, was part of the deal if he was to stay as a volunteer, and he'd been working hard at it.

He had dropped the bucket and rake, and now gestured helplessly, pointing at the ground. 'Well, what do you *want* me to call it?!'

And that's when the slight breeze shifted towards her. Felicia felt the bile rise in her throat.

'Is it just me, or is he sinking into the ground?' Debbie

asked as Felicia took off towards him. The caterer's final words trailed after her: 'Whew, something's kind of stinky. Time to clean those cages, huh?'

'Preliminary report from John is that the main sewer pipe burst,' Katherine said, referring to the Sanctuary's handyman. 'We've got City Sanitation on their way.'

The emergency conference in the teaching room, the only place big enough for the small staff, was attended by her, Felicia, Alan, Lance, José ... and Gabe.

Dammit. Why did he have to be here to witness this?

'Any idea why it happened?' Gabe asked.

Felicia stared at the poster on the wall showing a cross-section of a cat's paw and how claws retracted. Anything to ignore the fact that they were sitting so close around the crowded child-sized round table that their thighs were an inch apart. She swore she could feel the heat from his leg against hers.

'John's still looking into that,' Katherine said. 'The main thing is, of course, that we've had to close for the rest of the day, and may be closed for longer, depending on how long this takes to fix. We'll have to figure out some alternative methods of waste disposal, at least until the city gives us their evaluation.'

'What about the lawn?' Felicia asked, thinking of the fundraiser.

'Once we've got the leak fixed, it shouldn't be too hard to re-sod that area,' Lance said. His sneakers and socks were in the Sanctuary's on-its-last-legs washing machine. 'The grass'll probably grow mega-green on that corner,' he added with a grin.

'We'll tell kids it's a fairy ring.' Felicia felt like she was randomly grasping at any sort of positive idea she could find, no matter how stupid. She was surprised when Gabe said, 'Especially if mushrooms grow, too.'

'Well,' Katherine said, clapping her hands once

together lightly to signal the end of the meeting, 'we'll just take it one step at a time. Thank you all for the emergency meeting. Let's get out there and keep working at whatever we need to. When we have a report from the city, I'll let you all know.'

Felicia watched her boss trot out of the teaching room, spine erect. She hadn't seen Katherine that confident and spry in days, although she wondered if Katherine's method of stress relief had involved working out, because she was walking a little funny.

She slid her chair out from under the table at the same time that Gabe did, and now their legs did brush together. They both jumped apart, but not before a spark of arousal skittered through her, up her thigh and lodged in her groin.

'Sorry,' Felicia said.

'No need to apologise,' Gabe said gallantly. He paused, as if trying to frame his next words. 'I wanted to thank you again for the other night.'

For showing up when he was almost naked? For thinking about jumping his bones? Dammit, all he said was thank you and she was right back in the mindset of the evening, images flashing in her mind.

He stepped towards her, and she stepped back, only to have her thighs connect with the table. He leant forwards, and a flutter started in her stomach.

But Katherine's was the next voice she heard. 'Felicia?'

They jumped apart again as Katherine came back into view, framed by the doorway. She'd put her glasses on, although the tiny gold wire frames were sliding down her nose. 'Could you write up a press release and fax it to the *Addison Independent* as soon as we have some info from the city? If we nip this in the bud, maybe we can keep it to a notice buried on page seven rather than a full story.'

'I'll get right on that,' Felicia said.

'Thanks.' Katherine smiled at Gabe. 'I'm sorry to say, you've visited us at a crazy time, Mr Sullivan.'

Felicia stared at Katherine. She was *way* too calm. Felicia wanted a shot of whatever relaxation drug her boss was taking, preferably a double dose.

'It gives me the opportunity to witness grace under pressure,' Gabe said easily.

Trying to muster her own share of grace under pressure, although she was feeling more flustered than graceful, Felicia took the opportunity to slip back to her office.

Gabe retreated to one of the covered tables outside. Despite the heat, he found himself using the area as a temporary office where he could spread out some paperwork, review his notes and messages – and also be at the centre of things.

The sewage leak was either stupid bad luck, or it spoke of something more serious. He would wait until he heard the City Sanitation Department's report before he came to a final decision, of course, but he couldn't help but ponder the possibilities.

He was used to facing opposition and resentment in his job, even from facilities that were entirely on the up and up, with multimillion-dollar budgets and exquisite amenities. His presence never failed to engender a level of suspicion and guilt. He was from a policing agency, and his job was to scrutinise every factor and detail of the operation. That naturally put people on the defensive.

The bottom line was that no person or facility was perfect. Even a place he'd give perfect marks to might have a cashier in the gift shop who was skimming from the till. He didn't take points away for an individual like that, although he hoped the facility appreciated that his review had brought the problem to their attention.

The SCCS staff was under a lot of stress, there was no question about that. It was his job to figure out if the stress was due to everyday causes or a deeper set of problems. And, if there were problems, it would be his job to write them up and recommend solutions that the Zoo Association would require SCCS to implement. Or it would be his job to ensure that the SCCS's licence be revoked and the facility shut down.

Yeah, he had the potential to not just be a bad guy, but to be the *really* bad guy.

So far here, he'd seen dedicated, passionate employees struggling to keep an out-of-the-way, underfunded facility going. So far, he'd seen that the animals were well cared for. The cages might be a little bare, but there was a level at which things like murals and fancy shelters were for the benefit of the visitors rather than the cats themselves. The cats wanted a dark, quiet place – it didn't matter if it looked like a natural stone cave or a big plywood box. The point was that they were well fed and properly looked after.

The vet, José, had been pleasant enough, but reserved. Again, Gabe could put it down to the usual resistance he encountered. If everything was fine, then José naturally would be defensive. If something was amiss, José was likely to want it covered up.

As far as Gabe could tell, the veterinary records were in order. José had shown marked reluctance to show him a recent injury report, although the injury itself seemed to have been a fairly minor one.

José's distraction could have stemmed from the recent birth of Amur leopard cubs. He'd excused himself from their meeting several times to check on the mama cat and her babies, and he looked flat-out exhausted.

Still, Gabe had made note of the injury in question;

something just didn't seem right, and he wanted to give it a closer look.

If the Sanctuary were a child, he might have dubbed it 'accident prone'. First there had been the false fire alarm – but there had been a horde and a half of children swarming around. 'Don't touch' was the most powerful sign to encourage a child to put his or her hands on something.

Now there was a sewage leak. Again, something that could happen to anyone, anywhere. The same set of school kids could have shoved something down a toilet. The sewage system could be old and corroded. Whatever.

But coming on the heels of the fire alarm – and, for that matter, the ocelot injury a few days before that … Was a curious pattern emerging? Was it a random series of unfortunate incidents, or something more?

Unbidden, his mind flashed back to Felicia's comment over dinner about the land being prime real estate, that someone had suggested selling the property and relocating the Sanctuary. There wasn't enough to bring him to any obvious conclusions. It was all just something he'd keep an eye out for.

'Hi!' a voice said brightly.

He looked up to see the buxom blonde caterer smiling down at him.

'Mind if I join you?' she asked.

Gabe tipped his head so he could view her over his sunglasses. 'Be my guest,' he said, gathering in his paperwork.

She slid on the bench sideways, straddling it with just enough of a hip thrust to make her intentions clear.

She wore a pink sleeveless halter-type shirt with wide lapels, sort of funky and retro and stylish all at once. She obviously wore a push-up bra beneath it, because a crevasse of shadowed cleavage was apparent between the lapels. He'd noticed earlier that her jeans rode a little low and the shirt a little high, showing off the tattoo at the small of her back, although he hadn't been close enough to make out what the tattoo depicted.

Felicia was also wearing a sleeveless, button-down top today, but revealing less cleavage. Hers had seams down the front to shape the shirt to her body without being clinging. It was elegant, professionally sexy, especially paired with the long, straight white skirt that had a high slit up the back.

Felicia, however, was off limits. It would compromise their working relationship and there was also the slightest niggle of concern that she might be involved with the problems plaguing the Sanctuary. Not that he could think of any reason to be suspicious except that, at this point, no one was ruled out and, knowing he was attracted to her, he had to go out of his way to be objective.

'We didn't really get a chance to chat the other day,' Debbie said. 'Talk about mayhem! Anyway, I just wanted to say hi again, and get out of the sun.' She grabbed a file off the table and fanned her cleavage, which, he noted, glistened attractively with a fine sheen of sweat.

Debbie made it blatantly obvious that she was interested in him. He felt the first stirrings of arousal in his groin: a normal, healthy reaction to an outrageously sexy, confident, willing woman. He'd probably suggest drinks after work, see where the evening led, in the hope that it would lead back to his hotel room, where they'd share a fun sweaty, uninhibited time together.

'I'm kind of stunned by the heat,' he admitted. 'I have to confess I thought California was all palm trees and inviting beaches.'

There was nothing wrong with blatant. With blatant,

you knew where you stood. Women were finally admitting that sometimes what they wanted was a night of hot sex with no strings attached, that they didn't always want or assume that a wedding dress and two-point-five kids would follow.

Not that there was anything wrong with a wedding dress, et cetera. Gabe figured he'd find Ms Right someday – in fact, he was looking forward to that. But Debbie Landstrom wasn't Ms Right and, as near as he could guess, didn't have any interest in being Ms Right. The option of Ms Right-Now, however, was something they could both agree on.

'The café is air conditioned,' Debbie said. 'We could cool down.' She leant forwards, allowing a greater view down her shirt, and batted her doe eyes at him. Her musky perfume insinuated itself into his nostrils.

He'd planned to stay here until the City Sanitation people showed up. But goodness knew how slow government employees could be. And it *was* really hot, and iced tea sounded wonderful. He shoved the files and phone into his briefcase and stood, a bit awkwardly in his condition.

It didn't even occur to him until they were inside the building that it would be empty of both tourists, who'd gone home because of the sewage leak, and the now unneeded employees.

Oh, she was good.

She opened the ice maker and scooped out a sliver, popping it between her red lips and sucking on it suggestively.

The blood drained from Gabe's head and pooled in his groin. He stuck his hand in the cold bin and found a piece of ice. Coming up behind Debbie, he lifted her hair and traced the ice along her neck. She squealed and backed into him, shimmying her hips so that her fine ass snugged up against his hardened cock.

Debbie's squeal turned into a breathy, appreciative 'Hel-lo'.

Creative foreplay be damned. He spun her around. She was already unbuttoning her shirt. Her lacy yellow bra was the kind that scooped low, and all he had to do was tug a little before her nipples popped out.

She hopped up on the counter and threaded her fingers through his hair, urging him closer even as he dove in, kneading and sucking. Definitely enhanced, but she made all manner of cooing happy noises, so it seemed to be a worthy endeavour. He imagined how it would feel to slide his cock, slick with her saliva, down the valley between her breasts, and his cock responded, pressing hard against the fly of his khakis.

He made swift work of his belt buckle and yanked down the zipper. Debbie joined in to help, tugging his trousers down so they pooled at his feet, and pulling down his underwear with only slightly less force.

At his feet now, she closed her hot mouth around his cock, taking him in with ravenous enthusiasm. Her long fingernails grazed his balls, and he groaned, close to the edge. Last night's session in the shower – or the one the night before – hadn't taken the edge off as much as he'd hoped.

Straightening, she shimmied out of one leg of her jeans. She wasn't wearing underwear, and she obviously spent time at the waxing salon – a narrow strip of groomed hair was all that stood between him and her pussy. She perched back on the counter and spread her legs, sliding one hand between her thighs to massage her bare, glistening lips.

'C'mon, baby, I need you inside me.'

Gabe didn't need further invitation.

Hot, wet and tight. It was a cliché, but it was true.

He varied the length and speed of his strokes, gauging her reaction to see what gave her the most pleasure. Then he felt a stiletto heel press into his back as she clamped her legs around him, urging him on. Well, that answered *that* question.

She was already carrying on a litany of raunchy encouragement and, as he sped up, her moans increased. Reaching down between them, his fingers sought out her clit. There wasn't much space for skilful manipulation, but his hips rhythmically bumped his hand and his fingers slid along her hard button, and it was enough. Her moans turned to shrieks, and she squeezed down around him, and her fingernails dug into his back, and he felt the come surge up inside him.

When he released his load into her, fast and hard, it was Felicia's face that he imagined.

Curious.

Debbie released her death grip from his back and he disengaged from her, pulled up his trousers and held them together. He refrained from looking over his shoulder to see if she'd punctured his shirt, or, for that matter, his skin.

Debbie casually reached across the counter and pulled a handful of paper napkins from a metal dispenser. She swiped herself clean, dropped the napkins on the counter, and hopped down to readjust her clothes. In less than a minute, her jeans were fastened, her bra was back in place, her shirt was buttoned, and she was fluffing out her hair and dabbing a finger at the corners of her mouth to fix any smudged lipstick.

'I hope they sanitise the countertop before they serve anyone food,' she commented, flicking at the napkins with her forefinger.

He started to laugh, assuming she was making a joke, but then he saw her moue of distaste.

Shaking his head, he rummaged in the supply closet

and found cleaning spray and rags. He dropped the napkins she'd used in the trash and wiped down the counter.

'Seriously, I mean, jeez, isn't that the type of thing you write places up for?' Debbie asked.

'No, generally I don't write them up for my having had sex in their cafeteria,' Gabe said lightly. As a food-service professional, Debbie had had safe food-preparation rules drilled into her brain. But she still seemed to be overreacting. As if it hadn't been her idea in the first place!

'Well, *I* wouldn't want to eat there,' she said. 'I hope they scrub this place down before I have to use it to prep the fundraiser food.'

'Then I assume you don't have sex on your own kitchen counters?' Gabe asked.

She stared at him for a minute, then smiled and batted her eyelashes. 'Inviting yourself over already?'

'I'll take a rain cheque,' Gabe said, grabbing his briefcase. The problem with fun, sweaty, uninhibited playtime was that sometimes the other person turned out to be someone you weren't sure you wanted to spend time with again.

Once again, his obstinate brain flashed to Felicia, suggesting that she'd be as much fun after a steamy session in the sack as she was during it.

And once again, his obstinate cock, which really should have been sated, twitched in appreciation.

9

'No sooner than that?' A silence, during which Katherine fumbled with the clicker on her pen. Felicia, Mel, Gabe and Lance (who seemed to have decided the problem was partly his to solve since he'd discovered it), gathered around her desk, held their breaths – in part from politeness, in part because the offices were downwind from the leak and the A/C was being particularly uncooperative. 'I know it's Friday afternoon,' Katherine responded to what she heard. 'That's why we need to get this fixed today. Weekends are our busiest time.'

It was clear from Katherine's face that whatever she was hearing wasn't good.

She got off the phone shaking her head. 'It looks like someone – probably some bored junior-high kid – flushed an entire box of tampons and followed it with the box. The older parts of the pipe just couldn't take the strain. The city only has a skeleton crew on over the weekend, so the repairs may not be finished until late on Sunday – and they'll have to shut off the plumbing everywhere but the areas that are critical for the animals for the whole time. We'll have a port-a-john within the hour for the essential staff, but we'll be closed until Monday, and then it'll be a mess. They'll have to do a lot of digging in the main courtyard and one of the bad sections is under the garden outside the front gate, so we're going to have to get new plants and re-landscape.'

Lance groaned – understandably, since he'd planted

that bed, directed by a couple of seventy-ish volunteers who had the horticultural know-how but not the muscle.

Then he got what he clearly thought was a brilliant idea, because his usual James Dean sneer turned into an actual smile that made him look like a particularly eager (and very well-built) puppy.

He opened his mouth then fell silent, looking from face to face. Mel had said she'd got him to be chatty one on one, but, then again, Mel looked about his age; he still seemed intimidated by the senior staff, especially Katherine.

'Please,' Katherine said, evidently sensing his discomfort. 'If you've got an idea, speak up. We need all the ideas we can get at this point.'

'Can we move the plants before they dig there? It'll be kind of gross, but we've got gloves and coveralls and sh—stuff,' he corrected himself quickly. 'And my sister's seeing this guy who works for a landscaper. Maybe he can get us some clean dirt.' He snorted. 'Clean dirt. That sounds weird. But maybe they'd, like, give it to us. It's just dirt, right? Can't cost them a lot.'

There was a brief silence, during which Felicia kicked herself for assuming the bad boy had no useful connections. There were times a landscaper with a tie to SCCS could come in handy – and this was one of them.

Katherine nodded. 'Thank you, Lance, but I really hate the thought of anyone doing too much in this heat.'

'They're saying the heat wave's gonna break tonight. It's just going to be normal hot tomorrow, not killer. So if I come in early tomorrow ... If that's OK, that is,' he added quickly. 'Saturday isn't one of my days, but I don't have anything going down so I could help.'

'I'll help,' Mel said. 'I was coming in anyway.'

'I'll help too,' Felicia volunteered instinctively.

Katherine shook her head. 'Thanks, but, if you're working tomorrow, we've got that National Science Foundation grant to finish. Maybe it'll actually be quiet enough so that we can get it done. People don't usually call on Saturday.'

Felicia felt a brief urge to argue. While gardening wasn't her thing, spending some time doing physical labour with Mel and one of the more decorative volunteers sounded like a good break from her desk. But Katherine was right. The grant had been on her agenda for the afternoon, but there was no way she'd get to it, not with trustees to contact about the leak, a press release to write and a list of phone calls about five miles long for the event.

Mel laughed. 'Besides, Felicia, I know what happened to that aloe I gave you. We want the plants to live!'

'If you need more hands,' Gabe said, 'I'm a pretty good gardener for a city boy.' He smiled a little oddly and Felicia remembered how he'd supposedly done community service on a farm.

It wasn't until the others left to go about their day that Felicia realised how quiet Gabe had been. He hadn't said a word other than to volunteer, and hadn't met her eyes for the whole discussion. And, since she'd been having trouble *not* staring at him, she was sure about that.

He'd been friendly earlier, if a little cautious. But that made sense. The whole not-exactly-a-date and caught-in-a-towel situation might make him unsure how to treat her, and they hadn't really had a chance to talk since. Now, it seemed like he was ashamed of something.

And what was he still doing here anyway, let alone volunteering to help out on Saturday? Most of the real staff had gone home, except for the ones who might as well stop paying rent and move into their offices.

She didn't like where her mind was going, but he'd said he was a former juvenile delinquent, a vandal. What if the damage to the pipes hadn't been accidental? He'd been here at some mighty odd hours.

Was he staying on site hoping for a chance to make more trouble? Or at least to poke around and see how much more dirt he could unearth while things were quiet?

All she knew for certain was that it was going to be a long weekend. An even longer one, if Gabe was on site for all of it.

Alan walked carefully through the dark Sanctuary. At least they'd got a lot of the contaminated soil out of the way during the day, and a fresh breeze was picking up, cutting through the heat and dispersing the stench, but the work had left large holes behind. They were marked off by caution tape, but he still had this fear that the ground might open up under his feet. Strange shapes loomed in the darkness – just a backhoe and some other equipment the Sanitation Department team had left behind, but they looked like something out of a monster movie.

He glanced behind him at the machinery and swore he saw movement. 'Who's there?' he yelled, and trained the beam of his Maglite on the destroyed courtyard.

Nothing.

And who the hell did he think would be there anyway? The Jolly Green Giant's smellier cousin? He was looking at a hole that led down to the sewer pipe.

Still, he investigated, checking around the construction equipment.

Nothing. Not a sign of life, not even a footprint other than the baked ones left by the work crew.

Ever since that incident with the open cage, he'd been on edge. Too many weird things had been happening at the Sanctuary, enough that he was starting to see a pattern when maybe there wasn't one.

Occam's Razor, they called it: the simplest explanation was usually best. The simplest explanation was that they'd just been having a run of bad luck. All the equipment was old and most of it was jerry-rigged – no wonder things broke down.

But he'd been a cop for thirty years, and something stank here besides the sewage. Occam, whoever he was, was no doubt a smart guy, but Alan was keeping his eyes peeled, just in case.

And, if he jumped at shadows, well, there was no one here to see him.

After crossing the courtyard and cutting behind the buildings, he began to patrol the area along the back fence. Away from the road, it was blessedly quiet. He could hear insects whirring and the night sounds of the cats.

And a voice and some rustling.

Maybe he was imagining things again, but he didn't think so. It sounded like they were coming from near the back corner, where the fence came close to a quiet cul-de-sac.

Cautiously, he approached, moving as quietly as a rather large older man could.

Yes, someone was definitely there. Maybe a few someones. They weren't talking much, but he heard movement and what sounded like the clink of metal on metal.

He wheeled around the corner, regretting he only had a Maglite and a security guard's uniform, not a gun and a whole department to call for back-up if he needed it. If the intruders were armed, it could be trouble.

'Hold it right there, buddy!' he said in his best cop's voice, illuminating the area.

Two figures were fleeing. He tried to give chase, but

in the dark lost them quickly. He hadn't got a good look at the punks, but they'd appeared to be young guys, maybe Lance's age, one white, one darker. And they'd left their wire cutters behind.

Lance stopped his work to watch Mel walk away, pushing a wheelbarrow full of plants. Sweet. That chick's ass was just about perfect, and even her baggy khaki shorts and the smears of dirt on her legs didn't hurt the scenic view.

He'd always had a thing for Asian girls, but he'd met two kinds: the snooty, college-bound type who didn't have time for guys like Lance Boudreaux and the tough type who hung out with the Vietnamese gang members. Some of them were pretty hot, but he liked keeping his skin intact, thanks. Besides, they probably wouldn't have time for him either. He didn't have a fancy ride or money to spoil a girl. Maybe someday, but not now, and the guys who ran with the gangs already had it.

Mel was different. She talked to him for real and, what's more, she listened. She was one of the smart ones – she'd gone to Stanford and you don't get there by being dumb – but her family didn't sound like rich snobs. More like normal people who'd produced some real brainy kids. And, smart as she was, she obviously didn't care about money or expensive stuff or she'd be ... oh, a lawyer or something.

Or a porn star. She could make a lot of money doing that. She was definitely hotter than Asia Carrera. Not as stacked, but what she had was obviously real, and that was nice. Oh yeah, he could picture her moaning and writhing before the camera ...

No, actually he couldn't. Despite the best efforts of what he liked to consider a pretty creatively dirty mind, he couldn't convince himself it was Mel's style, although some of the images he came up with in his efforts were worth remembering.

Now that blonde chick, the one he'd heard was the new caterer, he could definitely imagine *her* as a porn star. She had the awesome body, the big hair, and even the right 'look at me' attitude.

And he'd caught her looking at him like he was ice cream or something. He wondered if she was really interested or just a flirt. She'd be fun to do – too high-maintenance to date, probably, but definitely fun to do. He'd love to get his cock between those tits to warm up, and then let her wrap those mile-long legs around him and drive into her hard. Maybe he'd come on her tits and her face, a real money shot, because she really did remind him of a porn star and he could picture her grinning lecherously as her tongue darted out to catch a few droplets.

Now with Mel it would be different. He'd be gentle, take his time, lick her until she was babbling and begging for his cock. She'd probably like to be on top. It wasn't his favourite position, but women seemed to enjoy it and, if you managed to get someone as special as Mel into bed, you'd want to make her real happy so she'd come back again. On the other hand, she was a little thing, but strong. They could try some exotic positions, standing up, holding her upside down, stuff like that.

Someone swatted him on the head. 'Hey, anyone home?'

He looked up into two very familiar faces. Just ('because Justin's a wuss name') and Dog were a couple of his oldest friends, but he hadn't been seeing a lot of them lately. Not since he'd been given a choice between cleaning up his act and spending some quality time in jail. Just was small and scrawny, but wiry, with no-colour hair and almost colourless eyes. Like Lance, he was white trash to the bone and, unlike Lance, proud of it. Dog, by contrast, was about six foot three, a solid muscular dark mixture of, as far as Lance could figure out, every race that had ever set foot in North America.

'Hey, guys.' He realised he should probably sound happier to see them, but they'd interrupted a really sweet fantasy.

'What's on your mind, dude? We've been standing here for like five minutes trying to talk to ya,' Just said.

'Look at his boner, man. What do you think's on his mind?'

'Quit looking at my crotch, Dog.' He glanced down, trying to be casual about it. Dog was always saying shit like that, so it was probably a lucky guess. How bad could it be under the baggy coveralls?

Oh. *That* bad. He felt his face getting red and decided he had to defend himself.

'Do you think I'd be out here playing with flowers if there wasn't a hot piece of ass involved?' He felt bad calling Mel a piece of ass, but it was the way the guys always talked when there were no girls around. But Mel would probably be mad if she heard him talking about her that way. And he wouldn't be surprised if she could kick his butt. He'd seen martial arts movies. It was the tiny pretty ones you needed to watch out for.

'So there's a hottie here?' Dog, in keeping with his nickname, was always interested in the ladies.

'Plenty of 'em,' he bragged. The caterer definitely fitted into that category, and Felicia was good-looking too, even if she was a suit. Even the director was cute in her way, although she was old, at least forty, and he was pretty sure she was a dyke. 'But one super-special hottie.' He raised an eyebrow and grinned, letting them think she was special as in his girl, not special as in, well, special.

Dog nodded knowingly. 'That explains it. We thought you'd gone all goody-goody on us or something. But, if you've got a new girl, maybe you've just been busy.' He thrust forwards with his hips, making Just snort with laughter.

'You might say.' It wasn't actually a lie. He had been busy, just not that way (which was a damn shame). It wouldn't occur to those guys that he might be busy working. He actually had a job now, plus the community service here and the classes he was taking. But they'd probably laugh if he told them that.

They snorted again, giving each other high fives.

And, for the first time ever, Lance looked at his friends and thought, Get some class, assholes.

Did *he* sound that dumb sometimes?

Yeah, maybe. At least he used to. He'd been trying, listening to some of the guys who worked at SCCS and at the restaurant, hoping it would help him make a good impression on Mel. And now that he had some idea of how ignorant he sounded, he was almost scared to talk sometimes.

At least with Just and Dog he could relax about that. Next to them, he'd sound like one of those brainy public-TV guys.

'So, what's up? This ain't your kind of cat house. They don't have that kind of pussy here.'

That got them. He knew it would.

Once they stopped laughing, Just said, 'We was looking for you. Your cell phone must have lost its buttons or something, so we went by your place and your mama said you were here.'

'Phone's dead. I gotta get a new one, but I put some moves on this geek girl at Best Buy and she said they'd have some sweet deals next week so I'm waiting.'

Actually the phone was fine. He just hadn't called

the guys back because ... well, he really wasn't sure why. Now that he saw them again, it seemed stupid. He'd missed them, even if they were asshats sometimes.

Dog looked around several times before he spoke. 'Isn't it about time for you to have a smoke?'

Lance had just about quit smoking – he couldn't do it here, at school or at work and by now he'd almost stopped jonesing – but he got the point immediately.

'Sure.' He stuck his head through the gate. Mel wasn't anywhere in sight, but Gabe was. (That guy was everywhere. What did he *do*, anyway? Right now he was helping with the plants, of course, but usually he was wandering around with a clipboard, looking busy but not actually working in any way Lance could recognise. Whatever it was, it left him with time to bug Lance about his plans for the future sometimes, like he was his social worker or something.) 'Hey, if you see Mel, tell her I'm taking a ciggy break. I'll be back in a few.'

He was gone before Gabe could react.

Instead of smoking, though, he headed down the street and climbed into Dog's car with the guys.

'So,' Just said bluntly, 'you want to help us on a job?'

He shook his head. 'I don't do jobs any more. Not while I'm on probation. It's not worth it.'

'It's not stealing or nothing,' Dog said quickly. 'Just kid stuff – breaking shit, a little tagging. Stuff we used to do for fun, only we're getting paid this time.'

'How much?' Money was tight. He'd like to move out of his mom's place, but that took cash. And Mel wasn't all about the bling, but girls always appreciated a nice dinner out, or real presents, not crap like the coffee mug from the Dollar Store he'd left on her desk the other day.

Just named a figure that sounded ridiculously large for what Dog had described.

Lance whistled. 'And I'd get a third of that?'

'Dude, that would be your cut!'

Forget taking Mel out to dinner. He could take her to Vegas for the weekend with that kind of cash and still have money left. (First he'd have to get her to agree, of course, but hey, she was single and he knew women liked his looks, and she'd been working hard and could use a vacation. Why would she say no?)

But something didn't sound right. Lance hadn't been a whiz kid in school, but money made sense to him. 'Wait a minute. If all you're doing is trashing some stuff, why do you need me? You're less likely to get caught with just two guys and you'd make a lot more.'

Dog put his hand on Lance's shoulder. 'We miss you, man. We want you running with us again.'

'And it's no big deal. No stealing, no messing people up,' Just emphasised. 'Just wrecking stuff and spray-painting. Almost no chance of getting caught. It's a no-brainer. We've done this a million times.'

'Only when we're done, we'll get some sweet money.'

Lance thought hard. He kind of liked the straight life, not that he'd admit it to the guys – no looking over his shoulder all the time, no worrying about the cops or about stepping on the toes of someone a lot bigger and meaner than he was, and actually getting to meet people like Mel instead of just stealing their wallets – but being goddamn broke all the time was getting to him.

'Let me think about it. I'll call you later. But I've got to get back to work before they ask too many questions.'

It was tempting. Seriously tempting. But why would someone pay so much for kid-stuff like vandalism? And what weren't the guys telling him?

10

Felicia called a meeting in the vet clinic – herself, José, Mel, and Alan. She checked outside the door before she joined the others, propping one hip on the examining table and trying not to think about the raucous sex she'd had on it less than a week ago. José sat on a metal rolling stool, and Mel had pulled out the desk chair and straddled it backwards. Alan stood in a corner, his expression serious; Felicia realised she rarely saw him sit when he was on duty.

'No Katherine?' José asked.

'She's got enough on her plate,' Felicia said. 'I want to reduce her stress, not add to it.' She turned to Alan. 'In no way am I questioning the work that you do – you're fantastic, and you almost caught the bastards last night. But you're only one man, and you can't be everywhere on site at the same time.'

'Could we get Brett to help out?' Alan referred to the college student who covered for him two nights a week. 'Not that I think he does much but hide in the office and do homework.'

'We can't afford to pay him for more hours, and he hasn't been here long enough that we can expect him to just volunteer.' She looked at all of them. 'It's up to us.'

'I'm already staying on site to watch over Noelle and the cubs,' José said. 'They need a couple more days' attention.'

'Which is the best thing you can be doing,' Felicia said. 'If Mel and I also stay on site tonight, we should be able to patrol effectively.'

'I'm in,' Mel said firmly, a determined look on her elfin face.

José nodded, looking like he was about to say something, but then didn't.

'I'm not offended – I appreciate the help,' Alan said. 'I've thought about calling in some favours, but I know you don't want word getting around that we have a problem.'

Felicia's jaw clenched. She took a deep breath and forced herself to relax before she gave herself another tension headache. 'It may be too late for that, but I appreciate the fact that you thought about it,' she said, and the security guard flushed, ducking his head to hide a shy smile. 'I want to keep things quiet – I don't want anyone else to know that we plan to stay tonight,' she said to the group. 'I hate to say it, but we don't know who we can trust.'

'Who there is trustworthy?' Tom asked.

Gabe scanned his surroundings before replying, making sure nobody was within hearing range. The tables in the centre of the Sanctuary green were perfect for keeping an eye on a fair radius, but not at all private, except for the fact that nobody could sneak up on him.

Christ. He sounded like a paranoid spy. A spy up to his eyeballs in shit – literally.

'I don't know,' he admitted. 'I haven't been here long enough to do psych profiles on the entire staff, OK? Most of them seem to be on the up and up and to really care about the place, but anybody could be a good enough actor when I'm around.'

He'd seen a semi-furtive enclave gather in the vet clinic. At this point, as much as he wanted to believe the people inside were the good guys, he had no proof either way. They could be plotting. They could be having an orgy, for all he knew.

He forced his mind away from that before his body joined the mental party. 'All I know is that there's been vandalism, and they don't have enough security to keep an eye on the whole place. Under normal circumstances, one or two people would be enough, but not now. Too much shit has been happening to be random, Tom.'

'It's not your job to play Superman,' Tom said.

Gabe rubbed a hand over his face, surprised to feel his palm rasp across more than a five-o'clock shadow. Had he shaved that morning? He couldn't even remember. Oh well. Women liked a roguish stubble, didn't they?

'I care about this place, too, Tom,' he admitted. 'Even if it's not going to make it, it needs to be protected from vandals. I don't want anything happening to the cats or to innocent staff members.'

Was Felicia part of that latter group? The question invaded his mind, not for the first time. She'd been secretive, evasive. Maybe it was just stress, or maybe it was just that he was considered The Enemy and she wasn't going to admit problems with the Sanctuary unless she was forced to.

He might find out the answer tonight.

'Don't get hurt,' Tom said. 'And don't get arrested.'

'You'll bail me out if I do, though.'

The vet clinic door opened, so Gabe ended the call, promising to call Tom again if anything major happened.

Now, all he had to do was find a way to get back in the facility after he made it obvious that he was leaving.

Katherine took them all out to dinner at a local Mexican restaurant where they often met after work for margaritas and chips and salsa. It made Felicia feel a little guilty for not telling her boss about their plan to stay on site, but she still felt it was for the best. If something went wrong, the blame wouldn't fall on Katherine.

'You've all been working so hard, such long hours,' Katherine said, forestalling their protests at her paying for everything. 'Overtime, coming in on your days off and today was really above and beyond the call of duty. I wanted to thank you all for that.'

The restaurant was crowded, unsurprising for a Saturday night. They were seated at a table in a far corner of the patio. Felicia realised they probably all reeked of sewer filth, even though they'd washed up before leaving the Sanctuary. Oh well, at least they were all in it together, so to speak.

Felicia sat as far away from Gabe as possible, not trusting her body's reaction if she sat next to him or across from him, with the possibility of their thighs brushing together again, of their hands bumping when they both reached to scoop salsa with a warm tortilla chip. But with only six of them, including John from maintenance, 'far away' just meant they were at opposite corners of a small rectangular table, and she was still keenly aware of his presence.

He asked Katherine some probing questions about how people might be sneaking into the facility, whether more security might be needed, or at least a change in the way the area was patrolled – and what was that exactly? His questions seemed constructive, but they put Felicia on edge. What did he really want? And, worse, could he be responsible for the latest crises plaguing the Sanctuary?

Magnolia had escaped from her cage the night before Gabe had shown up on site (but he would have flown in the day before, so he was already in the area), and the rest of the vandalism and strange occurrences had happened since. He'd admitted to the temptation of causing problems at facilities that he couldn't substantively prove should be shut down.

She didn't want to believe he was involved. But she couldn't shake the nagging suspicion prompted by his questions. Anybody she didn't know well loomed as a suspect in her mind.

'I really need a shower,' Gabe said as they wandered out to the parking lot, pleasantly full and tired after a day of hard work and an evening of burritos and tacos. 'I'll see you all tomorrow.'

'I'll drop you off so you can pick up your car,' José said to Mel, a plausible excuse because they had driven to the restaurant together.

Felicia offered to deliver the take-out they'd ordered for Alan, who'd obviously stayed on site. Katherine didn't seem to notice anything amiss, and Felicia sighed with relief as she watched her boss's car's tail lights grow smaller in her rear-view mirror.

The Sanctuary was quiet and mostly dark when she got there. Only Alan's truck was in the parking lot. The plan was that José and Mel would enter via the service entrance in the back, leaving their cars a few blocks away.

Felicia slipped inside, resetting the alarm for the front door and windows of the administrative building, and ducked into the ladies' room. She'd worn black jeans, and now she changed from her grubby T-shirt into a black long-sleeved knit top. She braided her hair back, relieved that the foul smell was no longer near her face.

Speaking of which ... She reviewed herself in the mirror. Her pale face was going to bob around like a disembodied ghostly head when she got outside. She had camo makeup somewhere in her apartment, bought on sale after Halloween and used once during sex games with a former boyfriend who had a minor

Navy SEAL fetish. She'd decided against going home and getting the makeup now, though. If something did go horribly wrong and the police showed up, she'd look even guiltier with her face smeared with olive green and tan paint, looking like a terrorist.

She sighed. Her muscles ached and she was exhausted. What she wouldn't give to go home and soak in a long, hot, jasmine-scented bath. Gabe's comment about a shower had really killed her and not just because a shower sounded like the most amazingly wonderful thing in the world right now.

But no. They had vandals to catch, and a Sanctuary to save. Super sleuths didn't have the luxury of long, hot, jasmine-scented baths (or long, lovingly detailed erotic fantasies) until the Bad Guys were behind bars.

'Here I come, to save the day,' she sang under her breath, and headed into the night.

She delivered Alan's supper to him. The security guard had just done a complete circle of the area and found nothing amiss.

'The cats are restless,' she said unnecessarily, for he'd just been outside himself. 'Something's upsetting them.'

Pancho Villa, the oft-vocal panther, had started the noise, a low growl that you could feel in your bones, occasionally punctuated by a louder roar that made your teeth rattle. Pancho's sounds were echoed by Brutus and Estella. It truly was a heart-stopping noise, especially at night when there was less of a sense that a sturdy enclosure separated you from the stunningly beautiful, but no less powerful and dangerous, panthers.

Then, Felicia had passed by the cheetah enclosure and Caramel had been pacing. That itself wasn't unusual. What was disturbing was when the cat stopped pacing and stared past Felicia with a frightening intensity she usually reserved for small crawling children who might turn out to be a tasty snack if only they would come just a little closer, oh please oh please. Felicia had looked over her shoulder, but hadn't seen anything. Caramel had excellent eyesight, so all it meant was that she was seeing something Felicia couldn't.

'They know when something's not right,' he said, unwrapping the foil from one end of the burrito. 'I don't think anyone's out there – at least, not yet – but they know things haven't been right for a while.'

'I meant to ask you,' Felicia said. 'What happened to the wire cutters you found?'

He swallowed his mouthful of tortilla, beef, rice and beans, and said, 'I gave 'em to a buddy of mine to dust for prints. He owed me a favour, and didn't ask any questions. Don't know how soon we'll hear back, though.'

'You rock, Alan,' she said, and stood. 'I have to check in with the others. You'll be back on patrol soon?'

He glanced at the clock. 'Inside of fifteen,' he said.

Gabe turned off his rental car headlights, and coasted slowly into the Sanctuary's parking lot. A lone street-lamp by the entrance walkway dimly illuminated two cars in the lot. He recognised the Cabriolet as Felicia's; the truck probably belonged to Alan.

He drove out of the lot and parked around the corner within sight of the parking lot exit, and waited. After about half an hour, he was convinced Felicia wasn't coming back out. There were any number of things she could be doing in there. And he was going to find out just what she was up to.

He left the car and hiked around to the back side of the facility. One of his tasks here had been to evaluate the security system, and he knew the service entrance wasn't alarmed, because too many deliveries were made after hours. Besides, if someone wanted to steal something, they were more likely to try and break in through the front, where the computers and cash register were, rather than deal with the hassles of getting through the loading dock.

Despite the lack of alarm, the service door was solid metal and heavily locked.

He paused, listening. He heard some of the big cats grumbling. He sympathised; he could feel the tension in the air, too.

He reached into the inner pocket of his jacket and withdrew several long thin metal rods. There were times when his chequered past came in handy.

The lock was a tough one, but he was a patient man. His large hands were surprisingly nimble – something more than one satisfied bed partner had commented on.

Finally, he felt the tumblers shift deep inside the lock. He eased the door open and slipped inside. The room was dark, and he turned on a penlight, holding it between his teeth while he ensured the door was firmly locked behind him.

He took a quick survey of the cavernous, warehouse-like room. Cement floors, metal walls. Metal roll-up door for large deliveries, locked firmly in place. Van for transporting big cats or bulky supplies. A couple of transport cages, broken down flat for storage. Metal shelving along one wall, half-full of boxes.

His footsteps echoed as he crossed the area and slipped into the attached storage room. From there he exited on to the Sanctuary grounds, turning off his flashlight. The storage-room door came out near a long building that ran along the back of a row of cages. You could go inside that building and access each cage, via a door into the cage itself. From the reinforced door that went into the long building hung an industrial padlock. He grasped it and pulled. Solidly locked. Good.

Just to be on the safe side, he was going to check every damn last one of them.

'See anything out of the ordinary?' José asked. They'd agreed to meet in the vet clinic at hourly intervals to check in with each other, and it was time.

Felicia shrugged. 'Nothing much. The cats are cranky, though.'

'They're not used to so many people here after – what was that?'

It had sounded like a clank, and then something or someone moving.

'Maybe it was Alan.' Mel didn't sound convinced. 'But I don't think so.'

'Mel, you stay here and be the point person,' José said, grabbing a Maglite. Felicia pulled her own flashlight out of her pocket. 'Where do you think you're going?' he asked. 'You should stay here, too.'

'Don't be ridiculous, and don't treat me like some simpering weakling,' she said. 'This was my idea, and I'm not going to be any help if I hide in here.'

He muttered under his breath in his native tongue.

'Yes, I'm stubborn, but I'm offended by that last part,' Felicia said, smirking as his jaw dropped and his dark skin flushed. In fluent Spanish, she told him not to be a chauvinistic pig.

Ignoring Felicia, José gave Mel a quick kiss, then reached for the door.

'Oh, fine, she gets a kiss, and all I get is an insult,' Felicia muttered, not really angry.

A small hand grabbed her forearm and tugged. She turned. Mel stood on tiptoes and planted a big wet one on her lips. 'Better?' Mel asked, fighting off a grin.

'Definitely,' Felicia said.

'Lock the door behind us,' José said.

Outside was a curious mix of silence and noise. They were far enough outside of town that they didn't catch the usual traffic noises; but the restless cats were drowning out the normal subtle desert noises, such as the scurry of small animals as they bedded down for the night.

It was a typical clear desert night, the stars shimmering in the clear air. Predictably, the temperature had dropped when the sun disappeared, and Felicia was glad she'd worn a long-sleeved shirt.

Felicia leant in close to José. He smelt of cat and antiseptic and sewer. Not exactly an erotic combination, although being near him still sent a sexual shiver through her. She *still* wasn't satisfied, dammit, despite the recent boost to her sex life. Sex with José and Mel had been full of orgasmic fun, but . . .

Dear lord, were Gabe's pheromones throwing her off whack? It would be just her luck that she'd be responding to the one man who stood to ruin her livelihood.

Her mouth a hair's breadth away from José's ear, Felicia whispered, 'You take the tiger enclosure; I'll loop past the main building and head towards the fishing cats.'

He nodded and moved away, blending into the darkness.

Felicia held the flashlight loosely in her hand. She kept it turned off, but ready to flick on at a moment's notice if she came upon anything suspicious. She knew the Sanctuary well enough to get around by the dim light of the three-quarter moon.

Something moved in the new plants, rustling the leaves, and her heart leapt. Cautiously, she directed her flashlight in that direction, suddenly aware of how feeble and ineffectual the beam of light seemed.

She smothered the laugh that threatened to burble forth out of the misplaced nervousness. One of the Sanctuary's three peacocks glared at her from the underbrush. After giving her one last haughty look, it stalked away, its sweeping tail trailing behind it.

She continued along, turning on the flashlight every so often to check for signs that someone had been there. Their primary goal was to catch the perpetrator(s) in the act, although scaring them away for good was a fine secondary goal.

She just prayed they did find out who was responsible, and that that person didn't turn out to be Gabe.

Lance huddled against the wall behind the cougar enclosure. He drew his hoodie farther over his head. Shit, it was cold. He'd declined going out to dinner with everyone, saying he had to get home. He'd helped Alan out with some last-minute clean-up of shovels and buckets, and then told him he was leaving just as the security guard was headed to the bathroom for his evening constitutional. Alan had said he'd lock up after Lance left.

Lance had simply unlocked the door, then circled back around and hidden in the narrow space between the main building and the supply shed until darkness fell.

He was still wearing the low-rider long jean shorts that had made a lot of sense when he was working out in the hot sun all day. Now, his bare legs pimpled with gooseflesh.

He hated sitting around. He hated waiting.

If Just and Dog didn't show up, he was going to kill them.

Gabe saw light streaming from the vet clinic window. Cautiously, he peered inside, expecting to see José. To his surprise, the petite Asian animal handler, Mel, was pacing the room, tapping her fingers on the metal examining table as she went by it.

He waited, feeling uncomfortably like a Peeping Tom, but José didn't emerge from the back room or the small bathroom. He frowned. If José had left Mel in charge of the newborn cubs for the whole night, he was in serious breach of protocol.

It was possible José was checking on the cubs himself, though, and Mel was hanging around for another reason. And of course she was probably the most knowledgeable person to leave in charge of the cubs if José had to step away for a short while. Gabe eased away from the window and continued his own surreptitious circuit of the Sanctuary.

Felicia crept behind the row of cages that housed the North American cats. Her stomach clenched and churned. Maybe Mexican food with a side order of nerves hadn't been the best choice.

A noise. She froze, heart in her throat. This one wasn't random – it was rhythmic. Someone walking.

She made a low noise like a night hawk, the pre-arranged signal.

No response.

Damn. She slid her flashlight on, masking the beam with her palm. Then, in one move, she turned the corner and started to raise the light. But before she could bring it all the way up, she slammed – hard – into someone.

A hand clapped over her mouth before she could draw the breath to scream. An arm wrapped around her, pinning her own arms to her sides, and her flashlight fell, thudding into the dirt beside the pathway.

Before full terror took hold, she saw her attacker's face in the moon's dim glow. It was Gabe.

She didn't know whether to be relieved or distraught. He shouldn't be here. But at least he wasn't a mad axe murderer.

She relaxed, just slightly, but enough that he took his hand from her mouth (and it was a good thing he did, too, because otherwise she would have bitten him), but he didn't let her go.

'Jesus, you nearly gave me a heart attack!' he growled.

'What the hell are you doing here?' she demanded.

'I could ask you the same thing. Development co-ordinators' job descriptions don't include skulking.'

'You'd be surprised at the lengths we have to go to,' Felicia muttered.

He didn't respond and, in the space of a heartbeat that pulsed deep in her groin, she realised why. She was pressed full-length against him: breasts to chest, thighs to thighs ... and soft belly to hard cock.

'Fuck,' he said.

She was entirely prepared to say 'OK' when his mouth came down on hers.

11

'Lance, my man! Wasn't sure you'd be here.' Just clapped Lance on the shoulder.

'How'd you get in?' Lance asked. 'This place is usually locked up tighter than a drum.' He knew, because he'd done the rounds with Alan before – plus now, they were being extra careful.

Both of his friends were dressed in all black, with black knit caps pulled low on their heads, Dog's also covered by a hoodie. Still, they walked and talked as if they owned the place; Lance wouldn't have been surprised if someone heard or saw them.

'That service gate, the one for machinery,' Dog said. 'We complained about not bein' able to get in last night, and the guy who hired us said he'd get us in. He called and told us where to go.'

Lance knew the gate in question. It was rarely used, but they'd opened it this morning for the backhoe to get through. He would swear Alan had locked it back up afterwards, though. But Dog seemed to be implying that whoever hired them had made sure the gate would be unlocked. Who had access? Who would hire them? Alan? José? Gabe?

'Who is this guy?' he asked.

'Like we're going to tell you,' Just said. 'Are you in or out?'

'He's in,' Dog said. 'Why else would he be here?'

'Yeah, why else?' Lance felt both relieved and guilty that Dog put such faith in him. Now he didn't have to answer the question. 'So, what's it gonna be? Tagging? Breaking stuff?'

A pair of cat eyes glittered as the pale moonlight caught them, giving Lance the sense that they were being watched, not just by those eyes, but by many, many more that they couldn't see.

'I dunno,' Just said thoughtfully, looking around. 'I'm bored. I'm thinkin' maybe we'll do something more fun.'

Pure bliss. Sensory overload. Like the finest chocolate in the world melting on her tongue while silk caressed her naked body and the sweetest symphony serenaded her ears.

She wanted more. Wanted – and needed. Felicia's breasts peaked, begging to be touched, squeezed, suckled. As if in response to her silent plea, Gabe skimmed his hands along her waist up her ribcage, to rest tantalisingly beneath her breasts. Slowly, maddeningly, he slid up and brushed his thumbs across her nipples. Even through a layer of shirt and another of bra, the sensation flashed through her, from nipples to groin. She gasped and instinctively pressed harder against him, and the movement of her hips ignited him.

The exquisite kisses, the sharp probe of his tongue, made her crave the feel of his mouth elsewhere, everywhere. Brushing across bare skin. Nibbling at her breasts. Licking insistently between her legs, where she was already wet and aching. Spreading her lower lips and flicking across her swollen clit.

She cupped her hands around his firm ass and pulled him even closer. He pulled back, then ducked his head to put his mouth where his fingers had been. Through her clothes, she felt the warm pull, the scrape of teeth, and then an aching chill as the moisture that wet the cloth hit the cool night air.

He tugged the hem of her shirt out of her trousers. Yes! Warm, strong hands on bare flesh, finally. She didn't care where they were. She only knew that she needed him. She reached for his belt buckle.

And froze.

'What was that?' she asked.

'What was what?' His voice sounded thick, distant.

She thought she'd heard something through the throbbing in her ears. Reluctantly, she swam up through the drugging layers of lust. As she neared the surface, a thought struck her so hard that she sobered, suddenly and immediately.

'Stop it,' she said, stepping back. Even though she knew it was for the best, her body felt bereft as his hands left her.

'I thought you wanted –'

'Are you just trying to distract me?' she asked, tugging her shirt down.

'What are you talking about?'

She found her flashlight, picked it up (aware all the time that he watched her bend over) and pointed it at him. 'You're not supposed to be on site,' she said. 'Are you distracting me while someone else tears things up? Or just trying to make me forget you shouldn't be here?'

'I could ask you the same thing,' he said. 'I saw you plotting with José and Mel.'

Felicia sputtered. 'What the hell would we be doing? We love this place! That's why we're here.'

He didn't have time to answer her. Shouts punctuated the night air, one sounding panicked.

They both took off at a run.

Lance tried to talk Just out of it, to no avail. Just swore he wasn't going to hurt the cheetah, just mess up the cage a little. For the high. To show that he couldn't just get in the facility, but he could also get into one of the cages.

Dog, being taller, gave Just a leg up. Just grabbed the chain link wall and hauled himself up further.

This was bad. Very bad. Lance didn't stop to think. He jumped and started to climb the wall himself, with the half-formed intent of pulling Just back down. The chain link rattled, and Caramel snarled.

He didn't have the boost Just had had, and Just's climbing motion made the cage wall shake, forcing Lance to hold on tighter and consider his moves carefully. So Just made it to the top first and swung a leg over.

Either Just's plans were less formed than Lance's, or Just simply hadn't realised that the covering at the top of the cage was just an open-weave mesh stretched loosely across. The cats couldn't climb or jump that high, so there was no need for a solid top, just something to keep the birds and debris out. The Sanctuary's peacocks enjoyed perching up there and taunting the cats into a frenzy.

Just, of course, ripped the mesh away from the wall. His leg plunged through the opening, and he shouted in shock and fear. Dog yelled something incomprehensible, either a useless suggestion or belated warning.

Lance redoubled his efforts, catching Just's ankle before his friend toppled into the cage. Cheetahs might be some of the most human accepting of the big cats, relatively speaking, but that didn't mean Caramel wouldn't lash out in fear and anger if Just landed in her private space.

Just's foot was tangled in the mesh and, now that Lance had caught and steadied him, Lance hauled himself the rest of the way up and fumbled around until Just's Doc Marten was freed.

Shouts, and the bobbing beams of flashlights. From all directions. It looked like the cavalry had arrived.

Just dropped to the ground ungracefully, but managed not to fall over. He and Dog took off towards the back of the facility, where the service gate was. They didn't give Lance a second glance – leaving Lance, his hoodie snagged on an exposed piece of metal, literally hoisted by his own petard. At least, he thought that was what that phrase meant.

Gabe was taller, but Felicia had the benefit of frequent gym visits, and she kept pace with him. She saw José approaching from a different direction. Behind them, she heard still more pounding footsteps. Felicia swung her flashlight in an arc, trying to find the source.

'North wall!' It was Alan, shouting and pointing. He'd been running, too, and was half-doubled over, gasping for air.

Gabe took off in the direction Alan indicated.

The cheetah enclosure rattled. Felicia swung around, pointing her flashlight. To her shock and dismay, Lance dropped to the ground from near the top of the wall.

Gabe ran into the night after one of the vandals. There was more than one of them – he could hear at least two other sets of running feet in the darkness near by, all headed in the same direction. He didn't take the time to look around, though. He was focused on the guy ahead of him.

The kid he was chasing had to be six three, six four, and most of that was leg. But that kid had been trying to hurt one of the cheetahs. Anger surged through Gabe, giving him a boost of added speed. Gradually, inexorably, he closed the gap.

Then the kid was stupid enough to look behind him.

It slowed him, just barely, but just enough. Gabe gathered his strength and leapt. He caught the tall kid around the waist, and they both went down, hard.

Gabe pulled on the waistband of the boy's jeans, trying to haul himself farther up the body. Unfortunately, the kid favoured the truly unpleasant fashion of low-rider jeans. Instead of giving Gabe the traction he needed, they slipped further down. A strip of white underwear flashed in the pale moonlight. Thank goodness he was wearing underwear, or it would have been a very different kind of moon.

The kid used the motion to his advantage, scrabbling in the dirt, squirming to evade Gabe's grasp. He twisted, and his knee caught Gabe squarely under the chin.

Stars replaced the moon as Gabe's head snapped back. He tasted the coppery scrape of blood and felt the flash of pain in his tongue. Dazed, he lost what little grip he had. The kid scrambled to his feet, hitched up his jeans and pelted away.

Gabe managed to get his hands beneath him and hauled himself up into a kneeling position, then upright on his knees. To his left, a flash of movement: the second boy, tailed by someone slight but lightning quick. The pursuer grabbed the boy's jacket. He stumbled and turned. The pursuer got the boy's arm twisted behind his back, but was too small to get an arm fully around his throat.

A moment later, the result was the same: a boy pounding away into the night and his pursuer bent at the waist, breathing heavily. And he heard a string of expletives in what sounded like ... Chinese?

'I got his hat, at least.' Waving the black knit cap, Mel straightened and flashed a wry pixie-grin.

'Are you two OK?' Felicia asked as Gabe and Mel approached out of the shadows.

'Nothing a hot soak with Epsom salts won't cure,' Mel answered.

'I told you to stay inside,' José said, a scowl creasing his handsome face.

'You did,' Mel agreed. 'But I saw what was happening, and came out to help. Don't worry, I locked the door, and Noelle is fine.'

'She was a firecracker!' Gabe said admiringly. 'She almost took him down – my money was on her.'

Felicia felt a tiny wave of jealousy. She comforted herself with the knowledge that she'd already had the opportunity to have sex with Mel, so there.

'You didn't tell me you knew self-defence,' José accused.

She shrugged. 'I did ROTC to pay for college,' she said. 'It was on my résumé. Don't tell me you hired me just for my looks?'

'It obviously didn't teach you to take orders,' José said.

Mel bristled but, before she could show José just what she thought of his orders, Felicia intervened. 'We have more important things to worry about,' she said. 'One of the cats could have been seriously hurt tonight – or one of the trespassers.'

'How did they get in?' Mel asked.

'The gate on the back fence, the one for service vehicles,' Alan said, returning to the group. He'd followed Gabe at a slower pace, and explained that he'd secured the gate after the boys had got away. 'I *know* I locked it after the city guy drove the backhoe in.'

'Someone else opened it again for them,' Lance said. He leant on the fence, rubbing his shoulder. He sounded resigned.

'You?' José asked. '*You* opened it for them?'

Lance shook his head. 'It wasn't me, man. I didn't know how they planned to get in.'

'But you knew they were coming.' Felicia pounced on his wording.

Lance sighed. In the flashlights' glow, he looked younger and yet somehow older, too, a world-weariness weighing on him.

'They came by earlier today and asked me if I wanted in on a job that paid really well,' he said. 'It was the stupid shit we used to pull – just busting things up, trashing stuff.'

'Someone was paying them?' Alan said. 'Who?'

'They wouldn't spill. I told them ... I said I'd think about it. It was stupid, and I didn't want to, but, fuck, man, the money! I coulda really used that much cash.'

Felicia let his bad language slide – there were more important things to worry about. 'What did you need the money for?'

He ducked his head, but not fast enough for her to miss the fact that his eyes slid towards Mel. 'Just ... stuff.'

'Drugs?' Gabe asked.

'No way! I don't do that shit any more.'

'I believe you,' Mel said, obviously having seen his shy look, too. 'Just start from the beginning and tell us what happened.'

He relayed the conversation he'd had with his friends earlier that day, and then tonight, explaining that, before they'd even arrived, he knew he needed to stop them, talk them out of it somehow, or at least try to minimise the damage they did. When they'd gone for the cheetah enclosure, his decision had been solidified.

'Just is an idiot,' he said. 'I should've let Caramel chew on him.'

Gabe rubbed his aching chin. 'I'm with you on that one,' he said.

'Are you OK?' Felicia asked.

'Insofar as the kid's knee and my chin have been intimate.'

She directed her flashlight beam at his face, and saw the spreading bruise. 'I'll get you something for that.'

'We'll meet you in the clinic,' José said. 'No sense standing out here in the cold.'

There was a First Aid kit in the main building, and ice packs in the fridge, but the café was closer. Felicia unlocked it and stepped inside, intending to grab a steak from the walk-in fridge. But, as she opened the door, she remembered the ice maker.

The fridge didn't seem as cold as usual, but she chalked it up to the desert night air that held a hint of chill even now at the height of summer. Wrapping some ice in a dish towel, she hurried back across to the clinic, pausing briefly at Caramel's cage, where the cheetah was sulking on top of her plywood 'cave'. Most of the cats had fallen silent, apart from the occasional grumble. The immediate danger was over.

She handed the ice to Gabe and hopped up on the examining table next to Mel. Someone had turned on the small coffee maker, and the smell itself warmed her.

'Why didn't you tell anyone what your friends were planning?' Alan was asking Lance.

Lance shrugged. 'I dunno. I guess I didn't want them to get into trouble. We go way back, you know? I thought maybe I could talk them out of being too stupid.'

'It's a good thing you were here,' Mel said soothingly. 'You prevented Caramel from getting hurt. But you should have told somebody.'

Felicia glanced around the room at the various men. José glowered, his male pride no doubt still bruised. Alan had his cop face on, assessing the situation without showing his thoughts or emotions. Gabe, the towel pressed to his jaw, looked thoughtful.

Felicia felt a wave of relief. Gabe hadn't been involved with the vandalism. He wouldn't have known to pay Lance's friends; if he'd wanted to hire someone, he would've gone straight to Lance himself.

'Well, I'm telling you now,' Lance said defensively, a hint of his former bad-boy self sneaking through.

'Why don't you tell us your friends' names?' Alan asked. To Felicia, he added, 'Maybe now is the time to go to the police.'

'I'm still not convinced,' Felicia said slowly. 'If Lance agrees to be a witness and identify his friends, the best we're going to do is get two vandals arrested. There's no guarantee they'll reveal who paid them – and *that* person is our real problem.'

'It confirms that nothing that's gone wrong recently has been random,' Gabe said. 'Now it's a matter of figuring out just how much this person has been involved and, most importantly, who the hell it is.'

'And why,' Alan added.

'Lance, do you think you can get your friends to tell you who paid them?' Mel asked. 'You could play the "I saved your life" card.'

'I'll try,' Lance said.

Felicia stifled a giggle. If she wasn't mistaken, his statement had an unspoken 'for you' following it. Their resident bad boy had a crush on Mel. Felicia didn't blame him. She knew firsthand just how hot Mel was.

But José was shaking his head. 'I don't know,' he said. 'How do we know Lance wasn't involved? If we let him go, he'll go running to his friends and they'll all tell whoever's at the heart of this – or maybe there isn't anybody else, and that's just their story to avoid getting into real trouble.'

Lance frowned, his expression darkening. He looked like he was going to get up and stalk out of the clinic.

Quickly, Felicia said, 'It makes sense that someone else is involved. Too much weirdness has been going on and, like Gabe said, it's not a surprise that it's all related. And, quite frankly, if Lance was involved, why would he be sitting in here with us?'

'How about this?' Alan suggested. 'You give me the names of your friends, and I'll have them checked out. Quietly, of course,' he added to Felicia. 'No official police involvement.'

'How many favours do you have left to call in?' Felicia asked.

He grinned, the expression changing his face from homely to endearing. 'Enough. I think I can find a couple of guys to swing by the boys' homes once in a while. Seeing the black-and-whites a few times might make 'em think twice about wandering out here.'

'Can't hurt,' Lance said. 'They'll do some stupid shit for money, but it won't be worth prison to them.'

'What about right now?' Mel asked.

'They won't be back again tonight,' Alan predicted. 'They know we've seen them. They'll lie low for a few days at least.'

'Just in case, I can patrol around this end of the site,' José said. 'Noelle doesn't need me here every second.'

'I can handle the rest of the rounds as usual,' Alan said.

'Sounds like we're in agreement, then,' Felicia said, sliding off the table. 'Now, how about a round of coffee before we head out?'

To her surprise, Lance followed her to the coffee maker and helped her prepare the drinks in a variety of mismatched mugs and a few Styrofoam cups.

'Thank you,' he said quietly.

'The best way you can thank me is by staying clean,' she said. 'Don't lie to any of us.'

He nodded, but his gaze was already across the room. Felicia bit back another smile. She wasn't sure if she should say something about his obvious crush, not wanting to dash his hopes. But then Mel looked up and flashed him a big smile, and Felicia decided that it was between Mel and Lance, and none of her business.

The group fell mostly silent while they sipped their coffee, the adrenalin having drained away now that the worst of the danger was over. Felicia was aware of just how bone-weary she was. It had been a long day of physical exertion followed by a night of unwanted excitement.

'I'd love to stay and chat, but a hot shower and my bed are better company right now,' she said, tossing her cup in the trash. 'I'll see you all tomorrow. Alan, José, be careful tonight.'

To her surprise, Gabe followed her outside. He wrapped a hand around her upper arm, not tightly, but with a caressing motion that she felt through her sweater to her nipples. 'No,' he said in a voice that brooked no argument, a voice that sent erotic thrills down her spine. 'You're coming back with me.'

12

This time, Felicia got to see the inside of Gabe's hotel room. To her surprise, it was a full suite, with a canopied king-sized bed, separate sitting area with comfortable chairs and a kitchenette, and what, at her quick glance, looked to be an extra-large bathroom. Everything was in shades of deep burgundy and gold, the bed canopy and swagged curtains a rich brocade. The art on the walls, rather than being generic hotel art, were prints of Italian Renaissance cities.

She commented, and he said, 'They were overbooked when I got here, so they gave me the honeymoon suite. And, since the Addison Radisson doesn't seem to be a big draw for honeymooners, they haven't kicked me out of it yet.'

'Handy, that,' she murmured, and was rewarded with another of his smouldering looks.

'I hadn't thought of it that way ... until now.'

Felicia dropped her bag on the long, low, pale wooden dresser and reached up to release her hair from its ponytail. As her hair tumbled around her face, she choked at the smell. *Shit*. Literally.

Gabe moved towards her, and she instinctively took a step back.

'Not changing your mind, are you?'

Good lord, no! If he didn't touch her soon, she'd implode. But she was still a woman, and vanity held sway. 'No, no! It's just –' Hell. She took a deep breath and plunged in. 'I haven't really cleaned up since this afternoon, and I'm – my hair is – kind of, um, smelly.'

His smile was wicked, but she wasn't prepared for what happened next. He moved faster than she anticipated, and all she could manage was a squeak of aroused surprise when he hoisted her into his arms.

'That's easy enough to fix,' he said. He nuzzled the sensitive spot between her neck and shoulder, the rasp of his five o'clock shadow making her catch her breath.

She closed her eyes, swimming on the sensation, and, when he set her down again, they were in the bathroom. He could distract her to the point that she didn't even know what room she was in. Impressive.

'I've already had fantasies about you in this shower,' he said between light, nibbling kisses. Then he broke away to turn on the water in the large glass-fronted shower. It was obviously built for two, with a shower head on each side and a tiled seat along one end.

In the time it took for him to adjust the temperature, she'd stripped out of her clothes. When he turned back, she was naked.

His eyes darkened, from slate blue to nearly black. His gaze travelled the length of her, down and then slowly up again, and she shivered, feeling it as keenly as if it were his hands traversing her bare flesh.

'You,' he said, 'are exquisite.' His gaze never leaving hers, he, too, began to strip.

She played his game, locking eyes with him, exchanging all the lustful thoughts they'd both been thinking over the past week. Only when he was also nude did she break his stare and admire him.

He was just as she'd imagined him that very first day: the dusting of hair on his chest was gold-tipped, mirroring the hair on his head. And his cock. Well. Oh my. Half-hard already, cut, thick at the base and tapering to the smooth mushroom-cap head. All she could think about was having it deep inside her.

After some long, excruciatingly exciting foreplay, that was.

In two steps she was right in front of him, and she could finally indulge in the fantasy she'd had when she first met him. Splaying her fingers, she slowly ran her hands up his chest, through the hair, and tugged gently on it. He didn't move. He just watched her, waiting to see what she would do next. She brushed her palms over his nipples, and was rewarded by his indrawn breath and the involuntary twitch of his hips. Oh good.

'I suggest,' he said, 'that you get your gorgeous ass into the shower, because in a minute I'm not going to be willing to wait for the shower, and the floor tiles are probably very cold.'

The shower was the perfect temperature and, after the sweaty stinky day and the chilly evening, Felicia couldn't stifle a moan of pure delight as the hot water cascaded down.

'Wow, and I've barely touched you yet,' Gabe said, shutting the glass door behind him.

'You're that good, obviously,' Felicia said, pulling him towards her.

Once again, they were pressed against each other, only this time there was no barrier of clothes between them and no frustrating stake-out to get back to. His chest hair grazed her nipples as he moved, running his tongue along her neck to swipe up water. She tossed her head back, letting the shower spray soak her hair and face as if she were under a waterfall. He took that as an invitation to work his way down to her breasts.

Felicia pressed one hand against the shower wall and grabbed a towel bar with the other, not trusting her legs to keep her upright. He pressed her breasts together and suckled both nipples at the same time, grazing the tender areolas with his facial hair. Her skin was so sensitised already that the water running down her body felt as if he touched her everywhere.

Her groping hands found a bar of blue-green soap with a scent like a fresh sea breeze. She lathered up her hands, then rubbed them along his shoulders and back.

In response, he released her breasts and grabbed a bottle of shampoo. 'Turn around,' he said.

Before she did, she couldn't resist running her soapy hands along the length of his now-hard cock, delighting in its weight and heat and the small noises he made.

He lathered up her hair with a shampoo that smelt of citrus and herbs, giving her a scalp massage at the same time, and even that felt damn good. She pressed back against him, and his soapy cock snuggled into the crack of her ass, rubbing against her tailbone. He responded by sliding up and down against her. Abandoning her hair, he reached for her nipples again, pinching and teasing as she ground back against him.

They broke apart long enough for her to rinse her hair before the shampoo dripped into her eyes. By the time she was done, he'd lathered up his hands with the ocean-scented soap and was sliding his hands here, there, everywhere, slipping across her sensitised flesh. Toying with her nipples. Dipping along her ass, teasing just a little farther down. Dropping to his knees, he encircled her legs and massaged them, starting at her ankles and ending at the juncture of her thighs, first one, then the other.

Excruciating. His touch was driving her wild, but he was touching everywhere except where she really wanted him to, where she *needed* him to.

He stood, just briefly, to unhook one of the shower heads and bring the nozzle back down with him, to sluice the soap off her legs.

Unable to bear it any longer, she rested one foot on the tiled bench, giving him access to her core. He ran a finger lightly over her pussy lips. 'You're drenched,' he said, 'and not just from the water.'

If he didn't touch her there soon, she was going to have to take matters into her own hands. She expected his fingers, or perhaps his mouth. She didn't expect him to raise the nozzle, directing the spray up the inside of her thigh, all the way up until the steady stream of water flowed over her needy clit. Then he adjusted the stream, so it pulsed rhythmically, urging her higher, closer.

Spirals of passion formed in her clit, radiating outwards. So close . . .

'Not yet,' he said, and she would have screamed if he hadn't added, 'The first time is on my tongue.' He dropped the nozzle and found her clit with his mouth, at the same time sliding a finger into her dark wetness. His tongue flicked across her swollen bud, again and again, and then she did scream as the orgasm melted her insides.

He stood, still keeping his hand against her, the finger inside her and his thumb against her clit urging her to another climax.

She reached blindly for his cock, wanting to return the favour, but he pulled her over to the bench and sat down.

'Turn around,' he said again.

She complied, easing her legs apart to straddle him, facing backwards, at the gentle insistence of his hands on her thighs.

'The very first day I met you, you bent over to pick something up, and all I could think about was doing this,' he said.

She tried to say 'yoga', but all that came out was a strangled gasp as he eased her down along the solid length of him. She guessed what he wanted. She bent forwards at the waist until her palms rested on the shower floor. Despite the yoga classes, she could feel the stretch in her thighs, the slight tension adding its own edge to her arousal.

'God, you're so limber,' he murmured.

Grasping her hips, he guided her up and down again, slowly. When he was buried in her, she couldn't resist a little hip twitch, grinding down. He groaned her name. Her thighs were still rubbery from the several orgasms, but she did her best, rising and falling on his cock, revelling in the sensation as she moved over it. One of his hands reached around, applying just the right amount of pressure to her clit.

'What an incredible view,' he panted. 'You have a stunning ass. I can see your pussy lips dragging along my penis, then swallowing me back inside. My God, Felicia.'

She barely heard him. Her head swam, not just from her upside-down position, but also from the rumbling approach of another orgasm from deep inside her. As relentless as a bullet train, it loomed, advancing, until she cried out again, grinding and bucking against the length of him inside her. A moment later, she felt him achieve his release.

He helped her up and they caught their breath, surrounded by the steam and pounding water. They spent a few minutes cleaning up again, and then patted each other dry with fluffy white towels, paying special attention to the most sensitive areas.

After leaving the towels on the bathroom floor, they collapsed on the bed.

'Hungry?' Gabe asked.

'Good lord, no, not after that Mexican food.'

'Thirsty?'

'What've you got?' she said.

He got up and opened the mini-fridge. 'Champagne,' he said, holding up a split bottle.

'Sold.'

They clinked glasses before drinking. 'Here's to a successful night of skulking,' Gabe said.

Felicia allowed herself a moment to savour the delicious bubbles. 'It certainly was an adventure.' She narrowed her eyes. 'How did you get into the Sanctuary, anyway?'

She wanted to be stern, wanted to be concerned, but his cheeky grin stripped away her reserve.

'I picked the lock on the service entrance door,' he admitted. 'A skill retained from my ill-spent youth. I did lock it behind me, though.'

The earnestness of his statement made her laugh. 'Did you know that Lance was planning something?' she asked.

He shook his head. 'I suspected something might happen, but I didn't know who. Just figured I'd be there to find out. What about you?'

'Same thing. We knew Alan needed back-up, but we couldn't afford to hire anyone, so José, Mel and I decided to stay on site and help.'

'Did you think I was involved?'

His quiet but direct question gave her pause. But she believed in ruthless truthfulness, and now was probably the best time to lay it all out. 'You were on my list,' she said. 'Things started happening just around the time you showed up.'

'Tell me everything that's happened that's been suspicious,' he said.

Naked, he walked across the room and grabbed his laptop. She lounged on the bed and ogled his butt, not even processing his question until he was back on the bed and the laptop was open.

She listed everything she could think of, from the ocelot cage being left open to the sewage leak to the vandalism, throwing in a few things that might or might not have been involved, such as the mysterious sprinkler problems.

'So much of it could have other explanations,' she said, running a frustrated hand through her half-dry hair. 'We had a passel of kids on site when the fire alarm went off. The sprinklers were just old. The sewage leak – well, there were kids on site that day too.'

'Anything else suspicious besides things breaking or going wrong?'

'Well, the donors have been kind of flaky recently; it's been an uphill battle to sell tickets to the fundraiser or get donations. But they could be reacting to what's been going wrong.'

'I thought you were trying to keep everything under wraps,' he pointed out.

'As much as we can, yes.' She sighed. 'Word still leaks out – the press catches wind of things here and there. Rumours start. It doesn't have to be anything specific. People sometimes just pick up on the vibes.'

'Now *that* sounds Californian, sweetheart,' he teased. 'Gonna read my aura next?'

Felicia had the pillow in her hand before he could react, smacking him on the head. He looked affronted. Carefully, he closed the laptop and set it on the night table. She was just starting to wonder if she'd overstepped her bounds when a pillow that had fallen off the bed at some point came flying at her.

She shrieked and pummelled him again, and he caught her arm, and they tussled. Very quickly, however, the tussling turned to a different kind of play and, very soon after that, her shrieks turned into cries of passion.

Alan set down his coffee cup, sighed like the weight of the world (or at least SCCS) was on his shoulders and said, 'Time to do another round. See you all later.' The vet-clinic door clanged heavily shut behind him.

'I'll do a round in this area in a minute,' José said.

Once the ex-cop was gone, he glanced at Mel. 'Hey, do you want to walk with me?' he asked in a tone of voice that, to Mel, clearly translated as: 'Hey, do you want to see if we can find a little privacy?'

She managed a tired ghost of a smile. 'I'm pretty beat. I'll see you tomorrow. Or later today – I'm pretty sure it's after midnight.'

To her own ears, her voice sounded a little strained from the effort of *not* sounding unreasonably pissy, but apparently José didn't notice. The vet just shrugged and said, 'Good night, Mel. Lance.' Then he wandered off.

As soon as the door closed behind him, Mel snorted, half in amusement, half in annoyance. 'That arrogant...' Mel glanced over at Lance, then switched to Vietnamese to add a few more choice adjectives. She knew she was overreacting, but the outburst seemed to relieve tension that had as much to do with all the evening's crazy events as with José. She cut herself off when she realised Lance was laughing hysterically. 'You speak Vietnamese?'

'Didn't need to. Some things sound the same in any language.' He grinned. 'Don't worry about him. I thought you were great out there. Girls who kick ass are hot.'

Normally, Mel wasn't crazy about being called a girl, but the compliment made her smile. 'Thank you, Lance. You were very brave yourself.'

He shrugged and looked away. 'You do what you gotta do. Besides, I ain't scared of Caramel. I feed her, so she likes me.'

'I meant telling us about your friends. That took guts.'

He shrugged again and took a great interest in the cracked vinyl flooring, or maybe his sneakers.

Of course this wasn't easy for him, Mel realised. By choosing to side with the Sanctuary, he'd turned his back on his earlier life completely. It was easy to say, from the outside, that he'd made the right decision. But part of him must be wondering if he had. She wanted him to know he had other friends. Real, solid friends. 'Hey,' she said. 'That coffee was pretty crap. Want to come back to my place for a real cup, and hang out for a bit?'

13

Any doubts Mel still harboured were dispelled when Lance met her pets. Phu Dog greeted him like a long-lost best friend, but that was nothing unusual. Everybody in Phu Dog's reality was his best friend ever. More importantly, while Lance was still cross-legged on the battered hardwood floor of the living room making friends and laughing over the curious appearance of a golden retriever/corgi cross, Gypsy crept out from under the futon couch.

The little grey tabby had come from an animal shelter, where she'd arrived with injuries consistent with having been kicked by someone large. The only other male visitor she'd reveal herself to at all was José, and she wouldn't get too close.

She slunk up towards Lance, but held back until he noticed her, said, 'Hi, little girl,' and held out his hand. One moment Gypsy was performing the curious-but-aloof-cat dance, the next she'd crawled into Lance's lap, purring.

Her heart melting, Mel tiptoed away to make the coffee.

When she returned, she set the lacquered tray on the low table in front of the sofa. He gently removed Gypsy from his lap and stood. As he shucked off his hoodie, he winced, and Mel was horrified to see a rusty smear on the back of his T-shirt. 'What happened?'

He twisted around to look over his shoulder. 'Oh, that. Happened when I got caught on the wall. It's nothin'.'

She heard the studied nonchalance in his voice, but his wince had already betrayed him. 'Let me get some hydrogen peroxide so we can get that cleaned up.'

When she re-entered the living room, she nearly dropped her First Aid kit. He'd stripped off the T-shirt. She'd expected a few tattoos, so the barbed wire around both biceps came as no surprise. The elaborate dragon whose head sent flames flickering around his left nipple and whose body trailed down his muscular chest and ripped belly, with the tail dipping under his trousers, on the other hand, was rather more than she'd expected.

'That's, uh, beautiful,' she managed.

Lance beamed at the admiration. 'Hurt like a bitch, but it was worth it. Gotta keep in shape, though – nothing worse than a sagging dragon.'

'Looks like you've been doing a good job,' she said weakly.

She tried to concentrate on his wound, she really did. Thankfully it was just a long shallow scratch; already crusting at the edges, it showed no sign of infection. She had basic First Aid training – with animals, at least – and that part of her brain kicked in and moved her hands where they needed to go, as opposed to where they *wanted* to go.

They wanted to roam across his smooth chest, tracing the intricacies of the tattoo. They wanted to slide down past his narrow hips and become intimately acquainted with the contents of his jeans. They wanted to clutch at the expanse of his back as he ...

Her fingers trembled, just a little, as she taped a gauze pad over the newly cleaned gash.

She meant to give him back his shirt, sit him down, drink some coffee and then boot him out. Really, honestly, she did.

'Hope that didn't hurt too much,' she said, moving around in front of him.

'Nah.'

'Good.' And that's when the reptile part of her brain, the part that always suggested that physical contact was A Good Thing, took over. There was no logical, rational thought involved when she slipped her arms around his waist, meaning to give him a quick big-sisterly hug.

OK, maybe not quite big-sisterly. Lance reminded her of the bad boys she'd always had crushes on in high school. If she happened to enjoy cuddling up to him, what was the harm?

He froze in confusion for a second, and she wondered if she'd offended him somehow. Then his arms locked around her and he lifted her slightly off the floor with the force of his response, pummelling her senses with young heated flesh and cheap aftershave, which he'd evidently used to cover the effects of the day. 'Oh my God, Mel,' he groaned, just before he kissed her.

Mel's body and her common sense got into a bit of a debate as to how to respond. Her common sense was pointing out that he was still a few months shy of nineteen. It reminded her that she liked older guys, like José. But, it argued right back that her relationship with José wasn't exclusive, and variety was, after all, the spice of life. Her body ignored the debate entirely and responded with complete enthusiasm.

Lance may have missed a few lessons on grammar or manners somewhere along the line, but he'd learnt a lot about putting his heart and soul into kissing. It was a little rough, a little awkward, and the aftershave was overwhelming. But it was impossible not to respond to the sheer force of his desire. He'd become hard against her almost instantly, taking her back to her teenage years and boys' amazing insta-erections that were the source of so much wonder and, frequently, embarrassment for all concerned.

Lance was certainly not embarrassed. He was doing his best to introduce her to what he had to offer, rubbing it against her, moving her small frame so she was straddling his crotch. Parts of her were liking this a lot. Even if her brain was still a little unsure, her nerve endings were tingling, her nipples were perking up and most of her blood seemed to be rushing between her legs, leaving her light-headed, unable to think clearly.

She remembered all the little gifts she'd been finding on her desk of late: wildflowers, a lottery scratch ticket, a cheap but cute mug, once a single red rose. Lance hadn't done what he did to help *us*, she realised. He did it to help *her*. And that was just too much.

Her judgement made one last-ditch effort to assert itself. She broke away from the kiss and said, a bit breathlessly, 'Lance, we can't do this.'

'No, I guess not,' he agreed with surprising ease. Then he added, 'Your coffee table doesn't look too sturdy, your sofa's not bad but a little small, the floor's not real comfortable, and I'm too beat to even try it standing up.'

She did her very best to look stern and serious, but the last bit was too much for her. She burst into sputtering laughter. And, as soon as she did, she knew she was lost. She wasn't laughing at him, but at the fact that she'd been making the same mental checklist.

'I have a nice big bed in the other room,' she said. 'Problem solved.'

By the time they got to her almost monastic bedroom, all black and white except for red pillows on the bed and the family photographs on the dresser, Mel felt thick and stupid with lust. She fumbled with her own clothes, fumbled with his, couldn't manage to undo her bra without his equally awkward help.

Lance wasn't wearing underwear, and his cock blossomed out of the fly of his shorts as soon as she unzipped him.

'Wow!' It wasn't his size that impressed her – he was unusually thick, but just about average length. What captured Mel's fascinated attention was the stud through the edge of the head, right where it would hit a G-spot in certain positions. She'd seen pierced eyebrows, pierced nipples and pierced tongues (although she hadn't been personally acquainted with the latter), but this was her first close encounter with a pierced dick.

'Like it?' He wriggled out of his shorts so she could get a better look.

She stared at it for a little while longer, considering the question. 'It's sexy. But I can't get past how much it must have hurt.' Thoughts of it teasing her G-spot almost blocked the picture of a needle going through that very sensitive territory, but not quite.

He shrugged. 'Wasn't so bad. It's fast, anyway. Me and the guys all dared each other. Dog said –' He fell silent.

He was obviously thinking about Dog and Just, and his lost expression was more than Mel could bear.

Well, certain activities might not solve a man's problems, but they made a great distraction. 'So, anything I need to know about handling the jewellery?'

'Handle away. It's healed. Just don't go all military on it.' The last few words came out a little brokenly as she wrapped her hand around the thick shaft and began to stroke. The cock jumped convulsively at her touch. With her other hand, she explored the piercing, delicately stroking, playing with the barbell.

'Sweet,' Lance breathed.

She paused just long enough to lick her palm for some lubrication, then returned to her explorations. It lay in her hands like a small animal, hot and hard and silky and very much alive. It twitched occasionally, adding to the impression of having a life of its own. As she stroked, enjoying the texture, his noises, even the smell rising off him (which even yet wasn't entirely free of hints of eau-de-sewage – then again, she suspected she wasn't either), her own body twitched in response.

Between Lance's thickness and the piercing, she had visions of chipping her teeth but, as his excitement grew, she couldn't resist tasting him. She knelt down, began to lick at the piercing with catlike lappings until Lance was moaning and squirming. Only then did she stretch her mouth around the head and begin to suck in earnest.

But she'd forgotten how short a fuse young guys could have. Just as she was settling into a rhythm, getting used to the odd but exciting feeling of the stud, within what seemed like seconds, and certainly wasn't more than a minute or two, he groaned, 'Gonna come.'

She could tell from the pulsing in her mouth and the tightening of his balls that she had seconds to make a decision. She enjoyed a cock exploding in her mouth – the heat, the taste, the intimacy – but she hadn't had what she liked to think of as a porn-star moment in a long time. If things might be abbreviated – and, given the exhausting day and night, Lance might just pass out on her after coming – she was going to milk all the pleasure from the situation that she could.

Keeping her hands on Lance's cock, she pulled back at the right moment. 'Come on my tits,' she commanded.

Lance looked a little confused, but the confusion was

displaced almost instantly by the happily contorted face of a man in the throes of orgasm.

Hot come sprayed on to her breasts and throat. While Lance still stared at her, slack jawed and glassy eyed, she rubbed his juices into her skin, paying particular attention to her throbbing nipples.

He started to mutter an apology, then registered her expression and did a double take. 'You like that?'

Mel smiled dreamily, playing with her slick nipples. 'Sometimes it's fun to be nasty. That always makes me feel like I'm in an X-rated movie.'

A grin that could only be described as 'shit eating' spread across his face. 'I win!' he crowed, striking a superhero pose.

Then he grabbed her hands, pulled her to her feet and all but threw her on to the bed.

Lance's tongue was pierced, too. Mel had noticed it when he was interviewed for the volunteer position, had asked him to get a Lucite stud so it would be less obvious to visitors and hadn't really given it any thought since. That changed quickly.

She'd heard that tongue piercings made a huge difference for oral sex – and, from other people, that they didn't. Mel was enough of a scientist at heart that she tried to maintain a certain objectivity and figure out the truth. She could definitely feel the stud, a hard ball slipping over her slippery flesh, tantalising the nerve endings in a slightly different way from the tongue itself.

But it's hard to stay objective for long when a gorgeous boy is licking your clit – with or without a pierced tongue – and pushing two fingers inside you. Maybe it was the piercing, the rush from the 'porn-star moment', the fulfilment of her long-time yearning for a down-and-dirty session with a bad boy. Or maybe Lance just liked eating pussy and did it well. All she could say for sure was that she was rapidly losing her mind.

When Lance tried to lift his head, she put one hand on the back of it, not forcefully, but enough to keep him where she needed him. The fingers of her other hand clenched into the firm muscles of his shoulder.

She was soaring. It was almost too much, the fingers working in and out, filling her (but not as nicely, alas, as that thick, studded cock would have done), the tongue working at her, the memory of his come searing into her skin and the stunned but triumphant look on his face when he realised she'd liked that. He must have thought she was all prim and proper like the tough guys back in high school did. If they could only see her now.

Her hips arched up. Her hands clenched involuntarily, digging her fingernails into Lance's skin.

The orgasm struck like a seizure. She didn't make a sound – she somehow couldn't – but every muscle in her body seemed to convulse.

Lance kissed his way up her body while she was still shaking until he was lying over her. Then she remembered the bonus side of younger guys: they might have short fuses, but they also had short recovery periods.

There were times when sex was a ballet, a delicate, intimate dance. This was not going to be one of them. As soon as she said something truly deep along the lines of 'Oh, yeah', he raised her legs and sheathed himself into her, one quick hard stroke that took Mel's breath away. Once he was in, he paused and looked down at her as if awaiting confirmation. 'Don't hold back,' she choked out. 'I'm tougher than I look.'

'I know. I like that.' He marked each word with a hard thrust.

She could feel the piercing stroking at her inner walls, an insistent, glorious pressure, just on the right side of the fine line between amazing and too much.

She didn't always like it this hard and fast. Before things got quite so crazy at the Sanctuary and there was such a thing as days off, she and José would sometimes spend a whole afternoon in bed seeing how long they could draw it out, a kind of homemade Tantra. But there were times when something close to brutality felt perfect and, after the stress of the night, she was ready for quick and rough and intense.

She whispered a suggestion. Lance moved to his knees, raised her up to meet his cock and then knelt up, arching her halfway off the bed. Gripping her hips, he slammed her against him, pounding into her straining body.

She loved this feeling: full and stretched, her body contorted, not at all in control. 'More,' she groaned, and he complied, shifting position a little so she was barely in contact with the bed.

It was all about his muscular arms directing her movement, his hips pounding against her so his balls slapped her ass, his cock moving in and out of her rippling pussy, the piercing stroking over and over against the most sensitive spot inside her.

More was the last recognisable word she managed to get out. She tried, a few times, to tell him how great it felt and to urge him on to something even more frenzied and athletic. But she couldn't make actual words come out, just noises.

They were nothing compared to the ones she made when she started to come though. If she'd been silent under his tongue, she made up for it now, sounding like a mating leopard, snarling and growling and shouting as convulsion after convulsion rocked her.

Sometime in the midst of all the screaming, Lance finished with a series of staccato thrusts and a howl.

Felicia woke, briefly disorientated by the unfamiliar hotel-room atmosphere, to the sound of Gabe's voice, a low murmur somewhere not too close. She was reminded of his cell phone ringing, late at night, and hated the flash of suspicion that bloomed in her stomach. She rolled over and watched him hang up the phone on the desk in the other room, admiring the muscles flexing in his back before he turned and saw her.

'I'm sorry. Did I wake you?' he asked. 'I was ordering room service. I'm starving.'

'Me, too,' she said vaguely

'It *was* a long night of wild sex,' he said easily. When she didn't respond, he narrowed his eyes. 'You OK? Not having morning-after second thoughts?'

'No, it's not that.' She caught her lower lip between her teeth, considering how to ask what she needed to know. 'The night we had dinner and you left your phone in my car, I found it because it rang. I saw the message from someone named Tom.'

'Tom's my boss,' he said.

'He was calling awfully late,' she said. 'It must've been after midnight in New York.'

'Tom,' Gabe said easily, leaning back against the pillows, 'is more of a workaholic than you are. Since I hadn't checked in earlier in the day, he decided to ping me.'

That made sense. It wasn't that she didn't believe him. It was that there were still unusual circumstances involved. 'He asked where you were on the problem so far. You've got to admit that could be read several ways.'

'Look, I'll be honest with you,' Gabe said, sitting back

up. 'You deserve nothing less. But you've got to keep this between us.'

'I'll do whatever's best for the Sanctuary,' she said.

He nodded. 'Fair enough. This wasn't just a random site visit. We were asked to come out and check on things.'

Felicia felt like she'd been doused with a bucket of icy water. 'Someone told the Zoological Association we needed to be monitored? Dammit!'

'No, no.' He took her hands in his. 'I can't tell you who it was, because we promised anonymity. But I can tell you that it was someone who wants the Sanctuary to succeed. Someone who loves the place and was worried. They thought a fresh pair of eyes might help, especially if someone working at the Sanctuary was part of the problem.'

She stared at him, desperately wanting to believe him. 'Really?'

'Really. And I'm willing to bet that if we join forces, rather than suspecting each other, we'll be able to figure this out.'

So very, very tempting. She'd been so tired and stressed for so long, trying to keep everything together. Oh, she could talk to Katherine or Mel or José, but they were just as busy and stressed as she was. The idea of teaming up with Gabe – and, more importantly, of having someone to share the problem with, someone to lean on – was close to exhilarating.

She either trusted him, or she didn't. She had to decide. 'You're on,' she said, and felt weak from the relief as she said it.

Gabe stalked over to the window and cracked the blinds, letting in a stream of brilliant sunlight. 'It's another gorgeous day – do you ever have any other kind here? Maybe we should get outside for at least a little while. There has to be someplace we could play outside, or where I could at least tease you. Nibble the back of your neck. Caress your breasts when no one was looking. Flip up your skirt and take you quickly from behind. That kind of thing.'

That delightful idea, unfortunately, immediately led her to think of all the reasons she should be doing other, far less pleasant things instead.

'What time is it?' She moved one of the many bed pillows that had gotten tossed around during their energetic frenzy, and found the digital alarm clock. She groaned.

'It's Sunday,' Gabe said. 'It's your day off.'

'Is it really Sunday? I've lost track of the days.' She rubbed her face, trying to think straight. 'And I don't have time for a day off until this damn fundraiser is over and the cheques are safely in the bank. And the bills are paid. I really should go in and check email and –'

'No,' Gabe said. In one swift move, he had captured both her wrists, pinning them down on the bed over her head.

A frisson of excitement skittered through her. She wasn't into hardcore S&M, but a little light frisky bondage was a nice diversion from the usual. She hadn't had a chance to wonder whether Gabe felt the same way.

'You're staying here,' he said. 'In my bed. I'm far from being through with ravishing your naked body. The only reason you can leave is if we decide to go exploring while we regain our strength, or you've got pets to feed at home – and if you do, I'm going with you, because I'm not letting you out of my sight.'

She insinuated a thigh between his, pressing against his crotch. 'Well, if you're going to be that insistent about it ... And no, there are no pets.' She could check email tonight.

As if reading her thoughts, he used his free hand to caress her breasts. 'All day,' he said. 'All night.'

Hmm. She liked the way he thought. He was certainly distracting her and goodness knows she hadn't felt less stressed in months. OK, she could handle emails in the morning.

'I just have a grant proposal to finish,' she said. 'If I don't email it by nine a.m. tomorrow, we'll lose it. Two hours, tops. We have to take a break sometime, right?'

He considered. 'You'll have to work for the time off,' he said, rolling her nipple between his thumb and forefinger and watching her shudder with delight.

'I'm a hard worker,' she said helpfully.

'So I've heard,' he said. 'And you're already making *me* hard.'

'I'm not even touching you,' she protested.

'I like watching you,' he said, his voice roughening with desire. 'Seeing how you respond when I do this –' He pinched her other nipple. 'Or this –' He leant closer and gently sank his teeth into that spot on her neck, the one he'd so ingeniously found the night before. 'Or this –' He slid his hand down her torso and cupped her mound. The tips of his fingers dipped between her legs, gently urging her to part them. He languidly toyed with her pussy lips, and she couldn't contain a mewl of pleasure, designed to encourage him to explore further.

'See?' he said, but she'd forgotten what he'd been talking about. She was already wet, already wanting him. 'How can I *not* react to the way you respond?'

She felt his hardening cock against her thigh and realised he was right. She spread her legs wider, hopeful, and he dipped a finger inside, just a little way. Then he moved his hand away, before raising it to his mouth and tasting her.

'Lick me,' she begged.

A knock sounded at the door.

With obvious reluctance, he released her. 'Room service,' he said.

Felicia considered screaming with unreleased tension, but decided it would probably scare the room-service waiter. Instead, she propped herself up and watched as Gabe dragged on a pair of faded jeans. They hung low on his hips, accentuating his taut stomach. His burgeoning erection pressed against the button fly. He almost looked yummier half-dressed than he did naked. Maybe it was because then she could strip his clothes off and start over. Unwrap him like the best birthday present in the world.

She was so entranced by the fantasies she was concocting that she almost forgot that she was hungry. But then he wheeled the tray into the room, and her senses were assaulted with the mouth-watering smells. Strawberries, brie and French bread. Scrambled eggs and bacon and sausages. Croissants and three kinds of jam. A delectable pastry assortment. Orange juice and champagne for mimosas, and coffee and cream.

She stared in amazement at the wide and varied assortment. Was he planning on feeding everyone on this floor of the hotel?

He saw her look and laughed. 'I didn't know what you liked, so I ordered a selection of things. We've had two dinners together, so I know you're not a vegetarian.'

His instinct to order a lot had proved right. Post-sex ravenous hunger drew them to replenish their lost energy. And then food became sex toys.

He swirled a strawberry around the entrance of her cunt, licked it clean as if it had been dipped in cream, and repeated the motion. The tiny rough spots on the fruit felt exquisite, and she was all the more gratified when he left the fruit there, drew it back out with his mouth, and then began licking her, until she was squirming and crying out and coming all over his face.

She returned the favour, dribbling champagne down along his twitching cock and then licking every inch of him clean. It wasn't easy, of course, because the more she licked, the more sweet pre-come oozed out, and then she had to lick *that* off ... Eventually, she just gave up and took him in her mouth, as deep as he would go, and used her hands and lips and tongue to bring him off.

And that was just breakfast...

Something licked at Mel's hand. 'Stop it, José,' she muttered. Then she came fully awake. Phu Dog sat by the side of the bed, his tongue lolling, looking worried as only a dog badly in need of food and walkies can. The light slanting under her white rice-paper shades said it was late morning, almost noon. On the northeast corner of the apartment building and facing the court-yard, her bedroom saw little sun before then.

Why was José still there? Oh, that's right, it wasn't José. (Always important to remember these things before you said a half-dazed good morning to the wrong lover.)

Somehow, they'd crawled from the bed long enough to run through a quick shower, but the last of their energy washed away with the sweat and splooge and they'd stumbled back, already more than half-asleep, while still wet.

Lance was sprawled on his side, still snoring. His normally spiky hair had formed tight curls because he hadn't done anything with it before he passed out. He'd probably hate the effect, but it was all she could do to keep from playing with them.

Let him sleep a little longer. He looked so adorable like that, all the toughness leached out of his face and replaced with an innocence he'd probably never had. Once he woke up, there were bound to be a few awkward moments as they tried to figure out what it meant. She was pretty sure it meant nothing much on her end except impulsive fun. But Lance had been interested in her for a while. She hoped that the interest was purely carnal. She could definitely see romping with him again. He was acrobatic, energetic – one hell of a good ride – and she genuinely liked the guy. But she was so not going all hearts and flowers with him.

She figured it was a bad sign for that sort of thing if, while she watched her handsome boy-toy sleep off some really hot sex, she was still thinking about calling the guy she was supposed to be mad at.

14

Felicia floated into work Monday morning on a cloud of hormones and the kind of high you hit just before you keel over from sleeplessness. Her thighs felt like she'd run a marathon over the weekend, her shoulders were sore from supporting herself in various acrobatic positions and she'd had to carefully choose a sleeveless, high-collared shirt to cover up a love bite just above her collarbone. Her abs ached from coming so much.

She'd never felt better.

She'd made a point of heading in early, leaving Gabe to follow at his usual time. It would be hard enough to be discreet without showing up at the same time sporting identical goofy grins and that 'I spent the last 24 hours having spectacular sex' spring in their step.

Some of that sex had happened shortly before she headed out, leaving her with damp hair and no makeup after a hurried second shower. She was still purring internally as she sat down at her desk, feasting upon happy thoughts of being caught from behind when she bent over to grab her bra off the floor.

She was doing her best to stomp on any thoughts about the fact Gabe was flying back to New York on the red-eye that evening. The timing sucked but, if it was just a fling, it was the best damn fling of her life, and that was something.

Given her to-do list, she wouldn't have time to worry about a possible future or (unfortunately) to replay the sizzling bits with possible variations. She'd finished the grant over the weekend at last, but she needed to check in with Debbie, call the temp agency to confirm the waiters, follow up with some of the corporate calls, push tickets and check in with the local classical radio station, who'd agreed to promote the benefit in exchange for a pair of tickets. The last would be a good place to start, as her contact got in early.

As she was reaching for the phone, it rang. Odd – usually getting in at 7.30 ensured her an hour or so of quiet.

'This is Bob Alfredi from Alfredi Motors. Is the benefit still on?'

Being dazed from sex and sleepless nights was, in this case, a good thing. Everything already seemed a little off-kilter to Felicia at the moment so the question didn't seem that odd. 'Yes. We've got you and your wife scheduled in the first group to go through and see Noelle's cubs.' Only after she replied did she wonder why he was asking.

'Good. I figured I should double-check after seeing the *Independent* this morning – it sounded like you guys had some major setbacks.'

She blinked in confusion. The Addison paper had mentioned the sewage leak briefly on Saturday, but, following the Sanctuary's press release, they'd stressed that it was fairly minor and that the Sanctuary would reopen by Monday. What now? Felicia faked it by smiling (smiling always helped, even if they couldn't see you) and saying, 'Nothing we couldn't handle. Everything's back on track.'

Once Mr Alfredi got off the phone, she checked the day's *Addison Independent*, which otherwise would have moved right from her briefcase to the ever-growing stack of unread newspapers on the floor next to the desk.

Nothing on the front page. She flipped through.

The lead headline on the editorial page was 'Bad

Things Come in Threes for Southern California Cat Sanctuary'.

The subhead was worse: 'Does Something Stink at SCCS?'

The 'Oh fuck' that popped out of her mouth was loud enough that Katherine (Felicia hadn't realised she was in yet but, then again, did her boss ever really leave these days?) popped her head in to see what was wrong.

Together, the two women read the editorial. Short as it was, it took a while, owing to several breaks to field more phone calls enquiring if the benefit was still on.

> Addison's own Southern California Cat Sanctuary is highly respected in zoo circles for its cutting-edge efforts in breeding the most endangered wild cats.
>
> It's also broke. And a major benefit scheduled for this Saturday has been plagued with setbacks, some of which have also affected the Sanctuary's much-needed gate revenue.

It went on to detail the Sanctuary's financial woes, the layoffs that had affected benefit planning along with so much else over the winter and the recent fire alarm and sewage leak.

> Something besides the sewage stinks here. We don't mean Executive Director Dr Katherine O'Dare (although some might say she's more a visionary than a manager) or her staff. We mean the circumstances, a chain of misfortunes severe enough that you can't help wondering if someone has it in for big cats. Will the beleaguered facility be able to pull things together by Saturday? And, if they do, will guests pay $200 a ticket to party in the recently excavated courtyard, site of Friday's leak?

With luck good things as well as bad come in threes. The recent birth of four Amur leopard cubs (they're the world's most endangered felines) and the city's fast response to Friday's smelly disaster were two blessings. We at the *Independent* hope a successful benefit on Saturday will be a third – if nothing else goes wrong.

'"More a visionary than a manager?"' Felicia threw the newspaper on her desk. A stack of already precarious files toppled to the floor. 'Can I just strangle this guy for you? Do they have any idea how hard –'

Katherine shook her head. 'Hey, there's some truth to it. I'm a scientist, not an MBA. If it weren't for some of our board members, we'd be in even worse shape.'

'Thank goodness for Mrs Turner,' Felicia said from behind her desk, trying to figure out in which folders the scattered spreadsheet printout and other paperwork belonged.

'I was thinking more of Richard Enoch and Sarah Wu. Valerie's even less of a number-cruncher than I am – even if she is the main reason we still have any finances left to deal with. And it could be worse,' Katherine continued. 'That's the only slam in here, other than the headline. It's really not that bad.' She didn't sound convinced. Especially when the phone rang again, with yet another potential donor wondering if the benefit was still on.

Between fielding incoming calls, contacting as many guests and potential guests as possible to reassure them, drafting yet another press release and still trying to squeeze in everything else on her checklist, Felicia hardly had a chance to think about Gabe until lunchtime. The only good news was that a few – not many, but she was being stubbornly optimistic – of the incoming calls were people who wanted to buy tickets, prompted by the editorial.

In a break between calls, Felicia was engrossed in trying to redo her budget projections with the new sales and the chair-rental prices she'd just got. Soft lips nuzzling the back of her neck roused her from her spreadsheet haze.

Her reaction – jumping in her seat enough that she practically head-butted Gabe – was probably not the one he'd been hoping for, but it did provoke a chuckle. 'You certainly are focused. I knocked, walked in, closed the door behind me and snuck up on you and you still didn't notice.'

'But now that I know you're here, I think I can ignore this mess for a second.' She stood up to give him what she meant to be a quick kiss.

It wasn't quick.

Felicia fought to keep a handle on propriety, but it was a losing battle. The simple kiss made her feel like butterflies were dancing on her skin, leaving her shivering in a delightful way. And if butterflies were dancing on her skin, her nipples were the main dance floor and her clit had to be the crowded spot right in front of the throbbing speakers.

She ground against him, feeling his hardness burgeoning beneath his tailored trousers. She was wearing a skirt and no stockings. It would be so easy to have a quickie, right here in her office.

'Does that door lock?' Gabe whispered. Two minds with a single dirty thought.

'I wish.' And she kissed him again, this time reaching down to cup his balls for the pleasure of feeling him shudder.

She was breathless by the time they broke apart, breathless and trembling. 'I put on special underwear for you this morning and it's already soaked!' She quickly lifted her skirt to flash her pearl-embroidered silk thong – the one she'd picked up at a very expensive lingerie store in LA and up to now had never worn. Dampness was spreading on the iridescent burgundy fabric. 'I hope you're satisfied.'

'Hardly.' His lazy grin made it clear that, while he might not be satisfied, he was enjoying the delicious torment as much as she was. 'I won't be satisfied until I can make you scream.'

Just hearing that made the sliver of silk even more saturated. Why did he have to go back to New York so soon?

'And you?' he added.

'Unfortunately, I don't think I'll be satisfied until the benefit's a success, and until I know who paid off those kids to vandalise us. Sated, if I'm lucky –' a knowing smile '– but not satisfied.'

'I can't help much with the benefit, but maybe if we put our heads together we can figure out something about our criminal mastermind. Want to talk about it over lunch?'

She was about to say an enthusiastic yes when the phone rang again. Once the call ended – it was a long-time donor who hadn't ordered tickets yet, but did by the end of the call, reassured that the event would take place – she shook her head. 'I wish I could, but all the would-be partygoers are calling on their lunch hour, which makes it hard to take mine.'

Gabe grinned. 'I know about pre-party panic, so I got us lunch.' He pointed to an In-n-Out Burger bag on her spare chair. 'Figured if you didn't even have time to talk I could at least make sure you ate.'

'I know what I'd like to eat.' She leered. 'But there's *really* no time for that. Maybe after work. Meanwhile, thanks for bringing lunch.'

She cleaned off a corner of her desk (no small feat, as it involved moving a hanging-file box, three used coffee cups and a framed photo of Pancho Villa) and they set up. What a difference a few days made – instead of trying to avoid each other's touch, they now sat thigh to thigh, revelling in the contact.

After eating, more flirting and feeding each other French fries (and two more phone calls), Gabe asked, 'So, have you had any time to think about suspects?'

She got out a pad and paper, not wanting to trust it to the work computer.

'First, Alan,' she ticked off. 'I don't think he'd be the mastermind, but a lot of the weird incidents happened on his watch. He knows the local gangs. Maybe he's been on the take all along, even when he was still a cop. Seriously, though, I can't imagine it. He's such a sweetheart.'

'How about Donovan? He's been really co-operative with me, but he could be using me as a red herring.'

She stroked his thigh. 'You don't feel like herring to me. You feel like one hundred per cent USDA Prime Beefcake.' Still, she added Donovan to the list.

'And if we're talking far-fetched,' he added, 'Valerie Turner.'

At that one, she snorted. 'No way!'

'You've said she's odd.'

'And how! But she's a good person. If someone had anonymously hired kids to dress up like leopards and go door to door for donations, I'd guess her, but she wouldn't do anything malicious.'

'I've heard she invests in land.'

Felicia snorted again. 'Not exactly *invests*. She buys it from under developers' noses and donates it to The Nature Conservancy. She and Richard Enoch have bumped heads about that because he wants Addison to grow and she wants to protect the desert.'

'OK, scratch her. Who suggested selling the land in the first place?'

She thought for a second. 'We had an offer from a

developer in Los Angeles; they're already on my list. A couple of board members were for it at first, but it was voted down. One was Bruce Schechter, which surprised me because he was new and I didn't think he'd go out on a limb like that. I'd have to look back in the minutes to see who the other one was; I wasn't actually there.'

She made a note to check it out, circling it three times and adding an exclamation point.

'What about the other board members?'

'Dr Jaxtimer is a no. Even more than Katherine, her life is all about big-cat conservation. Besides, she's been in Nepal studying snow leopards for the past four months. David Abrams and Sarah Wu seem honest enough. They're both entrepreneurs, though, and some deal might have tempted one of them too much.' She added them. 'Richard was great until this year, but he let the ball drop with the corporate fundraising. I have to cut him some slack there because I didn't keep on him. Volunteers need a lot of reminders or things slip through the cracks.'

'Add him.'

'I like Richard! But I suppose he should go on the list anyway, even if he found us Debbie, who's about the only good thing the benefit has going for it.'

'Besides you.' Gabe's hand ran up her bare arm and brushed across her breasts before returning to safer territory.

Felicia blushed and arched her back like a happy cat. 'Back to business! Let's see, there were the people we laid off when we lost the Barbery grant. Revenge is a classic motive. I'm adding a few other real estate developers who might be interested in the place, but there are so many others that we can't consider them all.'

'Any other enemies? Could your bank be trying to foreclose now that the land's worth so much?' He was stroking her throat and collarbone idly as he talked.

'If we want to look at all the angles – oh, that feels way too good – the Denver Zoo was upset that we got a clouded leopard breeding pair they'd wanted. I don't think their director's ever forgiven Katherine for that.' She drew a line, then wrote BANK??? and DENVER ZOO???. Gabe's hands strayed lower again, and Felicia drew a deep breath. 'That's not fair. I'm busy writing! Where was I? Oh, Denver Zoo and the bank. I think they're both pretty far out there, but you never know.'

'What's our next step? Other than seeing if we can find someplace to have our wicked way with each other. I'm hoping we can get together this evening before I leave, but I don't know if I can wait that long.'

'Web research on our suspects in our copious spare time – as if either of us have any. But, as for that privacy, there's a supply closet in the basement where we keep event stuff, and I'm the only one with a key. And right now, the phone seems to be pretty quiet.' She glared at the offending object as if daring it to defy her by ringing. It didn't, but she set it straight to the 'I'm in a meeting' voicemail for outside calls just to be sure.

They made it downstairs in record time.

She pulled an ancient cord that turned on a bare light bulb. 'It's not exactly the honeymoon suite.' The dim light illuminated stacks of boxes, one of which was ripped open and spewing paper napkins, some folding tables and a rack of chairs jauntily adorned with cardboard tiger ears left over from a family open house. The air smelt of dust and old paper.

'We'll make do.' Gabe shut the door and drew her close.

'It's been forever,' she whispered, knowing it had only been a few hours. But she needed his touch so badly, not just the teasing caresses they'd stolen in the office. 'Please.'

For a few seconds they clung together, breathing

each other's scent, revelling in the contact. Gabe kissed her gently – forehead, eyelids, lips.

Then all pretence of gentleness flew out the non-existent window. Felicia fumbled with Gabe's belt buckle. He worked frantically at the buttons on her shirt, somehow managing not to rip off any as he exposed her breasts, which were barely covered with a silk triangle bra that matched the thong.

His mouth closed over a silk-clad nipple. Wet heat transmitted and magnified by silk. He suckled, sending the tugging sensation rocketing down her body. Already sensitised, Felicia felt her lower lips swelling and pouting. She throbbed to the rhythm of his mouth.

His cock, still covered by soft cotton, was rigid in her hand, as hard and demanding of attention as if this morning (and everything before) had never happened.

His hand slipped under her skirt. The minuscule thong was already drenched. He pushed it aside, not bothering with subtlety, going directly for her slick clit.

'Please,' she whispered, rocking her hips against his hand.

Two fingers made concentrated small circles exactly where she needed the pressure, adding to the delicious tugging and suckling. She was already close – Gabe's teasing in the office had had her worked up and the playing-hooky aspect of sneaking off made her hotter. Gabe's fingers only needed to finish off what his lips, his words and both their imaginations had already done.

It didn't take long at all before she was bucking against him, biting her lip to keep from crying out, working his cock mechanically as she became lost in her own sensations.

While she was still shuddering, Gabe pulled out his cock, its head graced with a drop of fluid, with hands made clumsy by haste. Then he hiked up her short skirt so it rode above her waist. A sharp tug and the ludicrously expensive thong was history.

Normally, Felicia wouldn't have been thrilled to lose a piece of lingerie that cost approximately $20 per square inch, but she didn't have time to think about that, not with Gabe lifting her bodily from the floor and lowering her on to his cock.

Joined, her legs around his waist, his big hands supporting her, they staggered a few steps to the wall.

This was sex as primal force. Each thrust slammed her back and ass against the wall but, high as she was, what should have been discomfort just added to the pleasure. Felicia gripped Gabe with her fingernails, with her legs, with her insistently convulsing pussy. Their mouths were locked together, tongues dancing. Everything was happening much too fast by normal standards, but knowing they had only a few stolen minutes twisted Felicia's libido into overdrive. The sheer mental rush pushed her over the edge.

Her orgasm bubbled up from nowhere. She closed her eyes against the white heat, cried Gabe's name into his mouth. He began pumping faster, carrying her along, and she couldn't say later whether what happened as he climaxed was another orgasm or the same one, spun out and embroidered.

There was no time for lingering in the afterglow, and the dingy supply room wasn't conducive to cuddling anyway. But Felicia returned to her endless to-do list with a smile on her face, a spring in her step, an enticing draft where her underwear used to be, and plans for dinner – and, with luck, more – with Gabe.

In the end, they skipped a sit-down dinner in favour of sushi to go, which they fed to each other in bed between rounds one and two. The bedroom was saturated with the musky smells of sex and sweat, with a sharp overtone of wasabi, and Felicia's precious Egyptian sheets now had soy sauce dribbled on them as well as other more intimate stains. Languid with sex, stuffed with maki and relaxed if not precisely tipsy from white wine, they lay together in the damp sheets.

'I've got to get moving,' Gabe said, not for the first time. This time, though, he looked over at the clock and realised they couldn't put it off any longer. 'Join me in the shower?'

She thought back to the hotel shower, feeling tingly again at the memory. 'Do you really want to miss that plane?'

Gabe grinned. 'Actually, yes. But I think you're safe for the moment; you've worn me out! Doesn't mean I won't enjoy the company.'

Felicia wouldn't have dared to say it herself, afraid that wanting to share those last few minutes together in the shower seemed too mushy, too much like she was putting a claim on him. But, if Gabe suggested it, she wasn't about to say no.

Given the time constraints, they really did stick to showering. Mostly. As she lathered his back with ginger-scented body wash, she reached around and got the front as well. Despite claiming to be worn out, he twitched and blossomed under her touch, tempting them both until he made himself pull away. Then Gabe returned the favour – if getting them both revved up again really *was* a favour – making sure her breasts and lower lips were good and clean.

In the end, though, they could only delay the inevitable for so long.

At the door, words failed them. Felicia could think of a hundred ways to say goodbye, ranging from an overly casual 'It's been great. See ya!' to clinging to him and crying, but none of them seemed right.

Gabe was equally tongue-tied. Finally, he fell back

on work. 'I'll have to be in touch anyway, so I'll definitely talk to you. You know, find out how the benefit goes and stuff.'

'And stuff,' she echoed. He'd never been that inarticulate before.

A long pause. 'But you know I'd call you anyway, don't you? And email you, send text messages ...'

'Only if I can do the same to you.'

'If you don't, I'll find something else I need to investigate at the Sanctuary so I have to come back here. Or maybe that's if you do.'

'Silly man.' She kissed him on the nose. 'Now go. How can you come back if you never leave?'

Felicia watched him drive away, watching his tail lights until they were out of sight.

Then she sighed, closed the blinds and went to turn on her laptop. Seriously in lust or not, she had to put on a successful benefit on Saturday and there was a lot of work to do.

15

Surveying the man kneeling at her feet, his dark, well-cut suit a stark contrast to the bright geometric patterns of her Turcoman carpet, Valerie conceded that Richard was the classic handsome older business-man, from his expensively styled grey hair to the soles of his shoes. His body wasn't soft – he clearly worked out regularly – but had settled. (To be fair, her own had as well, although she was at least ten years younger than he was and time hadn't taken as much of a toll yet.) He had pronounced crow's feet around his sharp blue-green eyes and the kind of perma-tan that California natives who grew up pre-sunscreen often had.

And he looked great. Probably could have younger women throwing themselves at him, drawn to his looks and his air of money, power and authority. That air of authority – or rather the way he was shedding more of it by the second – was the only reason Valerie was finding his presence titillating.

She circled him again, inspecting him, letting him get a good look at her, because he wasn't closing his eyes under the intensity of her gaze or glancing down to study the carpet. She couldn't decide if he wasn't fully into a submissive frame of mind yet or if he so enjoyed looking at her that he forgot his manners.

With long-time playmates, she opted for comfort, but she'd suspected that Richard would respond best to the classic domme gear: thigh-high boots, fishnets and a burgundy and gold silk brocade corset that cinched her waist and made the most of her bust. Judging from his hungry expression, she'd guessed right.

She hadn't said a word since 'Hello, Richard. Kneel.' They'd worked out their negotiations beforehand – his likes, dislikes, absolute limits and his safeword. He'd said he enjoyed an edge of uncertainty and mental discomfort, and she was glad to provide it.

Besides, the silent stalking gave her a time to think things through.

This had seemed like a brilliant idea at 3.30 a.m. after a lovely night with Katherine, and had still sounded reasonable as she and Richard chatted back and forth. She was wondering, though, now that he was actually at her house, whether this might be another one of those notions like the raw-game dinner: brilliant on paper, but flawed.

Richard was attractive but there was something about him that didn't work for her on a visceral panty-dampening level. She could top him – at least if it might help Katherine – but neither her heart nor her body was in it.

He liked mild pain, anal play, humiliation, all games she'd played with near-strangers at play parties. But in order to devastate him, break him and reassemble him the way she'd need to in order to get what she wanted for Katherine, she'd need to find some emotional connection.

She mentally reviewed their earlier conversations without getting especially inspired.

Well, at least *he* was inspired. The front of his slacks already looked like a slate-grey silk circus tent and she hadn't even touched him yet.

Circus tent . . .

Well, he had said he didn't have a problem with dressing up if it made her hot. He'd probably had something else in mind; it was amazing how many take-charge male executives had inner French maids or naughty children just dying to get out. But he'd made the mistake of not being specific.

She smiled, a private evil smile that made the man kneeling before her shudder and finally lower his eyes.

He looked much better that way, less like someone who was still thinking about running his multimillion-dollar company and more like someone she could bend to her will in a way they'd both appreciate.

This might be fun after all.

She ran the slapper of her riding crop down the side of Richard's face, a painless caress that still made him flinch as if he'd been struck. She placed it under his chin, used it to nudge his head up. The air of command she was used to seeing in him had left the building. There was still some reserve in his expression, but she knew how to take care of that. 'Get up and strip,' she ordered. 'I want you naked – now.'

After the Armani was in a crumpled heap on the floor, she looked him up and down critically. 'Your legs are too spindly. And suck in that gut. You should be ashamed of your posture. But,' she conceded, 'I suppose you'll do.'

In truth, she thought Richard was in good shape for a sixtyish fellow who spent a lot of time behind a desk and had a reputation as a gourmet. But he'd said he liked verbal abuse. From his reaction – his face fell and his cock rose – it was true.

'Come along.' Using the riding crop, she herded him along towards the dungeon.

Richard's eyes widened at what she pulled out of the armoire in the dungeon. He opened his mouth and closed it, then opened it again.

'Do you have something to say, boy, or do you just enjoy imitating a fish out of water?'

He gaped again. His erection, so jaunty before, was flagging.

'Put it on,' she ordered.

She smacked him with the crop, rather hard. He remained frozen in place. Had she hit a limit at such a simple thing? 'Put it on or say red.'

'I'll put it on,' he said quickly, picking up the proffered garments from the floor. 'But, Mistress, I don't think I'll be able to keep a straight face.'

'Are you laughing at my request?'

He was struggling into the baggy striped pants and couldn't answer immediately, but when he did, he was definitely choking back chuckles. 'No, Mistress.'

A sharp slap to the face cut off the incipient laughter. 'You're lying to me.'

He hung his head (which must have given him a good look at an interesting big-top effect forming in the baggy pants). 'I'm sorry. I wasn't laughing at you, but I *was* laughing at the outfit. And because I just remembered you'd wanted a circus theme for the fundraiser. I couldn't help myself, Mistress.'

'Laughing is all right. Clowns are supposed to laugh. On the other hand, they're not supposed to lie to the ringmaster. Bad, bad clown!'

She put on her ringmaster's top hat, slipped on a gaudy brocade tailcoat and began to laugh evilly. Through the laughter, she managed to say, 'Put the nose on, boy. The nose is the most important part!'

Fifteen minutes later, Richard, in a clown costume, giant shoes and a bright red Bozo nose, was trussed up, ass in the air. If he'd had any doubts about why the clown pants had a drop seat, he didn't any more. Circus music was playing in the background, a sprightly melody that always made Valerie feel happy. And, when she was happy, she did her best work.

Richard's face was a study. He was fighting her on

some level, confused by the costume and the unexpected turn events were taking. On the other hand, his breathing was ragged, eager, and, as she'd restrained him, his cock had been at attention.

'You're not used to truly giving up control,' Valerie said, pitching her voice at a low dark whisper. 'You've played at it. You like the sensations, the release that pain and humiliation bring you. But usually it's been following *your* script. Am I right?'

He nodded. 'Yes, Mistress.' His blotchy flush almost looked like the traditional clown makeup she hadn't taken time to apply to him.

'You're not sure what to make of this. On the one hand, you're nervous, maybe resentful. On the other hand, you pursued me for a long time for a reason, right?'

He nodded again, a much tighter nod.

'And what is that?'

He took a deep breath and seemed to think before answering. 'They say you're the real deal. And that you play safe, but you're really unpredictable. You give people what they need, not what they want.'

'And?'

He gulped audibly before he answered. 'I never imagined . . . being like this, Mistress. But if it pleases you . . .'

'Oh, it does.'

'Then it must be what I needed.'

'Very good.' She stroked his hair almost tenderly. He looked so much better now that he was helpless – and especially with the red nose and oversized orange bowtie, which were her favourite parts of the costume.

Grinning, she snapped at the air over Richard's head with her singletail. It didn't land anywhere near him, but the sharp crack made him gasp and arch against his bonds. Nice reaction. Was it just surprise or did the sound of a whip do something for him? She repeated the experiment and was rewarded by more shuddering. Yes – apparently Richard was audio-activated.

She repeated the process a few more times, until it was clear that Richard's brain was short-circuiting in the best possible way. Then she bent down and whispered in his ear, 'Do you want to feel this on your skin, boy?'

An almost imperceptible nod.

'Are you sure?'

He nodded again.

She had to think briefly. She'd enjoy doing it, but she didn't have the impression that Richard wanted that much pain. He got off on a woman putting him through mental hoops, not on the kind of heavy pain that a singletail could dish out. But there was a way she could use the whip to put him through hoops – and, with luck, through the ceiling.

She took a few steps back, targeted carefully and struck. The whip cracked resoundingly – well behind his ass. Moving at a much gentler pace, the lash continued its journey, reaching Richard's skin with a fraction of its original force. It didn't even turn his skin pink. But to Richard, mesmerised by the sound, it clearly struck like erotic fire. He jumped in his bonds, yelped, and then began babbling thank-yous.

It was gratifying enough that she kept going. Each time, she let a little more force land on his skin, until the last couple of blows raised small bee-sting welts. It was nothing compared to what she'd do to a practised pain-slut, but definitely stingy, and it made him gasp, 'Yellow!' through clenched teeth, signalling he was reaching the edge of his endurance.

Letting the whip down, she walked around so she could see his face. That expression – poised on the brink between agony and ecstasy – was so beautiful, especially coupled with the clown nose.

'Do you want to take one more hard stroke, clown? For me?'

'I want to, Mistress. But I don't know...' He couldn't finish the sentence, but she knew what he meant.

'You can,' she assured him. She knew what she intended to do, even if he didn't. 'It's what you need. What you deserve. You were a very bad clown, you know, being cheeky to the ringmaster.'

'I'll try.'

'And, remember, there's no shame in using your safeword.' She knew he wouldn't. Scared as he was, he was too proud.

She'd brought a cool drink downstairs with her. While she let Richard stew, waiting for the blow he feared, she secreted an ice cube in her left hand. When she lashed at nothing with a tremendous crack, she touched the ice cube against his skin.

And Richard flew into space.

Once he'd calmed down enough to speak again, she asked, 'Am I going to have to get the clown suit dry-cleaned?'

He took a deep breath. His expression was still a little vacant, but his eyes were more or less focused on her. 'No, Mistress, but it was a near thing.'

'That shows some restraint, clown. I'm pleased enough by that to say I'll let you come later. Danny has to make a dry-cleaning run tomorrow anyway. It would be a shame if he had to go just to pick up one dress.'

Richard's face flamed almost the colour of the rubber nose.

'What? Does it embarrass you to think that my slave will be helping clean up your spunk?'

Richard nodded tightly.

'He'll enjoy hearing about this afternoon. Not who you are, of course, but a few select details. Danny's bisexual and he has a weakness for good-looking older men. He won't know which one of us to envy more: you for getting my attention or me for getting to play with you.'

She couldn't read Richard's expression, but it certainly wasn't distaste. She decided to push it. 'For all he's so submissive, Danny's not a passive boy.' She leant close, whispering in Richard's ear, 'I think he'd love fucking your ass while I watched. What do you think about that?'

She had no idea if Danny would actually enjoy Richard. She liked the image, though, so she was going to play out the fantasy and see how Richard reacted.

'I like something in my ass, Mistress.' Richard was having trouble talking. 'But –'

'But you don't like men.'

He nodded, clearly relieved she'd taken the words from him.

'You'd probably like Danny if you let yourself. He's lovely when I dress him up, almost like a pretty girl with a cock. And that's what you like, isn't it, a girl with a big rubber cock doing evil things to your ass?'

Richard gulped.

'Wouldn't it be better if it were flesh and blood? It wouldn't make you gay if I ordered you to take it, and you'd get to try something you've been curious about. Because, admit it, you have been.'

He tried to shake his head no, but failed. One of the frequent effects of sub space was an inability to lie. 'I'm not really attracted to men. I just can't help wondering –' he took a deep breath '– what it would feel like. If it feels any different with something real.'

Valerie smiled. 'Maybe you'll find out someday, if you ask me nicely.' (That'd be the day. Everyone had at least one fantasy that seemed a little too out there to fulfil. This – for all that some people might think it tame compared to some of the things he did regularly –

was clearly Richard's.) 'As for real, if silicone doesn't seem real to you, someone hasn't done you right in the past.'

With those words, she stepped away for a few minutes.

He couldn't see her well, tied as he was, but she could keep an eye on him. She could almost feel desire and tension flowing off of him in waves. He needed this badly.

And to her surprise, she did too. Richard in his cool, detached businessman persona might not do much for her, but Richard bare-assed in a clown costume, vulnerable and confessing his secret queer fantasies, did.

After slithering out of her thong, she selected a strap-on harness that allowed two attachments – one for her. The dildo sank into her easily, its stubby thickness stretching her lips, arousing her further. The weight of the one she would use on Richard pressed against her clit. Neither in itself would be enough to get her off, but Richard's reactions – and the vibrations she'd kick in for both of them at the critical moment – ought to do it.

The strap-on was burgundy, like the corset. She took a quick look in the mirror to adjust the angle, grabbed the lube and returned to Richard.

After a proper greasing, she tested him with one finger, which penetrated easily. 'So open,' she purred.

'More. Please,' he begged as she moved the lubed finger slowly in and out. Soon another finger followed, and another.

You could have all the toys in the world – and Valerie pretty much did – but sometimes there was nothing better than this simple thing, feeling the heat from inside a man's body while you opened him up with your fingers. 'You're a slut,' she said as she worked him.

He was pushing back as best he could, wanting more, grunting inarticulately.

'Say it. Say "I'm a slut." ' He didn't, at least not quickly enough for her liking. 'Say it or you won't get any more.' She started to withdraw her fingers.

That did the trick. 'I'm a slut, Mistress.'

'Are you an ass-fucked slut?'

'I am your ass-fucked slut.'

'Then get ready for me to use your ass.' Valerie eased it in, a bit at a time, to a chorus of inarticulate grunts and moans.

Once it was seated, she flicked the remote attached to the harness.

Oh my God. Two sets of vibrations, one inside her, the other working on her clit even through the leather of the harness, were doing some extraordinary things to her.

She worked in and out, varying the rhythm in response to his reactions. Her own body was shimmering with sensation, a wonderful plateau on the way to orgasm.

'Do you want to come, clown slut?' Stupid question. Of course he wanted to come. But it was part of the ritual.

'Yes ... if you'd like that.'

'What would you do for me if I said you could come now?'

'Anything!' They always said *anything* when they were desperate to come.

'Would you let Danny fuck you so I could watch?'

A brief hesitation and then a soft 'Yes'.

'Would you let me take you to a party dressed like this?'

'Good God, yes!' No hesitation there.

The idea – and his apparent eagerness for it – went straight to her clit. Wouldn't that be something, to show up at one of the select LA fetish parties with Richard as her very own clown on a leash?

'Maybe I'll let people feed you cotton candy.'

'Yes! Please!'

For some reason that image really got to her: Richard on his knees in a clown costume, hands clasped behind his back, eating cotton candy like he was sucking cock. Her legs were quivering. She clamped down on the toy inside her, working at it involuntarily, ready to lose her own control.

'Come for me, then!' she ordered. As he was coming, she threw in, 'And will you write large cheques to the Sanctuary?' but she couldn't tell if his 'Yes' was a response or just an exclamation. And at that point Valerie was too lost in the waves of sensations pouring over her to care.

Before he left, he asked – with an attitude somewhere between the abject sub and the confident businessman – whether he could have the privilege of playing with her again.

This time, she was a little more clear-headed. 'It's been grand and I'd like to see you again. You make a darling clown. But I warned you before we started: I have my conditions.'

'I meant it when I said I'd do anything.' He smiled nervously at her raised eyebrow. 'All right, not anything! Pre-discussed limits and all that, and I'm still not sure about Danny. But I'd go through a lot for you. Name your price!'

'You know how much the Sanctuary means to me, Richard. Pop a nice fat cheque off to them in the morning. Then we'll talk.'

She expected a nod, a thank-you, ma'am, some sign of compliance. Instead, he looked away for a moment before turning back to her. 'Things are a little tight right now. I've got a business deal in the works that's tying up a lot of my cash.'

Against a rush of anger, Valerie fought to maintain

a stony demeanour. She knew that Richard did put a lot back into his businesses, but she also knew that he was unlikely to be as cash-strapped as all that. 'I guess,' she said coolly, 'that you're just not that interested in seeing me again. "Anything" must mean "Anything that turns you on" not "Anything that pleases me." And that's not the way I operate.' She turned and stalked away.

Richard was after her in a flash, clutching at her. When she turned, he hit the floor, kneeling so abruptly that she winced for his knees. 'No. Please, Valerie, I didn't mean it that way. I'll send them something tomorrow. I'm sorry, Valerie ... Mistress.'

'I haven't given you permission to call me that out of scene.' But her voice was gentler now. It was presumptuous, but also flattering.

'I'm sorry. But I can hope, can't I?'

'Of course you can,' she said, thinking as she did that pigs might fly someday thanks to genetic engineering, but she wouldn't hold her breath. 'Now get that money to them and we'll talk about seeing you again. And believe me: I'll be checking with Felicia to see if it's arrived.'

He nodded, looking a little glassy eyed and frantic. 'And once this deal goes down, Valerie, I promise I'll take care of them properly.'

16

With Gabe gone, Felicia found herself with a curious
energy. Somehow, he'd sated her restless desire –
mostly. She still craved sex, but she figured she could
probably live for a few days without crawling out of
her skin.

Instead, she channelled the energy into work. Tuesday morning found her pounding through email that
had piled up overnight. She followed that up by an
hour of focused office cleaning, finally filing the paperwork strewn across her desk, putting the various books
in order on her credenza, opening and dealing with all
her mail. She even – with great regret – admitted that
the aloe was a lost cause, and gave it a hero's burial in
her trash can.

She was especially glad she'd taken the time to purge
and organise because, soon after she finished, Richard
Enoch paid the Sanctuary a surprise visit.

Board members didn't often come to the Sanctuary,
and almost never unannounced. If they were going to
make a visit, they scheduled it in advance so the staff
could give them their full attention – and frantically
whip into shape any areas that had fallen into disarray.

'Richard!' she said, holding out her hands as she met
him in the gift shop. 'So lovely to see you.'

There was something about Richard, something she'd
never been able to put her finger on. On the one hand,
he was a handsome older man, with silver hair and
natural wrinkles around his striking blue eyes that
hadn't been Botoxed into submission. He reminded

Felicia a little of George Hamilton. She'd seen *Love at First Bite* as a girl and had never lost the mild fascination with the actor. Plus, Richard was charming and attentive, remembering details about people and sounding sincere when he asked how things were going with this or that.

On the other hand, well, there was no spark, nothing that made her feel, even in her wildest fantasies, anything but calm appreciation for his looks and charm. She always sensed that he was holding something of himself back, hiding a secret. She often wondered if he were gay, and of a generation that made him unwilling to reveal the fact – if he'd even accepted it about himself.

In her previous erotically charged state, she might have felt some twinges but, right now, she felt nothing but business.

'Felicia, you look stunning as always,' Richard greeted her. Without making her feel slighted, he added, 'I'm surprised not to see Katherine.'

'She's on a conference call with the Lincoln Park Zoo in Chicago and some geneticist from the Felid Taxon Advisory Group – the group that keeps the studbooks on endangered species,' Felicia explained, leading him down the short hall to her office. 'Lincoln Park is discussing loaning us a snow leopard to breed with one of ours. It would be a major coup for both facilities if the mating is successful.'

'Really?' A look Felicia couldn't quite identify – surprise, perhaps? – crossed Richard's craggy face. 'I didn't think you were prepared to take on more animals.'

'We might have to do a little reshuffling, and the final decision will be made after we know how much money we've raised. Plus, when the new leopard cubs are old enough, we'll parcel some of them out to other breeding centres.'

'I see.' Richard sat in her newly cleaned-off guest chair (a bit gingerly, Felicia thought, and hoped he wasn't feeling unwell). 'So things are going well?'

'As well as can be expected.' She flashed him a wry smile. 'By that, I mean the week before a major fund-raiser is always a chaotic time. All told, we're doing quite well. We've sold seventy per cent of the tickets, and already received several generous pledges for the new cubs.'

'Oh! Oh . . . that's wonderful, Felicia. Congratulations.' Richard reached into the inner pocket of his suit jacket. 'In fact, that's why I'm here. I decided it was high time I made another donation myself. Baby cubs need new shoes, and all that.'

Felicia smiled gamely at his terrible joke. Her expression changed into a genuine grin of delight, however, when she looked at the cheque he'd just handed her. 'Richard! This is wonderful. Thank you so much!'

He shifted in his seat. 'Well. I'm glad I could help, given everything that's happened recently. You know, I'd love to take a walk around the site before I go. Would it be possible for you to escort me?'

He was so delightfully formal sometimes. She really didn't have the time, but you never said no to a board member.

As they strolled along the central green, he asked about how the sewage leak repairs were going.

Felicia gleefully swept her hand in a wide arc. 'Look! You can barely tell where they had to dig up the line.' Even she found it hard to believe that the leak had happened last Friday. It was only Tuesday and the place looked great. 'You can see a few obvious lines there, and there, where they laid new sod, but those will be smoothed away by this weekend – and, once chairs are put out and twilight has fallen, no one will ever notice.

I have to credit the entire staff, because everyone pitched in some major overtime, gratis, to get things cleaned up, including Lance here.'

Lance happened to be walking by with a cart they used to schlep around the pounds of meat for feeding time. She briefly introduced him to Richard, explaining Lance's contribution of landscaping plants thanks to a connection. She watched Lance head towards the café, noting that he had an extra spring in his step. She hoped it wasn't because he'd successfully pulled the wool over everybody's eyes.

To Richard, she continued, 'We've already sent a huge letter of thanks to the Sanitation Department, because they jumped on the problem as quickly as they could, and their guys were great.'

'Hmm, good,' Richard said. He sounded a little vague, and Felicia noticed he seemed to be scanning the area, as if looking for something. He glanced past the jaguar enclosure, and Felicia felt a flash of guilt. They were keeping an awful lot from the board right now. She was worried that she'd slip up and mention the vandalism. If they had any hard evidence, it would be different.

Richard seemed to shake himself out of his reverie. 'Glad to hear everything's pulling together. I was a bit concerned after that editorial in the paper yesterday.'

Felicia subtly steered him away from the cheetah enclosure; Caramel was still cranky and Felicia just didn't want the reminder anyway.

'It wasn't the best publicity,' she said, 'but in the end it was pretty positive, saying they wanted us to succeed. That's always nice to hear. As a result, some of the donors have even chipped in a few dollars to help cover the costs of the re-landscaping. This whole experience is really showing us how much people support the Sanctuary. I wouldn't be surprised if we had an extra-successful benefit!'

'Who would have thought?' Richard said. 'You certainly have a way of turning lemons into lemonade. Well, I must be off. Give my regards to Katherine, and I'll see you Friday at the benefit.'

'Saturday,' Felicia reminded him.

He gave a short laugh. 'Of course. Saturday. Take care, Felicia.'

Frowning, she watched him walk quickly away. That was strange. Such a sudden turnaround.

Oh well. Not her problem. He'd brought them a nice cheque, and she'd write up a thank-you note for Katherine to sign, and make sure she listed him in the benefit booklet – which she had to finish designing and get to Kinko's by 8 p.m. that night. Back to work.

There was a message from Valerie Turner when she got back. More ticket sales – great! – and, she said, another fabulous idea. Oh. Dear.

Felicia considered putting off the return call, but it was possible one of the guests had bought an entire table and would have to be listed in the booklet.

'Safari theme!' was all Valerie said at first.

'Safari?' she echoed weakly.

'African decorations, mosquito netting, jungle plants, leopard-print accents, and pith helmets as souvenirs for the guests. Maybe we could get the menus written out on huge leaves. I found my old pith helmet today, the one Horace got me before our first trip to Africa, and I knew as soon as I saw it that it was the perfect theme.'

Felicia blinked, unbelieving. This was actually a great idea if they could pull it together on time. Certainly better than the generic flowers and votives that had been what their budget seemed to dictate. She already had leopard-print cocktail napkins on order because they'd been on sale and she thought they'd be cute.

'Mrs Turner, I love it! The only problem I see is

getting what we need on time – and without spending too much money.'

'Pish-posh, darling. You just find some mosquito netting and get me a copy of the menu so I can get it to the calligrapher I know. I'll take care of the rest. And see if you can find some landscaper to loan us some potted palms. If not, one of my friends might be willing to clear out her greenhouse.'

All Felicia could say was 'Thank you'.

After confirming a few details and getting some information on the latest additions to Valerie's guest list, Felicia said good-bye.

'Oh, one more thing,' Mrs Turner said before she could hang up the phone. 'Felicia, dear, did Richard Enoch talk to you about a donation?'

'As a matter of fact he dropped off a cheque this morning – why?'

She could practically hear the shrug. 'Oh, he mentioned he was planning to, but I thought he might have been full of hot air. Good to know he came through. Ta!'

There was something curious about this, Felicia reflected, but, if Valerie and Richard were butting heads again, it was no business of hers.

No, her business at the moment was coming up with a benefit booklet that looked vaguely safari-like without actually costing them extra money.

Lance pushed open the café door. Mel was sitting at a table chatting with two visitors, women in their thirties who, Lance noticed, despite their advanced age hadn't completely let themselves go. Mel was explaining something about the fishing cats. She finished up, and the statuesque redhead and shorter curly-haired brunette thanked her, bussed their own table and walked out hand-in-hand, although not before giving Lance an appraising glance that left him slightly confused. Were they gay or not? Or maybe they swung both ways?

He would have loved some time to think about that, in private, but he had a list a mile long of things to do before the benefit that weekend.

Plus Mel was standing there, looking cute and sexy, and his brain promptly provided him with detailed memories of how cuter and sexier she looked with her clothes off and her face screwed up as she came all over his cock.

Down, boy.

'I brought the cart; I'll help you load it,' he said.

'Thanks,' she said with a smile.

He followed her into the fridge, hoping the cold air would cool him down. They hadn't indulged in any on-site humping, which he figured was something she wasn't comfortable doing. They hadn't even really talked much about the other night. He wasn't sure what to think about that. Was she playing hard to get? Was she just professional at work?

He did entertain a small hope that the privacy of the fridge would inspire her, but instead she stopped inside, hands on her hips and her brow furrowed. 'Is it warm in here?'

He focused. 'It doesn't seem as cold as usual.'

They went back out and closed the door.

'It's not closing all the way,' Mel said, trying to push the door shut. It would go almost all the way – far enough that no gap was visually obvious – but the heavy door didn't completely seal. Mel bent over and examined the floor by the opening. Lance admired her trim little butt.

'Ah ha!' she said. Having borrowed a knife from Gina, the café worker, she used it to pry a small rock out from the track in the wall that the door fit into. She tried the door again. This time it closed securely.

'Good going,' Lance said, and was rewarded with a triumphant smile from Mel.

They went back inside.

'Um, I don't think that was the whole problem,' he said.

'What do you mean?'

'Listen.'

She cocked her head, then shrugged. 'I don't hear anything.'

'Exactly,' he said. 'There's no hum. The fridge isn't on.'

'Is the cats' meat OK?' was José's first question.

Another confab in the vet clinic, this time including Lance in the conversation.

'A few pieces were starting to get dodgy, but we caught it in time,' Mel said.

'It would have been worse if we hadn't caught it until the benefit,' Felicia said. 'Debbie needs to use the fridge, too, and the smell of spoilt meat wouldn't exactly go over well with the hors d'oeuvres, not to mention that the hors d'oeuvres themselves could've gone bad.'

'Not to mention the cost of replacing the meat – or treating a cat with food poisoning,' José said. He turned to Lance. 'Are you sure,' he asked, 'that you didn't know about this?'

Lance held up his hands in a back-off gesture. 'No way! If Just or Dog did it, they didn't tell me about it. And *I* sure as hell didn't do it!'

'Anybody could get access to the circuit breaker,' Felicia said. 'It's not locked. If it hadn't been for the fact that it was only the fridge that was flipped off, I would've thought it was some kids messing around.'

'The rock easily could have been an accident, if it wasn't for the circuit breaker, too,' Mel added. 'The circuit breaker could have overloaded and tripped on its own, but the fact that the rock was there means neither was an accident.'

'So what do we do?' Lance asked.

'We keep our eyes peeled,' Alan said. 'We've got to be extra-vigilant about everything.'

'How about if we break down the Sanctuary into quadrants,' Felicia said, 'and we'll each be responsible for one area?'

'That's good,' Alan said. 'In the morning and before you leave, at the very least, police your quadrant – check anything you can think of.'

'I'll make the list,' Felicia said.

'I'll go feed the cats,' Mel said. 'There are some very grumpy kitties out there.'

And I'm going to find out who turned off the fridge, dammit, Lance decided.

After the fridge incident, Felicia thought she was prepared for anything. Maybe she should dig out her camo makeup, because this was war. Someone wasn't backing down, and she was on her guard for anything.

Except for what hit her desk on Wednesday morning.

This time, the Sanctuary was on the front page of the *Addison Independent*.

And it was really, really bad.

SCCS TO BE SHUT DOWN?

Addison, CA – The Southern California Cat Sanctuary is being investigated by the Zoological Association, an anonymous source said yesterday.

The local big-cat breeding facility and zoo has had a representative from the watchdog group on site in the past week, the source said.

Unconfirmed reports are that the SCCS's recent

problems caught the Zoological Association's notice, and they sent an investigator to the site for a review.

A bad report – which the source says is likely – could mean the SCCS will be shut down.

The Zoological Association's job is to monitor zoos, aquariums and other animal facilities to ensure they comply with federal and state regulations and that all animals are receiving quality treatment.

Furious, Felicia reached for the telephone.

After the high heat but low moisture of the California desert, the humidity of the New York summer was a heavy change of pace. But Gabe was humming as he opened his office window, letting in the whir and bustle of the street below and at least some air movement, even if it wasn't cooler.

The window protested at first. The building was at least fifty years old and, while it had the charm of fancy cornices and mouldings, charming light fixtures and walls of built-in bookshelves, it sometimes acted as if it just wanted to be left alone so it could take a long nap.

He'd been in meetings all morning, and had escaped long enough to pick up a coffee and a bagel with lox and cream cheese from the deli on the corner. Now he settled in to do his expense report from the California trip.

The California trip. He couldn't stop himself from grinning. That had certainly been one of the most ... enjoyable site visits he'd done. Oh, he'd had women (and one or two men) try to seduce him before, to convince him to write a good report. He'd always seen right through them. It didn't mean he didn't occasionally enjoy messing with their heads – but that was only when they were outright nasty to their animals and he was poised to shut their facilities down so fast their heads spun.

Felicia, on the other hand, had waited until she was sure *he* wasn't the bad guy, until they had joined forces against a common enemy. Even if they didn't know who that enemy was yet.

He'd tried to review the SCCS's financial reports on the flight home but, thanks to the combination of way too much incredible sex, a red-eye flight and the extraordinary lack of excitement inherent in spreadsheets, he'd pretty much passed out until the plane's landing gear had hit the tarmac at JFK.

He didn't want to think about financial reports. He wanted to think about Felicia and those outrageous panties with pearls sewn into them. So, when his phone rang and he saw the caller ID, he couldn't have been happier. 'Felicia! I was just thinking about you.'

'I just bet you were.'

That didn't sound positive. It sounded like she was gritting her teeth. He hoped nothing else had gone wrong. 'Is everything OK?'

And off she went.

Eventually he managed to sort through the how-could-yous and why-didn't-you-have-the-courtesy-to-tell-mes and what-the-hells, and wait for her to get it out of her system and calm down a little bit.

'OK, slow down,' he said. '*What* report are you talking about?'

'Your report, you bonehead! The negative one!'

'Felicia, I haven't written my report yet. For one thing, I can't finish it until after the numbers come back from the benefit, just to make sure you bring in enough. More importantly, my report isn't going to be negative. I can't tell you anything more, but the Sanctuary is in great shape from what I saw.' He blew out his breath and ran a hand through his hair. It had gotten hotter in his office, that was for sure – and not for any of the right reasons. 'I'll recommend some areas of improvement, but you're nowhere near the problems I'd need to recommend you be shut down.'

'We're not? Really?' Her voice sounded small.

'Really.' He put every ounce of conviction he could muster into the word. 'What made you think the report was going to be so bad?'

She told him about the newspaper article, reading it to him over the phone, punctuated by several sniffles and one very descriptive expletive. He found himself grinning at that, although he didn't let her know. She was a firecracker, all right. She might be down for a few minutes, but she always came back fighting.

His grin faded in seconds, though, to be replaced by a tightening in his jaw. 'That's insane,' he said. 'Where did they get that information? It's all speculation.'

'An anonymous source,' she quoted. 'Unconfirmed reports.'

'They didn't even try to contact me. Is that even legal?' he asked, but it was a rhetorical question and the more important thing was that, across the phone lines, he heard an audible gulp. 'Are you OK?'

'People are calling. They're getting bounced to my voicemail right now, but I'm going to have to hang up and deal with them.'

Gabe thought fast. 'Don't. Don't call them back. Give me half an hour to sort this out, OK? I'll call you. Don't pick up the phone for anyone but me.'

As soon as he'd severed the connection, he was out his office door, bellowing Tom's name.

Felicia had heard the phrase 'the longest half-hour of her life', but she'd never really understood it until now. She spent most of it explaining the situation to Katherine and convincing *her* not to answer the phone, and passing on the same information to the gift-shop clerk and the volunteer who took group reservations. In truth, the board members should have been contacted so they could do some damage control, but Felicia gave Gabe his half-hour.

When she saw Gabe's number on her caller ID, she lunged at the phone. Katherine leant in expectantly as Felicia put the call on speakerphone.

'Tom is *livid*,' Gabe said. 'The newspaper apparently made some half-assed attempt to contact him last night after he'd left the office. As far as he's concerned, the newspaper article was libellous. They'll be printing a retraction tomorrow, and right now I'm not sure if he's still planning to sue or not. He's still in his office screaming at the editor.'

Felicia's stomach lurched and then settled. Across from her desk, Katherine sagged into the guest chair.

'I've got the Zoological Association's official statement here that you can give to anyone who calls or writes,' he said.

She grabbed a pen and began scribbling, only half-hearing phrases like 'preliminary assessment is extremely favourable' and 'in no danger of closure' through the ringing in her ears as the adrenalin oozed out of her system.

'Gabe, thank you,' Felicia said. 'I'm so sorry I went ballistic on you.'

'It's OK. You had good reason to be upset,' he said. 'But there's one more thing.'

The ice re-formed in her gut at the sombre tone in his voice. Her fingers clenched around the pen. 'What is it?'

'Tom got the editor to reveal his anonymous source,' Gabe said. 'It was Richard Enoch.'

17

Gabe got up from his laptop and paced the few yards into the narrow ship's-galley kitchen of his apartment. Even with the air conditioning on and him stripped down to his skivvies, he felt sticky.

Or maybe he just felt dirty. He'd been digging deep into public records via the Lexis-Nexis legal database that the Zoological Association used for research. Usually, it was to figure out how much you could reasonably ask someone to donate. This time he was trying to figure out if someone was a crook, but all he'd learnt so far was that he wasn't cut out to be a private detective. He'd been at it for hours, but hadn't found anything useful. Poking through the records of Richard Enoch's business transactions (none of them connected to commercial real estate), David Abrams's divorce (uncontested and not involving alimony on either side) and the bankruptcy of one of Sarah Wu's software startups (which looked like a motive until he realised the failed startup was the spin-off of a very successful established company) felt wrong.

Not as wrong as what someone was trying to do to SCCS, though.

He grabbed a Sam Adams from the fridge and headed back to the computer. He'd done some research into the developers who'd made the offer on the Sanctuary property but hadn't gotten very far. Nothing turned up on any of the business databases.

He sipped the sweating bottle of beer and stared at the computer screen at the list of options for business research. Maybe he was missing something. Fictitious business names and D/B/As? Why not? He'd tried everything else.

Twenty minutes and many layers of search later, he jumped up and yelled 'Eureka!' to the empty apartment. He'd traced the business name back to another company, which traced back to another company, which listed ownership.

Of course, the names weren't on their suspect list. A quick Google turned up nothing to help pin down the right Joseph Estabrook and unearthed one Lindsay Chamaine in California, a photographer specialising in artistic but racy lesbian imagery. Not likely to be the same person, but Gabe bookmarked the site just in case.

Maybe the names were familiar to Felicia. And, even if they weren't, it gave him a good excuse to call. A few minutes of looking at pictures of women kissing each other, tying each other up and preparing to do still more interesting things to each other had got his blood racing. There'd been one petite blonde with short-cropped hair who looked like a slacker elf. She and her curvy, coffee-coloured, strap-on-wielding partner would have normally started a very distracting chain of fantasies.

But lately, even if he started getting horny because of some random image, his fantasies all wound back to Felicia.

Felicia relaxed back on her bed, a glass of oaky white wine on her nightstand. She'd snuck out early enough tonight to have time to have a hot bath. The benefit was two days away, and she'd been going into work earlier and earlier each day this week.

Gabe had called while she was in the bath, leaving a message for her to call, no matter how late it was. She'd towelled off, slipped into a spaghetti-strapped, sage-green satin nightgown that skimmed the tops of her thighs, and made herself comfortable before calling. He'd sounded like he was in a good mood, and she hoped to take advantage of it.

She was pretty sure he'd be feeling frisky. After all, her wake-up call from him that morning had been a text message suggesting what thong she wear that day.

She'd taken extra care in the bath, gently scrubbing every inch of her skin with a loofah puff until she tingled. She hadn't been able to resist brushing the rough puff over her nipples, and now they rose again, making small bumps beneath the smooth satin.

Her skin was still damp, smelling of the gardenia-scented bath bomb she'd used. She was already growing damp between her legs, just thinking about Gabe, remembering the acrobatic sex they'd had in this very bed and anticipating hearing his voice.

She took a sip of wine, savouring the crisp flavours, and slipped the earbud of her phone into place before dialling Gabe's number.

He answered on the second ring. 'How was your day?' he asked.

'Blissfully uneventful,' she said. 'The *Independent* printed the retraction – it was very humble, by the way; I should fax you a copy – and five people called to buy tickets to the benefit specifically because they felt sorry that the newspaper had screwed up. So I was crazy-busy, but nothing went obviously wrong.'

'Maybe we scared Richard off?' he suggested.

She hesitated. 'I know we're ninety-nine per cent sure Richard's involved,' she said. 'But it just doesn't make sense. He's been making a lot of stupid mistakes recently, but that doesn't make him a criminal master-mind who organises nightly vandalism raids.'

'It's not the first time someone assumed that the presence of the Zoo Association on site meant that the facility was going to be shut down,' he admitted. 'Put all together, though, Richard looks suspicious.'

'Extremely suspicious,' she agreed. 'He just doesn't have a motive. Why would he donate so much money the other day if he wanted us to be shut down?'

'Good question,' Gabe said. 'I managed to get time to do some research on the corporation who made the offer to buy the Sanctuary land.'

Felicia sat up, her heart pounding. 'And?'

'And Richard's not attached to it – at least, not in any way I could find.'

'Oh.' She flopped back against the pillows.

'Let me give you the information anyway, in case it sparks any ideas for you.'

She grabbed pen and paper off her nightstand. 'Shoot.'

He relayed the company's Los Angeles address, which she probably already had in her files somewhere, and the names of the owners.

'Joseph Estabrook owns a chain of fancy restaurants – he's a bigwig in the city,' she said after taking another sip of wine. 'I assume it's him. He used to donate heavily to the AIDS foundation I worked for. I don't remember him ever giving to the SCCS, though – too small for him, I'd guess. Lindsay Chamaine – that name sounds familiar.' Tapping her pen against her teeth, she considered. 'I'll go in early tomorrow and check the donor records on her.'

'Don't work too hard,' Gabe said.

'I won't . . . after the benefit is over.'

'Are you going to take some time off afterwards?'

She hadn't really had time to think about it. 'You know, I probably should. Once the thank-you notes are in the mail.'

'Good,' he said. 'Take at least half the week.'

'What are you, my vacation planner now?'

She heard the laughter in his voice. 'If that's what it takes you to relax.'

'I know how to relax,' she protested. 'I even took a long bath tonight.'

He was silent for a moment. 'Bubbles?'

'Bath bomb.'

'Scent?'

'Gardenia.'

He took a deep, not entirely steady breath. 'Still in a towel?'

'No, I changed.' She described the short nightgown, from the narrow strip of matching green lace around the top to the way one of the straps kept falling off her shoulder. 'How about you – what are you wearing?'

'Hold on.' There was a crackle as he put the phone down, and then she heard rustling before he picked up again.

'You stripped, didn't you?' she asked, laughing. 'That's not fair.'

'I was only wearing my underwear, anyway,' he said. 'And it's not as though you're here to help.'

Her fingers itched to unbutton his shirt and part it to reveal the gold-tipped hair on his chest. To unbuckle his belt and push his trousers and briefs down in one quick motion. OK, so maybe it was a good thing he was already naked. She obviously wasn't in the mood for subtlety.

'So what would we be doing if I were there?' she prompted him.

'I'd stand behind you and lift up your hair and smell the gardenias on the back of your neck,' he said. 'Then I'd nibble, right at the nape. You'd shiver, brushing that satin across my crotch.'

If she hadn't been leaning back against pillows, she would've raised her hand to her neck, to the spot that tingled from his promised lovebite. 'Go on.'

'I'd pull you back against me so you could feel me growing hard. Hands on your hips, rubbing along you. Sink my teeth into your shoulder. I remember how you reacted to that last time, how you cried out and you grabbed on to me and your hips arched as if I was touching you there.'

Oh God, she remembered, too. He'd bitten, gently but firmly, and then laved the area with his tongue as if to soothe the erotic hurt.

Her hips shifted restlessly on the bed, the nightie rising a little higher on her thighs.

'Are your nipples hard?' he asked.

She described how they were plainly visible through the nightgown. 'Touch them? Please.'

'Just try and stop me,' he growled. 'Would you like it if I rubbed the satin on them?'

'Yes.' Was that her voice? It sounded like a whimper.

'Do it. Drag the satin across them. Use your finger-nails to graze them through the satin.'

She did, her breathing growing heavier. 'It feels so good,' she said. 'But it's not enough.'

'What do you want?'

'Harder.'

He fell silent again. She knew he was toying with her. She gritted her teeth, promising herself she wouldn't give in, wouldn't beg.

'Pinch them.' His voice was rough through the phone. 'Twist them, as hard as you like. Tell me how it feels.'

'Good, really good.' How could she describe the sensations rippling through her? 'It gets me so hot.'

'Do you think you could come that way, just from having your nipples played with?'

'I don't know. Maybe.' Maybe with you. But she didn't say it, because she wasn't sure. The use of the phone, as well as the fact that they were separated by thousands of miles, made it easier to talk about some things. Made it easier to whisper honestly into the darkness. 'I'm willing to give it a try, next time. If there's a next time.'

'Oh yes,' he breathed. 'There'll be a next time. You can count on it. But for now – stop.'

Stop? She didn't want to stop.

'I want you to lick your fingers,' he said. 'Then play with your nipples again. Get the fabric wet. Use your nails, too.'

She complied, still not sure what he was getting at. He didn't keep her in the dark for long.

'That's my mouth on you, sucking and nibbling through the satin.'

This time she moaned, imagining the feel of his hands and mouth on her. Her nipples peaked harder, the moisture on the satin reacting to the air conditioning. Cold and hot. Ice and fire. She told him.

'Good,' he said. 'I wish I was there to do it myself. God, yes. Your breasts feel so good in my hands. I can practically smell the gardenias.'

'Can you feel my hands on your head, urging you closer?'

'Absolutely. Show me what you want. Tell me what you want.' Then, as if the thought suddenly struck him, 'Would you want to try nipple clamps sometime?'

'Not – not very painful ones.' Given how charged she was right now, though, she doubted she would complain if he snapped a pair of tight ones on her. The hurt would throb like the blood pounding in her clit.

'Just the kind that add pressure,' he agreed. 'I'd love to see you wearing ones with little bells dangling off them. Pretty jewellery for such pretty breasts. If you were on top, I could close my eyes and listen to them jingle as you came all over my cock.'

'Oh, yes.' Felicia's pussy clenched futilely around nothing as she imagined his cock inside her. She leant over and fumbled to get her nightstand drawer open.

'What are you doing?' he asked.

'Do you mind if I get a toy out? It's not the same as having you inside me, but –'

'Sure, get it out,' he said. 'But don't use it until I tell you to.'

She bit her lip. She wanted it inside her so bad. She could just ease it in, quietly, not turning on the vibrator . . . No. Perversely, she wanted him to run the show, to tease her. She wanted to be helpless to his whims, to put her pleasure in his imaginative hands. Even if she went insane from needing to come.

'Are you wearing panties?' When she told him no, he said, 'Spread your legs.'

Cool air slithered between her thighs, but it wasn't nearly enough to cut the heat she swore she could feel radiating out from between her legs.

'Use your hands to part your lips.'

She could smell the spicy-sweet scent of her own arousal as she did so. 'I'm so wet,' she said. 'Already. Slippery with my own juices.'

'Taste yourself,' he said. 'Let me hear you suck the juices off your fingers. You taste so good, Felicia. I could just feast on you for hours.'

He'd already shown her his cunnilingual prowess. The thought of him doing it for hours, while she came and came and came again under his ministrations, made her toes curl.

She missed him.

'What about you?' she asked. 'What are you doing? Tell me. Let me see.'

'I'm naked,' he said, a hint of laughter in his voice. 'I'm hard. Talking to you, thinking about what you're doing to yourself – that makes me so damn hard.'

'Are you stroking yourself?' Felicia loved the mental picture of his hand sliding up and down the length of his cock.

'Lightly. There's some pre-come, and I'm rubbing that on the head. But I'm not ready to come any time soon. This one's for you, Felicia. How hot can I make you, over the phone, telling you where to touch yourself, and how?'

'Pretty damn hot,' she admitted. 'I'm wet, and needing you inside me.'

'Stroke your clit, gently,' he instructed. 'Don't come yet. While you're doing that, tell me what the toy looks like. I want to imagine you using it on yourself.'

'It's bright blue,' she said, holding it as if she'd never really seen it before. Truth be told, she was usually pressing it against her clit or impatiently pushing it up inside of her, and neither of those positions provided a good angle for her to watch. 'The shape is pretty realistic, with some shaping and veins. There's another part that extends from the base, and it comes up into a shape like a bunny's head. The ears vibrate.'

'I've seen those,' he murmured. 'I'll bet you like those ears buzzing against your clit, don't you? It probably makes you shoot off like a rocket.'

'Mm hm,' Felicia agreed. 'I call him Mr Twitchy.'

Over the phone lines, she heard a strange noise. Gabe was either choking or laughing. It was probably the latter. Well, she didn't care: Mr Twitchy had been making her happy a lot longer than Gabe had.

She wanted Gabe to make her happy, though. She wanted him to tell her she could come soon. She wasn't used to holding back when she masturbated, and the slow maddening movement of her own fingers, one on either side of her wet clit, was driving her crazy.

She told him. 'I need to come soon,' she added.

'OK,' he said, much to her surprise. 'But not quite yet.'

Dammit!

'Put Mr Twitchy's head –' and she could tell he made a great effort not to laugh when he said that '– just inside you.'

She was so wet that the tip slid in easily. Her thighs trembled from the strain as she resisted the urge to plunge the vibrator deep inside her. He continued to instruct her to feed it in, inch by excruciating inch, until it was buried up to the hilt.

'God, I wish that was me inside of you,' he said.

She couldn't fashion a coherent response. She wished it was him, too, but a fake cock was the next best thing, filling her up.

His next words almost sent her over the brink. 'Turn on the vibrator.'

With the dildo portion all the way in, the bunny ears nestled against her aching clit. A flick of the switch, and they hummed and buzzed against her.

She was so close, so charged, that it was only a moment before the orgasm peaked, tumbling her over the edge as it spiralled out through her belly and down her legs. She pulsed around the vibrator, pressing the fake cock deeper inside to trigger a second intense orgasm. Dimly, over her own cries of passion, she heard Gabe shout his own release.

Exhausted, she fell back against the pillows.

Even thousands of miles away, he still had the power to rock her world.

Lindsay Chamaine sounded hauntingly familiar but, after searching the donor database, Felicia still couldn't find her.

Not for the first time, Felicia yearned for the more sophisticated database they'd had at the AIDS organisation. This one was pretty bare-bones, programmed in

Access by a high-school student doing a community service project, and they had to keep a lot of information in paper files.

She'd just have to check paper files. And, like it or not, she'd have to start with Richard Enoch.

Her palms were sweating as she pulled the file. Funny, some detached part of her brain thought, she'd heard that expression a million times but it was the first time she'd ever noticed it happening to her. Sweaty palms and a sick sensation in her stomach.

The file was thick. Richard had been involved with them almost from the beginning. She started from the current stuff and worked down. Buried deep in the stack, she found a note in Katherine's handwriting: 'Divorced from Lindsay Chamaine June 2001. Need to update database.'

That was why the name was familiar. Lindsay and Richard had been long divorced by the time she'd started at SCCS, but she must have seen it in the file or in some old event materials. Did that make Richard guilty or innocent? Part of a convoluted plot involving his ex or a victim of it?

Rummaging further in the files told her nothing useful. Apparently, Lindsay had never been deeply involved in SCCS.

Someone must know more.

Valerie Turner.

She knew everyone. If there was dirt on Lindsay or on the divorce, she'd know.

Felicia was glad Mrs Turner was on her speed dial, because her hands were shaking.

'Felicia, darling, I was just about to call and see how my tables were coming together. I'm sorry it's all so last minute, but some of my friends can be very naughty if I don't keep on them.' Her voice was husky and amused, and definitely not the voice of someone just waking up.

(Unless she'd been waking up slowly and in good company, but that didn't seem likely.)

'You're up to twenty-three guests so far. I'll fill you in on that later, but I'm hoping you can help with a delicate question.'

'I'm all ears. Always glad to help out.'

How to phrase this? She trusted Mrs Turner, but she had little idea how deep loyalties and friendships ran in her circle. 'A name's come up a few times lately as a board candidate, but it could get touchy and I wanted your opinion. It's Lindsay Chamaine.'

'Lindsay? How curious she hasn't said anything to me about moving back to the area. She moved to San Francisco after she and Richard split up.'

'I heard she'd started a business in Los Angeles. Real estate development, I think.'

Valerie snorted. 'Hardly! She's a photographer, a fine one, but no business sense whatsoever; Richard still has one of his people taking care of the financial end of the photography for her or she'd be lost. The closest she's come to being a businesswoman is being the paper owner of some of Richard's firms for tax purposes. The dry-cleaning chain, maybe a few others.'

'Still? They've been divorced for years.'

'Longer than they were married. She just wasn't cut out to be a society wife. But they're better friends now than they ever were. Funny how it works that way sometimes.'

Felicia took a deep calming breath. For a few minutes, she'd had hopes of a vengeful ex scenario, something that would make a man she'd come to respect a victim, not a villain. Unfortunately, that didn't seem to be the case.

If Richard had walked into her office, she'd have clubbed him with her laptop.

She forced herself to sound casual. 'Can't imagine

what scrambled story I heard. A new husband who's in real estate, maybe?'

A laugh from the other end of the phone. 'When I said Lindsay wasn't cut out to be a society wife, what I meant was she left Richard for a massage therapist named Inge. But you didn't hear this from me, of course.'

'Of course,' Felicia muttered, too distracted to enjoy what would normally have been a delicious piece of gossip. 'Is Richard involved in real estate development?'

'Richard knows how I feel about preserving the desert, so he'd probably not tell me just to spare himself the lectures. It's possible. He dabbles in everything, as long as there's money in it.'

A more thoughtful tone had crept into her voice as she talked. Then she paused, such a pregnant pause that Felicia held her breath. Felicia's heart raced, feeling as if it wanted to break free of her rib cage.

'This isn't about getting Lindsay on to the board, is it? This has to do with all the problems SCCS has been having. You've figured something out.'

For about half a second, Felicia considered lying. Valerie was impulsive and eccentric. But she was far from stupid and would probably sense the lie.

She was also, at this point, the board member Felicia knew was most loyal to the organisation. 'Lindsay's the paper owner of the firm who tried to buy our land, along with Joseph Estabrook the restaurateur.'

'Whose sister recently married a Barbery Foundation trustee. I was at the wedding – and so was Richard.'

Felicia used several words she would have normally avoided in front of a board member. Then she apologised.

'Quite all right. I was thinking far worse things; these are people I fancied were my friends.'

'The problem is, the connections are all there, but

how do we prove wrongdoing?' She sagged in her chair. She had answers now, but she still didn't know what to do with them.

'Leave the next step to me, Felicia,' Valerie said, her voice laced with polite venom. 'I know Richard well. I have a plan.'

Normally, Felicia would shudder at those words out of Valerie's lips, but she certainly didn't have a plan herself. And, in a strange situation like this, maybe Valerie's weird ideas were just what they'd need.

18

One good thing about throwing an outdoor benefit in the southern California desert in summer: you could count on clear weather.

Felicia believed in counting her blessings, so she was clinging to that thought. It was the only completely positive thing she could think of at eight on Saturday morning while all hell was breaking loose around her.

'I know the tents aren't ready yet,' she said to the irate man from the rental company. 'The truck from the tent company broke down on the highway last night. They got here as early as they could this morning.' Which meant she'd had to be on site at dawn so they could try to get as much of the chaos as possible settled before the day's tourists began to arrive, but she doubted that would earn her much sympathy from the chair rental guy, who'd probably been at work that long too.

'Lady, I'm sure they did. But I'm on a schedule. If that tent isn't up fast we're throwing everything in the courtyard and it's your problem from there.'

'Give me ten minutes.' She got on her cell. 'John, as soon as the restrooms are clean, get the cleaning crew over to help with the tents. And grab anyone else who looks big enough to be useful. I'll meet you there.'

'How about me? Am I big enough to be useful?'

Felicia wheeled around at the sound of the unexpected voice. It couldn't be.

It was.

Gabe was rumpled from the top of his sandy hair

down to his socks, which were sagging into his sneak-ers. His eyes were shadowed, he was unshaven and he was clutching a Starbucks travel mug like a holy relic.

He looked gorgeous.

'I am too old,' he said, 'for two red-eyes in a week. But I hope I'll be some help.'

And then he didn't say anything else because Felicia (figuring Chair Rental Guy didn't matter and everyone else was too busy to care) gave him something better to do with his mouth.

There was no awkwardness or hesitation. He folded her into his arms, pulled her close against a body that suddenly wasn't sagging with fatigue – in fact, parts of it were jumping to attention – and everything was more than all right. Heat radiated out from her belly, setting her nipples alight, setting her juices flowing. Her whole body pulsed and throbbed with want, but at the same time she felt peaceful, as if Gabe's body were her home and she'd arrived after a long absence.

There was no one in the office building. Even Kath-erine was outside dealing with setup. They could sneak in and fool around. The schedule for the day was too tight to allow time for anything very involved, but she could see herself sinking to her knees and taking Gabe's cock deep into her mouth. She'd got off herself the night before with Mr Twitchy and thoughts of what she'd like Gabe to do to her. It seemed more urgent now to taste him, feel his come flooding her mouth.

Someone tapped her on the back. She jumped about a mile and turned to see Irate Chair Rental Guy, looking more irate than before. 'Love is grand and everything, but I need somewhere to unload my truck.'

They pulled apart. 'Come on,' she said, tugging on Gabe's hand. 'Let's go set up a huge tent.'

As they headed towards the tent, a woman in a Feehan's Flowers shirt blocked her path. 'I know you weren't expecting us until later,' she said, 'but there's this wedding in Braeburn that's messing up our schedule.'

Felicia just laughed. It was easier to laugh now that Gabe was here.

While Felicia was still dealing with that, one of the volunteers ran up. 'Some of the food's being delivered. Where does it go?'

And her cell phone began to ring. Valerie Turner. She answered it while trotting towards the tent and grabbing a random animal care staff member to show the food service where the walk-in was.

'Darling,' Valerie exclaimed, 'I was at a party in LA last night and sold another twelve tickets!' The woman had too much energy. What was she even doing awake at this hour, let alone so perky, if she'd been at a party the night before?

'Wonderful!' Felicia forced a smile, hoping the muscle memory would make her voice sound cheerful. 'We can certainly use the money.' Even if it would mean she'd have to redo the seating chart for the fourth damn time. 'May I call you later for the names? We're in the middle of deliveries and I can't grab a pen.'

Fortunately, Valerie seemed to understand, because she said, 'You know I detest email, but I'll give in to the twenty-first century for once and send them to you. Try to stay calm, dear!'

'Hi!' Sounding ever breathless, Debbie bounced up to her. Her very blonde hair was piled haphazardly on her head, and yet somehow it looked artful and casual. 'Sorry to bother you – I know you're absolutely insane right now – but the café's locked; do you have the key?'

Felicia did, but it was on a keyring with about fifty thousand other keys to various parts of the Sanctuary, and she wouldn't have handed them all over to her own mother at this point.

She glanced across the green. Gabe had apparently convinced Irate Chair Rental Guy that things would go faster if he helped set up the tent. Amazing.

'I'll unlock the door for you,' Felicia said.

As soon as Felicia got the door open and the lights on, Debbie walked into the fridge. Felicia assumed she was checking on space, or the ostrich and steaks she'd left there a few days before. But then she heard Debbie swear.

'What's wrong?' Felicia asked, peering in.

Debbie didn't answer at first. Then she shook herself and said, 'It's so cold.'

'It's supposed to be!' Felicia said with a laugh. But she couldn't help but be reminded of Wednesday and Mel finding the circuit breaker thrown and the fridge door being blocked open. Could Debbie have been responsible?

No, that was absurd. Debbie was a caterer, for God's sake! And a good one. Felicia obviously had suspect-on-the-brain syndrome.

'You probably need to get set up,' she said. 'I'll send someone over to help you carry stuff in from your van. Can I get you anything else?'

Debbie shook her head. 'No.'

'Let me know if you need anything.'

Her cell phone rang again, and she dashed out.

Everyone was running around like their hair was on fire. Lance knew the benefit was a big deal, but he didn't understand getting *that* stressed about it.

His way of dealing with the mayhem was to stay calm, stay out of people's way unless they needed something from him, and to get his work done swiftly and efficiently. So far, so good. José had praised him for the work he'd done cleaning out some of the cat enclosures, and José didn't even trust him much.

Now Felicia had sent him to haul stuff for the big-titted caterer – now, that was a welcome change from shovelling highly toxic cat poop! He pushed open the door of the café, and frowned. Where was she?

Then he saw that the door from the kitchen to the private walkway behind the building was ajar. He glanced through the opening and found Debbie.

She was smoking, the smell making him crave a cigarette himself. Already, there were several butts at her feet. He thought it might be a fire hazard – wouldn't a fire be just the last straw today? – but then she dropped the cigarette she was holding and ground it firmly into the dirt next to the other ones.

He was sorry that she wasn't wearing spike heels today. But he knew from working in a restaurant himself that there were rules about what kind of shoes you had to wear and, sadly, open-toed stilettos didn't conform to those rules.

As he watched, unsure what to do (thanks in part to the woody that was already growing in his pants, because spike heels or no she was still hot hot hot), she pulled out her cell phone and stabbed at it.

'It's Debbie,' she said when the other person answered. 'Yes, of course I'm here. We have a problem. They found out the fridge was turned off.'

Whoa. Lance eased back slightly so there was less chance he'd be seen. This wasn't good. It didn't make a lot of sense, but he knew that he should pay attention. Felicia would want to hear about this.

'The stuff I left here didn't go bad.' Debbie tapped another cigarette out of the pack and juggled it, the phone and a lighter. 'Yes, I *know* we have to do something else to fuck up the meal. Think of something? Yeah, well, I was hoping *you* might have a suggestion.' She took a long drag on the cigarette, tapped out the ashes nervously. 'Oh thanks, thanks a lot. It can't be anything obvious. You know, I still have a reputation to uphold. What the fuck do you mean, you'll ruin my reputation?'

Her voice had risen above its usual breathiness by the end, taking on a harsh, grating note, and Lance briefly wondered if she was going to punch the rough adobe wall.

'Well, fuck you, too.' She jabbed the phone off. 'Bastard,' she muttered. She dragged a hand through her hair, took one last suck of the cigarette and disposed of the butt.

Lance quickly tiptoed his way back to the front door of the café and eased it open a little. Letting it fall shut, he called out, 'Hey, Ms Landstrom, you here?'

Debbie popped in the back door, all smiles and jiggles. He noticed she'd repaired her lipstick – brilliant pink to match her T-shirt. Which, he also noticed, was plain and basic, something you wouldn't mind hiding under chef's whites, but which still managed to show a boatload of cleavage.

'Well, hey there, cutie,' she said. 'I was just grabbing a cigarette. Can't smoke once I've started with the cooking.'

'I'm s'posed to help you haul sh– er, stuff,' he said.

'Great!'

As they walked out the door, he added, 'Um, I've been working over at Bella Lugosi – it's the Italian place out on State. If you need any help today . . .' If he could stick around, he could keep an eye on her, catch her in the act of whatever she was going to do to fuck up the food.

She regarded him with a mixture of surprise and shrewd assessment. 'Really?'

He nodded.

'Well, then, cutie, you are *so* hired. I'm short-staffed today and I could totally use another pair of hands.'

Lance trotted after her, admiring her butt encased in jeans so tight he could tell there was no panty line. No matter what else happened, at least he'd have a nice view for a while. Debbie might be evil, but she certainly knew how to look good doing it.

And, if everything worked out, he'd have another chance to make a good impression on Mel. Playing hero had helped him get lucky before. Saving a couple of hundred rich old farts from being poisoned ought to be good for some more hot sex.

Normally, Valerie wouldn't have set up a scene in the early afternoon on the day of a big benefit. A good scene took time and concentration, and there was simply too much to do. But, instead of being at SCCS helping where she could, or even spending some quality time with her massage therapist and hairdresser, she was in her dungeon.

Priorities. Whatever help she could offer with setup was nothing compared to what she might be able to accomplish in this space of burgundy leather.

If she could pull it off.

Richard was in the clown costume again, this time in full Bozo face paint. He'd begged for it this time, naked and with his cheek pressed against Valerie's booted foot.

If she hadn't been so suspicious of him, she'd have been thrilled to see how malleable he'd become after only one scene. He obviously didn't have a thing for clowns himself, but he was letting himself be guided by her desires. Exactly as it should be, in theory, but in practice it usually took more time to build trust.

So sad that the trust was one-sided – and probably misplaced. Today, she planned to blow 25 years of self-control and respect for other people's boundaries right out the window.

If Richard weren't really plotting against SCCS, he'd be entirely open to her after she finished with him, broken apart and vulnerable. After breaking him open, she'd owe it to him to take him on as a sub for a while. (It could be worse. The clown costume really suited him.)

And if he *was* up to something ... well, he'd still be broken and vulnerable, but she wouldn't much care.

So far, everything had gone well. Heavy verbal humiliation. Face-slapping. 'Forced' oral sex – she'd guessed he'd be especially enthusiastic if she tied him to the table and then sat on his face. (She'd been right. She hadn't actually expected to come during this session, all things considered, but Richard's clever tongue had sent rockets through her body even while her brain was considering the best way to deal with a traitor.) Moving him to the spanking bench, securing him again, and then spanking his ass to the limits of his tolerance. Red now, it clashed charmingly with the orange and purple stripes of the clown outfit.

And, now, it was time for the finishing touch.

'Still with me?' she asked.

Richard nodded, his eyes vacant, his expression fixed in a blissed-out grin. He was with her, but barely. Large parts of his brain had left the building.

Excellent.

She took the clown nose and wig off him and pulled a leather hood over his head. He made a startled noise, or maybe a questioning one, but didn't actually say anything.

'I believe in discretion,' she said, an explanation that deliberately raised more questions than it answered.

She walked around him, letting her nails rake lightly over his sensitised skin. When she got behind him, she removed the butt plug and lubed him up some more. She began working her fingers in and out of him.

'Danny's been such a good boy lately, working very hard and putting up with a certain amount of neglect since I've been busy helping with the benefit. Don't you think a good slave like that deserves some reward?'

Under the hood, Richard made a small noise that might have been a yes.

Here she thrust a little harder. 'I want to hear you.'

'You're right, Mistress,' he said in a small voice.

'So glad you agree.' She pressed the intercom button on the nearby wall. 'Danny, please come downstairs.'

'With pleasure, Mistress!'

The noise that came from under the hood was apprehensive, but it wasn't a safeword or even a protest.

'I told you he loves fucking older men.' She drizzled more lube in the crack of Richard's ass. The way he shivered, she surmised, was not because the lube was cold. 'So I figured I'd give him a treat.'

Footsteps echoed on the stairs. Valerie grinned to herself. Danny could move quietly as a cat, but he was making sure Richard heard him.

Richard was twitching visibly. She checked his dick. Hard as hot marble.

Danny drew close. He grinned and winked at Valerie and said 'Delicious!' in a voice laced with far more toppy evil than Valerie would have deemed possible.

Valerie withdrew her fingers and let Danny position himself carefully, gripping Richard's hips with his strong hands. Richard let out a strangled moan.

'Are you ready?' She waited for a safeword, a no, anything that sounded like a protest. Instead, Richard raised his ass a little higher.

'This is going to be fun,' Danny said, still in that unfamiliar evil voice. He spread Richard's cheeks, letting him feel the large masculine hands on his flesh. Then, still holding him open, Danny inched to the side and let Valerie in with a good-sized dildo, the expensive kind with a fairly realistic texture. She'd been lubing it up and strapping it on while Richard was distracted.

Richard hit the roof as soon as the head nudged against his opening, pushing backwards against it and muttering a half-coherent litany of 'Please, please, please. Fuck me. Please.'

She pushed inside him, finding no resistance. As soon as the dildo entered him, he began to cry, the painful choked sobs of a man who never allowed himself that release. For a second Valerie worried she might have gone too far. But even through the tears he was begging for more.

He didn't seem to notice when the hands on his ass were replaced by small, female ones or when Danny slipped away. Some part of him, she figured, must register the truth, but, as soon as his mind and body gave in to his scariest fantasy, Richard started flying. Lights on, but nobody home.

She pushed, fucking him hard, working him with all the skill she possessed to push him right to the edge of explosion.

Then she stopped. And switched on the tiny tape recorder concealed in her bodice. She wasn't sure the tape would be admissible in court, but at least she'd be able to prove he'd confessed to her – *if* he did.

'Richard, what game are you playing?'

'I . . . don't know.' His voice sounded far away. 'Whatever you want.'

'I want you to tell me the truth now. Does Lindsay own that real estate development company for you, the one that tried to buy the Sanctuary?'

Silence, broken only by a soft sob.

'You can imagine how surprised I was to hear Lindsay was dabbling in real estate. It's not her thing at all. So of course I guessed you had to be involved somehow, and you know how curious I am. You'll tell me, won't you?' She twitched her hips, pushing deeper into him.

'Yes,' he answered almost inaudibly. 'She's so nice . . . helping with the taxes. Just have to slip her a little to keep her and Inge living in style.'

She felt queasy. Just knowing that all but confirmed her suspicions – if he hadn't revealed he was involved with the company and abstained from the vote in the first place, he was already in such a legal and ethical quagmire that the rest didn't seem like a stretch. But she pressed on.

She wriggled again, just to keep him on edge. 'Why did you volunteer to do so much for the benefit? You couldn't get it all done and we had to pull everything together last minute.'

'Didn't want Felicia to do it. She's too good. And you care too much.' That was ambiguous; it would be easy to argue that he'd meant to spare her and the busy development co-ordinator trouble. She could push him for something more definitive, but even the most spaced-out sub had a few brain cells left functional and Richard in his normal state was an exceptionally sharp man.

She tried one more tactic. Beginning to fuck him again, she waited until he was building back to orgasm and remarked, 'Katherine told me that some kids broke in the other night and almost hurt one of the cheetahs.'

'Idiots. Told them to keep away from the animals.'

'You little piece of shit!' she hissed, pounding into him with all the force of fury. 'You're vile! And I hope you end up in jail sharing a cell with someone named Bubba who wants you to be his bitch.'

'Thank you, Mistress!' Richard exclaimed as he came.

I must remember to erase that part of the tape, Valerie thought grimly, just in case it *is* admissible as evidence.

Straining to keep her expression and body language normal, she slipped the dildo out of his ass and began loosening Richard's restraints. If she could manage to keep him blissed out for a few more hours, he might never realise what he'd said until it was too late.

Pity this would involve interacting with the little shit, but, fortunately, he got off on women's contempt.

19

Mel careened into the rear entrance of the fishing cat enclosure, heavy buckets of food in each hand.

Wait a minute. The gate was supposed to be locked but she'd just bumped it and it had swung open.

She set one bucket down, dipped the other so she could swing it like a weapon, got into a defensive stance – then laughed nervously when she saw José. 'Everything OK?' she asked.

'Just checking on Fidget. She's about ready to go into her first heat and Katherine doesn't want to breed her, so we'll want to separate her and Chachi.'

'You're not telling me anything I don't know.' She'd been monitoring the young fishing cat's gallop towards puberty for several weeks and José knew it. Clearly, he'd been lying in wait for her.

'Well, I *was* checking on her. But mostly I hadn't been able to catch you alone in days and you haven't called. You're not still mad, are you?'

This time Mel's laugh was even more nervous. 'I've just been crazy-busy – and I was never that mad in the first place. But we have to talk.' She set down the bucket and looked around – not likely that anyone else would be passing, since this area was off limits to visitors and she knew all her staff were busy dealing with visitors or setting for tonight. Her voice dropped. 'The other night Lance and I –'

'You screwed Lance?' He sounded more amused than upset, but Mel still felt herself blushing.

'It was a fling. But even though you and I never talked about sleeping with other people –'

José drew a few steps closer. 'What do you mean? We talk about it all the time. Felicia. That old boyfriend you saw when you went to Washington to deliver Khan. Denise – and I got an email from her this week. The next exotic-animal vet conference is in San Diego.'

Mel was momentarily derailed from her attempted confession. 'So I'll get more stories?' Mel's curiosity had been piqued by tales of José's long-distance friend and lover, a redheaded bisexual reptile specialist who knew some very creative uses for vet wrap.

'From the way she's talking, you may get to be in the next story. She likes what I told her about you.'

But Mel was on a roll, determined that she should feel guilty. 'That's different. When I played with Lance –'

José put his arms around her. 'You were pissed at me. I know. But did you do it to get back at me or because you thought it would be fun?'

'Fun. OK, ninety-nine per cent fun and one per cent pissiness.'

'And did you have a good time?'

At this point, Mel couldn't manage to keep making herself feel bad. José was smiling at her too warmly, and his hands running over her body felt too good – and the jaunty erection poking at her leg confirmed that he was far from angry. 'Hell, yes! I'd do him again as long as you didn't mind.'

'Why would I mind? As long as you tell me all the details, that is. Or let me in on the fun. I'd love to see how you'd react to the two of us together – his cock in your mouth and mine in your sweet little pussy.' His voice dropped to a sultry purr that hit Mel directly between the legs.

Dragging him off into the bushes and making like cats in heat sounded like a fine option, until a real feline noise intruded. To a human, it sounded like an annoying yowl but, to another fishing cat, it was the equivalent of sultry music.

'Sounds like Fidget'll be needing some private time.'

José reached for the protective gloves he carried on his belt at all times. 'It's all those pheromones you put off, Mel. You just pushed the poor creature over the edge. Say, are you doing anything after the benefit?'

Mel kissed him, then ducked away to grab the catch-pole they kept at the back of the enclosure for such emergencies. 'Telling you a bedtime story about a bad boy.'

Felicia grabbed a few spare but crucial minutes to change out of shorts and into her cocktail dress. It had been an unusual purchase, but it had been on sale, and she couldn't resist. The mandarin-cut dress was made of fiery Chinese silk and had a subtle red-on-red Asian dragon print and gold piping. The high collar was balanced by an open back, and the narrow knee-length skirt had high slits on both sides that allowed her to walk normally.

She'd had Mel braid her hair right after she'd got on site, into a plait that wound around her head like a crown. Cool, and almost impossible to mess up even when she changed clothes.

She finished the outfit with a pair of kitten-heeled backless red shoes. High heels would look better, but she'd be on her feet all evening and needed to be able to move quickly.

She was in the jungle-decorated visitors' centre giving last-minute instructions to the three college students staffing the check-in table when Valerie Turner descended upon her.

Damn. Too late to duck.

'Felicia, darling, I need to talk with you!' Valerie

exclaimed in her usual extravagant manner. She looked rather surreal in a black-and-burgundy corseted Gaultier gown adorned with buckles and straps (rather edgy for a woman her age, but she somehow pulled it off) and a battered pith helmet that was probably as old as Felicia.

'Just one moment. Let me finish up here and I'll be right with you.' Felicia turned her attention back to the students. 'When anyone on this list checks in, one of you go find Dr O'Dare – they're VIPs. And when press people show up, use the two-way radio to get me.'

'Felicia . . .' Valerie touched her arm, but Felicia took a deep breath and kept going. Valerie probably wanted to rearrange the guests at her tables, in which case she could just move the place cards herself and let her friends figure it out.

'You all understand how the auction pre-checkout works?' Felicia asked the volunteers.

Valerie moved so she was between Felicia and the students. 'Felicia, I insist. Apologies, girls, this will take two minutes.' She took Felicia's arm and whisked her into the ladies' room.

Once in there, Valerie's manner changed abruptly from high-handed but charming socialite to something much scarier. Contained fury combined with her severe gown to make her look like a dangerous sorceress from a fantasy movie. (The pith helmet added a bizarre touch.)

Felicia backed away, trying to inch between Valerie and the door. She'd seen Mrs Turner as a harmless if sometimes annoying flake, but that was not the face of a harmless woman. And if she'd misjudged the other woman's character that badly, had she also misjudged her intentions? What if, by asking her about Richard's ex, she'd tipped Valerie off that Felicia was on to some elaborate scheme in which Valerie was also involved?

And what if the plotters had picked Valerie, the one nobody would suspect, to take care of the problem?

She inched closer to the door.

Valerie grabbed her wrist. Felicia wheeled, trying to take a swing with the other hand. Before she was sure what was happening to her, she found herself immobilised, both hands pinned behind her, pressed against the bathroom wall with Valerie leaning against her.

'Are you ready to listen now?' Valerie whispered, her voice intense and menacing. 'This is important.' My God, the woman even smelt dangerous, her perfume something sharp and almost masculine, yet sexual. She was leaning in closer, a predatory look in her eyes. Felicia's heart began to race. She trembled, feeling like a rabbit with a snake. To her horror, not all the reaction was fearful. Already primed from a long day of flirting with Gabe at every possible opportunity and feasting on his nearness when she couldn't actually flirt, her traitorous body seemed intrigued by the idea of being imprisoned by the evil witch.

Then Valerie blinked, loosened her grip on Felicia's wrists and took a few deep breaths. 'I'm so sorry, Felicia. I didn't mean to alarm you. But I've been trying to get you alone ever since I got here and I simply couldn't catch up with you.'

Her voice was something between the familiar 'eccentric heiress from a screwball comedy' inflections and the scary sorceress. Felicia had a feeling that she was hearing Valerie's real voice for the first time.

'Talk to me.' She was trying hard to regulate her breathing, and to ignore the embarrassing dampness of her red silk panties.

'Richard confessed to being behind some of the problems here, including the break-in that Katherine told me about. I got it on tape.'

'He confessed to you? How did you –? No, don't tell

me.' After the little demonstration just now, she guessed as much as she needed to. Her brain said 'la la la' and slammed the door on that line of thinking. 'Is it enough that we can go to the police?'

Valerie nodded, and Felicia reached for her cell.

'Wait until after the party, dear. We can't have Addison's finest barging in and arresting him in front of all the guests. I asked him to be my date tonight so I could keep an eye on him.'

Until two minutes ago, Felicia would have scoffed at the idea of Valerie keeping an eye on anybody. Now she was relatively sure that Richard wouldn't try anything under the older woman's watchful gaze.

'After all, how much trouble could he cause at this point? Everything's in place already and –' Everything started to click into place, audible tumblers turning in a lock that opened the door to all the clues. Felicia could actually feel all the colour draining out of her face. 'Oh my God. Mrs Turner, Richard hired the caterer! For all we know, she's going to poison everyone!'

Felicia's cell rang just as she was reaching for it to call the police. It was Mel. 'Felicia, we have a problem in the kitchen – a big problem. Get to the vet centre now and I'll fill you in.'

Before she ran out, Felicia turned and appealed to Valerie. 'Distract Katherine. She'll have a breakdown if she figures out what's going on.'

A strange smile played over Valerie's face. 'No problem.'

It took every ounce of control for Felicia not to take off her shoes and race across the lawn. It took every shred of restraint she had to smile and chat briefly with the guests who stopped her. It was all she could do not to laugh in sheer amazement as Valerie managed to intervene in every situation, delicately steering each person away from Felicia without ever giving away that Felicia needed to be somewhere else *right now*. Felicia owed Valerie one big huge thank-you bouquet. Of African lilies, or something equally fitting.

Alan met her just as she got to the vet clinic. Mel was pacing the room when they entered. No José – he was either still showing off the cubs to the last tour group or making sure Noelle and her little family hadn't been too upset by all the commotion.

'Richard Enoch's behind the problems and the sabotage,' Felicia said without preamble, 'and he hired the caterer. What's wrong in the kitchen?'

'Debbie's going to sabotage the dinner,' Mel said. 'Lance found out. He's been working in a restaurant – who knew? – and recognised what she was doing.'

'Fuck,' Felicia said. She caught herself just before she dragged a hand through her hair; even the carefully braided updo wouldn't handle that. 'What's she doing?'

'Lance said she's still worried about her career, so she's being subtle. She's spraying dish soap on the salad plates. Lance got pictures.' Mel held out a cell phone. There, in full (albeit small) digital incrimination, was Debbie and a plate and a spray bottle. The next picture was a close-up of the bottle and plate.

Felicia didn't need to see any more.

'Lance said it won't kill anybody, but it'll make them sick by the time the meal is over,' Mel added. 'Who knows what else she'll do if we give her time?'

'Where's Lance now?' Alan asked.

'Still in the kitchen,' Mel said. 'He's trying to stall her. But we have to do something quick.'

'I'll take care of it,' Alan said. He had a strange glint in his eyes. 'Let's go.'

As they hurried back across the green, Felicia was relieved to see the guests were just settling into their seats. They had drinks from the bar, and they'd been nibbling hors d'oeuvres, so with luck they wouldn't notice that their meals didn't start with salads. She just prayed Debbie hadn't tainted the appetisers.

Now that the big night was finally here, Katherine could almost breathe again. The corporate donations weren't where they'd hoped, but Felicia had managed to pull enough together so their costs were covered and then some, so all the ticket sales were profit. Ticket sales had spiked at the last minute, thanks, in part, to Valerie going utterly insane with her own selling efforts. And they had some great auction items – again thanks in part to Valerie, who'd called in every connection she had. These included her travel agent ('I happened to call to book my trip to Vietnam this fall and got a brainstorm'), who'd given a South Pacific cruise, and some random friend of a friend, who was donating the use of her villa in Tuscany for two weeks.

'You'd never know so much of the decoration was free,' Katherine whispered to Valerie. 'It looks beautiful in here.'

It had been easy enough to pull together the safari theme. The waitstaff and about half the guests were wearing pith helmets jauntily decorated with a leopard-print band, which had magically appeared on Friday morning. Lance's landscaper friend had provided dozens of potted palms; both Valerie and Sarah Wu had loaned souvenirs collected in their travels; and the promise of a private tour for the manager of a local fabric store had yielded many yards of free 'mosquito netting' to drape from the tent rafters, disguise the plain white linens that had been all they could afford and soften the stark interior of the visitors' centre. (The netting was prom-season leftovers, mostly pale pink and lime green, but in the dim lighting you couldn't tell.)

'Nonsense,' Valerie said. 'Those African masks and

batiks weren't free, although I'm sure we paid far less than the artists deserved. Horace adored bargaining in bazaars.'

Horace Turner had been dead almost twenty years. Katherine wished she could have met him, though; from the little Valerie said about him, he seemed like another free spirit in Valerie's mould.

'You know, some day I should ask Manny what the collection's actually worth.' Valerie pointed to one of the tuxedoed gentlemen who were there on her invitation. 'He works for Sotheby's.'

'How do you know all these people?'

Valerie made one of her 1930s-movie-star gestures. 'Oh, here and there.' Then she looked around as if seeing who was nearby. Seeing no one paying attention, she put her arm around Katherine's shoulder as if trying to draw her closer to whisper. She pressed her fingernails into Katherine's upper back as she did so, galvanising her attention and making her struggle to maintain composure.

'Some of them are old friends from our LA days and some of them I know from when I was on the board of The Nature Conservancy. But others I know from more interesting contexts. You see that group, for example?' Valerie pointed towards three men and two women, the men elegant in tuxedos, the women in gowns straight from the pages of *Vogue*. 'One of them is a full-time slave and another is the slave-owner. One of them is into the adult-baby thing. Another likes to mummify people in plastic wrap, and the last is wearing a chastity belt. Would you like one of those, my dear? I'd enjoy knowing you were suffering for me. And I'd make it up to you later.'

Katherine bit her lip as heat surged through her. A paradox, but the idea of a chastity belt turned her on.

Valerie added, 'I'll leave it up to you to chat with

them and figure out which is which. There will be a quiz later. You'd better pass it.' She smiled evilly. Then she looked towards the door and her evil smile faded. 'Oh dear, Richard's arrived already. I was hoping he'd be running late. Teasing you here is such fun.' She lowered her voice even more. 'As soon as you can, go into the bathroom and take your panties off. I'll check on you later.' Then she raised her voice back to a normal pitch. 'Must dash and mingle! Ta!'

She pulled Katherine's hair surreptitiously and melted away into the crowd.

Knees weak, Katherine leant on the bar for support. She might as well take the panties off. They were soaked through anyway.

They burst into the café. Felicia was in the lead, trying to look like her furious mood was no more than normal event-planner frenzy. Alan and Mel were close behind.

Despite the air conditioning, the room was sweat-inducingly hot thanks to the row of chafing dishes along the counter. All of the tables and chairs had been piled along one wall, except for a row of tables that was being used as a staging and food-prep area. Small dishes of shrimp cocktail were lined up, ready to go. For a kitchen where nefarious plots were taking place, it smelt remarkably good.

Debbie wasn't enough of an actress to disguise the panic that bloomed in her eyes. Lance quickly dropped his eyes and busied himself washing something in the sink behind the counter.

'Debbie, can I talk to you for a moment? In private?' Felicia asked evenly. She didn't want to panic the two chef's assistants that Debbie had brought with her.

'I'm *insanely* busy!' Debbie said, plastering a false smile on her face. 'Really, no time. Can it wait until the main courses are out?'

'No, it can't,' Felicia said. 'This is important.' She gestured to the back door.

'But I really can't –'

'Yes, you can,' Alan said in such a strident tone that Felicia jumped.

'I love it when he uses his cop voice,' Mel whispered to her.

In two strides he was next to Debbie, simultaneously unhooking the handcuffs from his belt and flicking them open. Debbie jerked in an attempt to bolt, but he had one hand behind her and cuffed before she got anywhere. In a blur of motion, he had her second wrist imprisoned.

'I've always enjoyed doing this to a hot blonde,' he commented to nobody in particular.

Felicia decided she was just *so* not going to go there.

'You can't do this!' Debbie protested.

'Yes, I can,' Alan said calmly. 'And, trust me, it's my pleasure. It's what's called a citizen's arrest. I'll turn you over to the cops when they arrive.'

'No, you've got it all wrong!' Debbie changed her tack. 'It wasn't me! It's him – he's the juvenile delinquent.' She jerked her chin at Lance.

Lance glanced from Debbie to Felicia. His expression was inscrutable, but Felicia guessed he was prepared to be accused – he'd dealt with the 'once a bad boy, always a bad boy' assumption enough in his life.

'Nice try, but now you've really pissed me off,' Felicia said. 'We already know he's on our team, honey. He's the one who took pictures of you doctoring the plates.' To Alan, she added, 'Take her out back until the police get here.' The area between the buildings was cordoned off so none of the guests could wander into the work area.

Lance stuck his tongue out at Debbie's departing back.

'You and you.' Felicia pointed to the two assistants. 'Were you in on this?'

Before they could answer, Lance broke in. 'They're not, unless she paid them off while I was in the bathroom. I know them – they're both from Bella Lugosi, where I work.'

'Well?' Felicia asked the two.

They both shook their heads, eyes wide.

'Good.' Hands on her hips, she surveyed the food all over the kitchen – any of which might have been messed with – and the meagre staff.

She should have been panicking. A very tiny voice in the far depths of her brain was screaming and running around in circles. But the truth was, she was calm. She could feel the adrenalin surging through her body. Fight or flight.

They were going to fight. And they were going to win.

'Here's the deal,' she said. 'I need to confer with Mrs Turner and make a phone call. I'm also going to get more help in here. Somehow, inexplicably, we're going to pull this thing off.'

Lance hesitatingly raised his hand.

She couldn't hold back the smile. 'This isn't detention, Lance,' she said. 'Toss out any ideas you have.'

'I'm, uh, taking cooking classes at the community college,' he said. 'And doing an online course in restaurant management. I think I know what we can do.'

'Excellent. Get started. I'll be right back.'

Stepping outside the café, she glanced along the rows of tables. When she found Valerie Turner, she saw the woman looking at her. Felicia nodded once. Valerie eased her chair back and stood.

Katherine, thankfully, was at the other end of the pavilion, chatting with somebody. Felicia knew she'd have to tell her boss what was going on soon, but this had to be done first.

The police arrived in record time. It must have been a slow night in Addison.

Felicia's calm had slipped when she imagined how the guests would react when two people – including a respected board member – were escorted out in handcuffs. There was no way to get Richard into the main building without him suspecting something was going on, and bolting.

Valerie told her not to fret, dear.

The older woman grabbed a wineglass and spoon, tapped until everyone quieted down and looked at her.

'We have a special treat for you all tonight,' she said. 'You've all been so very generous, and I know there's some frantic bidding going on with some of the items in the silent auction, too. But we have one final fun way for you to play with your money.'

She couldn't have timed it more perfectly if she'd tried. Or maybe she had. Felicia was slowly falling in awe of Valerie Turner. Maybe – just maybe – she wasn't such a loon after all.

As she was making her speech, the police walked up.

Valerie continued, 'You've probably all heard of this fundraising activity before. We throw someone in "jail" –' she waggled her fingers in the universal symbol for quotation marks '– and you have to pledge money to raise bail to get the person out of jail. Sound like fun?'

She asked the question in such a way that nobody dared answer in the negative. There was applause and even a few shouts from those who had already made good use of the bar.

'Excellent! I'm delighted to announce that our prisoner of the hour is our very own board member, Richard Enoch!' Richard was sitting at a small cocktail table near her. She blew a flamboyant kiss at him and winked, every inch the dizzy society lady who'd had maybe a little too much of the champagne.

Felicia thought it was a little dicey, announcing him before the police officers were very close to him. But Richard rose, made an awkward half-hearted attempt to run, stumbled and was in custody pretty much before he knew what hit him. He started struggling ineffectually against the burly officers and shot a dismayed glance in Valerie's direction. She cooed and patted him on the cheek as some of the more inebriated guests got into the spirit of things and shouted, 'Lock 'im up and throw away the key!' It probably looked like cute byplay, but Felicia could just imagine what he'd seen in Valerie's eyes.

He sagged and let the officers lead him away.

Felicia glanced over her shoulder and saw Alan hand Debbie over to the police as well. There went the caterer . . .

Crap. The food.

20

Katherine had made her way through the crowd, a worried crease furrowing her brow, and Felicia simply dragged her into the café, leaving the crowd in Valerie's hands. (Hands that were more capable than Felicia ever expected. Either that, or Valerie's moment of sane clarity would end as swiftly as it had begun, and chaos would reign once again. Right now, Felicia didn't have time to worry about it.)

At the same time, Gabe returned from his run to get more ice. The bag slung over his shoulder, he cast a curious glance at the departing officers, dropped the ice unceremoniously on the bar, then followed Felicia and Katherine into the café, eyebrows raised. 'So it *was* Richard all along!' he said.

'What was Richard all along?' Katherine demanded. 'And why did they arrest the caterer, too?'

'We only have time for the short version,' Felicia said briskly. 'We can worry about details after the benefit is over. Richard was behind all the sabotage and donor messes, because he's part-owner in the company that wanted to buy the land. He hired Debbie to cook the food, and she tried to poison the guests. Lance, bless his heart, caught her before it was too late.'

Lance, hearing his name, glanced up from where he was chopping watermelons. He'd stripped off his shirt, and hints of a tattoo on his muscled chest peered around the white chef's apron he was wearing. He wiped sweat off his brow with his forearm, saluted them with the wicked-looking cleaver, and went back to work.

'Are those the cats' watermelons?' Katherine asked weakly.

Watermelons were one of the tigers' favourite toys, and people often donated them to the Sanctuary.

'I washed them off,' Mel said without glancing up from the chafing dish she was stirring. She had a chef's hat perched jauntily on her pixyish hair. 'The salads were trashed, thanks to that bitch, but Lance had the idea of serving fruit as a starter course. It'll buy us some time.'

'She hadn't mixed up the dressing yet.' Lance didn't miss a beat in his chopping. 'So I did a sweet and hot thing. Saw it on the Food Network the other day, only they used fresh chillies so I winged it with some of the chipotle dipping sauce from the appetisers. Now I just need to get it portioned. About a third of a cup into each bowl.'

Since he was still chopping, it was clearly a plea for help. Felicia picked up a spoon and gingerly began filling small bowls with the watermelon chunks. She'd hardly call herself a culinary whiz but, if Mel (who kept nothing but pet food and coffee in her kitchen) could tend the chafing dish, she could plate things – as long as she had very clear directions.

'What about the dessert?' the smaller and younger of the cook's assistants asked out of the blue. 'I mean, she brought that with her, and it's this dark-chocolate mousse cake flavoured with Amaretto. You could hide anything in that.'

'Toss it,' Lance said, his voice surprisingly confident. 'Anyone who's ever watched a murder mystery knows cyanide tastes like almonds. I don't think the bitch would be that crazy, but why risk it? And there's always chocolate Ex-Lax and shit like that. Someone should go get like fifty gallons of ice cream and some good hot fudge sauce.'

This time no one bothered correcting his language. Felicia, for one, was too busy being stunned by the way Lance seemed so in his element in a busy kitchen.

Mel stopped stirring for a second and looked imploringly at Gabe. 'I'll go if you take over this sauce.'

He shrugged and slipped out of his suit jacket. She handed him her chef's hat, and he put it on with a flourish and winked at Felicia as he took over stirring the sauce. They were now almost shoulder to shoulder at the counter.

Felicia inched over so they were brushing against each other. It wasn't much, but the contact was reassuring. And she loved the way he'd calmly jumped into the breach.

'Use the supply credit card.' Katherine said. 'We'll figure out the bookkeeping later.'

Speaking was a mistake. It drew attention to the director, who'd been hovering by the door, clearly hoping to escape the chaos and get back to chatting up donors. 'Hey, you with the red hair,' the other cooks' helper, a round, motherly-looking black woman, said to Katherine. 'You look like you know your way around a grill. Keep an eye on the steaks, OK? The vegetarian entrée needs me.'

Evening gown and all, Katherine shrugged and obeyed.

It was a good thing she'd moved out of the doorway then. A small herd of waiters filed in looking for the starter course, which wasn't quite ready. Felicia began spooning faster, trying to keep it neat and keep low-flying watermelon away from her silk dress, but not succeeding completely at either.

'How can I help?' someone said, and José squeezed in between her and Lance. 'Mel left a note saying to get over here as soon as I could. So here I am.'

He was talking to Felicia, but Lance answered. 'Help her.'

Felicia sensed a few seconds of tension as José tried to process Lance actually being in charge. Then he smiled and grabbed a spoon.

The first trays of watermelon salad were whisked out of the kitchen.

And under the cover of that ruckus, Gabe stroked his fingers down Felicia's bare back, making her shiver with delight.

Maybe cooking for several hundred wasn't so bad – in the right company.

A check-in volunteer appeared, still clutching a plastic glass of red wine. 'I thought we could mingle once the party started,' the girl said, 'but some older lady in a Gothy dress said to go to the kitchen and tell Dr O'Dare it's time for her speech. And you're Dr O'Dare so I guess I'm ... grilling?' She looked as confused as someone who'd been whisked out of a cushy volunteer job mingling with local high society to cook very well might.

The assistant who'd originally been manning the grill swooped down and poked at a steak with a fork. 'No, you'll be plating. After Dr O'Dare gives her speech, the main course has to go out.' Then her eyes grew wide, realising she'd commandeered the executive director to tend the steaks.

Katherine grinned and fled.

And the other assistant took over Gabe's sauce, freeing him to start plating. As he moved away, he brushed Felicia's hand, blew her a kiss.

Melt.

Yeah, even a crisis had merits, with the right people.

* * *

Felicia shoved the last of the leftover food – there wasn't much, thanks to guests who'd been either ravenous or unable to resist 'free' food, or both – on to a shelf in the fridge. She closed the door firmly behind her and blew out a long breath. The café looked like a food fight had occurred.

However, José, Mel and Lance had all volunteered to do a massive washing-up session the next day. (It was odd – they seemed to be almost looking forward to it.) On Monday, Felicia would track down where all the chafing dishes and other cookware needed to be returned, given that Debbie wasn't going to be in a position to do so.

She ticked off the rest of the mental list in her head. The tents and chairs would get picked up Monday morning as well; right now, the menfolk were stacking tables and chairs and otherwise making the lawn pre-sentable again. She'd tackle thank-you notes and book-keeping Monday afternoon.

Was that it? Was that really it? Was the benefit-from-hell, except for the paperwork, for all intents and pur-poses, really and truly over?

Insanely, she felt a curious sense of loss. The damn thing had been dominating her life for so long. Now, with the adrenalin finally draining away, she felt almost bereft. What would she do with herself now?

Her spirits perked up considerably when the door opened and Gabe walked in, carrying a bottle of champagne.

'That looks heavenly,' she said as he grabbed plastic cups from next to the soda dispenser.

'We deserve it,' he said. His shirt was unbuttoned at the throat, and he looked delectable.

She hadn't yet asked him when he was flying back to New York. She hoped it wasn't until tomorrow night (although there was the chance that yet another red-eye flight would, in fact, kill him). She still had enough energy in her for a romp, and she couldn't think of anything more heavenly than the idea of sleeping in and then spending the rest of the day in bed, leaving it only to answer the door to pay the food-delivery person. And maybe to take a shower.

Yeah. She liked showering with him.

She tossed back the first cup of champagne giddily, registering crispness and nose-tickling bubbles but not really tasting it. 'Just half,' she said when she held it out for a second helping. 'I still have to get myself home, and I'm just now realising how little I've eaten today. We can take the rest with us – unless there's another bottle or two we can make off with.'

'Felicia, we need to talk,' Gabe said.

Her spirits plummeted again. He looked really, really serious. And everyone knew 'we need to talk' meant 'I'm going to say something that you're not going to like'. Now he was going to tell her about the wife back in New York. The wife and passel of children, all with gold-tipped hair like their daddy.

'I know it's kind of soon, but it's something I've been thinking about for a while,' he said. 'Well, part of it, anyway. I hadn't met you yet. I just don't want you to get scared that things are moving too fast, or –'

He hadn't said 'wife' or 'kids', which was a good sign. The bad sign was that she didn't understand any of it.

'Gabe,' Felicia said patiently, 'what the hell are you babbling about?'

He took her hands in his. 'The Zoological Association has been discussing opening a branch office in LA. One of the reasons I got the assignment to check out the Sanctuary was so that I could also look at office space and decide if I wanted the promotion.'

'Promotion?' Felicia echoed. OK, now her head was

really swimming. Did he mean what she thought he meant? 'You're ... moving out here?'

'I was already considering it before I even met you,' he said. 'I'm not trying to scare you away, or let things get too serious too fast.' He brushed the back of his hand against her cheek. 'But I'll be honest: you're definitely one of the reasons I told Tom I'd take the job. I'd like the opportunity to get to know you better.'

'Um, OK,' she said, unable to formulate a clearer response. Sunshine filled her, and it wasn't from the champagne. He *still* hadn't said 'wife' or 'kids', and she was now pretty darn sure he wasn't going to.

'We can take things as slow as we need to,' he said.

'Yes, let's take it slow,' she agreed cheerfully, and snaked her hand into his trousers.

'Felicia!' He sounded surprised, but not particularly shocked – and certainly not upset.

'We can take the relationship as slow as we want to,' she said, delighted to feel him twitch beneath her palm. 'But we've already had a head start on the sex and, while slow has its merits, there's nothing wrong with a quickie.'

'Good point.' The kiss he gave her sent shockwaves through her body. 'Can't get caught, though. I still haven't finished my report – had to wait 'til after the benefit – and we don't want anyone thinking that you unduly influenced me.'

Before she could ask where he proposed they go, he'd pulled her into the walk-in fridge, leaving the door open just a crack so they didn't accidentally get locked in, and started kissing her again.

Felicia's nipples budded from the cold of the fridge and the heat of arousal. No stress, no worries – no more benefit! – just intense, immediate desire.

She hadn't bothered to find a longline bra to go with

the dress, and her arousal was clear. Gabe brushed his thumbs over the peaks, sending a thrill through her.

'Just like when we talked,' he murmured. 'But now I'm here.' He dipped his head and sucked one of the nipples into his mouth, tugging and nipping in a rhythm that her clit picked up, pulsing in time. When he switched to her other breast, the cold air and wet silk felt like fire and ice, sending echoes between her legs.

He stopped long enough to drop his trousers and briefs. His erect cock jerked in the cold but lost none of its hardness. 'I've missed you,' he said, then groaned when she wrapped her hand around him and stroked.

He turned her around, and she obligingly grabbed hold of the shelf in front of her, tilted her hips back and wiggled her ass at him. Normally, the icy metal shelf would have felt almost painful under her warm hands, but she was so heated now that the intense sensation became part of the experience. He shimmied her skirt up her hips to her waist and whistled at the sight of her mostly bare ass, which was bisected by a little fire-engine-red thong.

'There's a part of me that's tempted to spend some time playing here,' he said, running his hands over her sensitive curves, 'turning your fine bottom as red as your thong. It would sting extra good in the cold, don't you think?'

The only response she could manage was a long low moan because, as he spoke, he slipped one hand around her and under the scant front of the thong. He fondled her clit with long skilled strokes, bringing her to the edge but not quite – not yet – over it.

'I think we'll have enough time to explore that later,' he continued. 'Right now we should probably hurry before someone comes in. Can you hurry for me, Felicia? I want to feel you come.'

His coaxing voice was the final trigger. Her hips jerked as she convulsed through her orgasm.

A moment later he was sliding inside of her, clutching her hips for traction as he pumped. He felt so good, the length of him filling her, pressing into her. She thrust her hips back to meet his strokes, and felt herself building up, a giant wave rising inside her towards a crescendoed release.

Then, over the hum of the fridge and their simultaneous panting, she heard the café door bang open. They both froze. Felicia wanted to cry, she was so close.

'Hello? Hello-oo!'

Oh no. She leant her forehead against the cold metal shelf in front of her. Valerie Turner.

'Felicia, dear, are you in here? Hmm, I could have sworn I saw you come in here, but I didn't see you leave.'

Gabe put his mouth right next to Felicia's ear. 'Don't. Make. A. Sound,' he said so quietly she almost couldn't hear him. Did he really not realise she had no interest in ending their encounter to talk to Mrs Turner? Then she felt his lips touch her ear, felt his warm breath as he nibbled on her lobe.

'Well,' called Valerie, 'I was just coming to say goodnight.' Something in the tone of her voice suggested that she knew perfectly well what Felicia was up to in the fridge.

Gabe was inside her to the hilt; she was stretched around him. She felt his hand worm its way around her and between her thighs to stroke her wet clit.

Staying quiet was getting harder by the second.

She fluttered and clenched around him, and felt his hips jerk in response. Well, if he was going to torture her, she was going to torture him back. Now a little roll while she tightened some more.

She bit her own lip. That had been a mistake, at least from a keeping-quiet point of view.

'Oh, and I wanted to let you in on a little secret,' Valerie continued, 'just between us girls, because I know how angry you are at Richard. I suggested to the police that Richard would probably need a thorough going-over, just in case he's hiding anything. Can you imagine how surprised they'll be when they find the butt plug that's stuffed in him? Ta ta, dear!'

The woman's delighted laugh, which didn't sound the least bit demented under the circumstances, faded as she left the café.

Felicia was so stunned by the revelation that, for a moment, her mind went blank. Then Gabe started moving again, thrusting into her and manipulating her clit at the same time. Felicia clutched the shelf so hard that she thought she might yank the bolts out of the wall.

'God, yes!' Gabe gasped, suddenly moving faster. The blood buzzed in Felicia's ears as she responded, clamping down around him and shuddering through another orgasm along with him.

Only then, spiralling down from her climax, did she start to giggle. Gabe leant against her, and she felt his chest rock with his own laughter.

'I think I can finally reveal that she's the one who suggested the Zoological Society come out here,' he said. 'You know, I'm really glad she's on our side.'

'I think the whole Sanctuary is glad,' Felicia agreed.

Visit the Black Lace website at
www.blacklace-books.co.uk

BLACK
LACE

FIND OUT THE LATEST INFORMATION AND TAKE
ADVANTAGE OF OUR FANTASTIC FREE BOOK OFFER!
ALSO VISIT THE SITE FOR . . .

• All Black Lace titles currently available
  and how to order online

• Great new offers

• Writers' guidelines

• Author interviews

• An erotica newsletter

• Features

• Cool links

BLACK LACE – THE LEADING IMPRINT
OF WOMEN'S SEXY FICTION

TAKING YOUR EROTIC READING
PLEASURE TO NEW HORIZONS

LOOK OUT FOR THE ALL-NEW BLACK LACE BOOKS – AVAILABLE NOW!

RUDE AWAKENING
Pamela Kyle
ISBN 0 352 33036 8

Alison is a control freak. There's nothing she enjoys more than swanning around her palatial home giving orders to her wealthy but masochistic husband and delighting in his humiliation. Her daily routine consists of shopping, dressing up and pursuing dark pleasures, along with her best friend, Belinda; that is until they are kidnapped and held to ransom. In the ensuing weeks both women are required to come to terms with their most secret selves. Stripped of their privileges and deprived of the luxury they are used to, they deal with their captivity in surprising and creative ways. For Alison, it is the catalyst to a whole new way of life.

Coming in April

ENTERTAINING MR STONE
Portia da Costa
ISBN 0 352 34029 0

When reforming bad girl Maria Lewis takes a drone job in local government back in her home town, the quiet life she was looking for is quickly disrupted by the enigmatic presence of her boss, Borough Director, Robert Stone. A dangerous and unlikely object of lust, Stone touches something deep in Maria's sensual psyche and attunes her to the erotic underworld that parallels life in the dusty offices of Borough Hall. But the charismatic Mr Stone isn't the only one interested in Maria – knowing lesbian Mel and cute young techno geek Greg both have designs on the newcomer, as does Human Resources Manager William Youngblood, who wants to prize the Borough's latest employee away from the arch-rival for whom he has ambiguous feelings.

DANGEROUS CONSEQUENCES
Pamela Rochford
ISBN 0 352 33185 2

When Rachel Kemp is in danger of losing her job at a London university, visiting academic Luke Holloway takes her for a sybaritic weekend in the country to cheer her up. Her encounters with Luke and his enigmatic friend Max open up a world of sensual possibilities and she is even offered a new job editing a sexually explicit Victorian diary. Life is looking good until Rachel returns to London, and, accused of smuggling papers out of the country, is sacked on the spot. In the meantime, Luke disappears and Rachel is left wondering about the connection between these elusive academics, their friends and the missing papers. When she tries to clear her name, she discovers her actions have dangerous – and highly erotic – consequences.

Coming in May

CIRCUS EXCITE
Nikki Magennis
ISBN 0 352 34033 9

Julia Spark is a professional dancer, newly graduated. Jobs are hard to find and after a curious audition she finds herself running away with the circus. It's not what she expected – the circus is an adult show full of bizarre performers forbidden from sex yet trained to turn people on. The ringmaster exerts a powerful influence over the performers, and seems to have taken a special interest in Julia. As the circus tours the UK, Julia plays the power games with Robert, finding herself drawn in to his world of erotic fantasy. He dares her to experiment, playing with her desires and encouraging Julia to explore the darker side of her own sexuality.

ELENA'S DESTINY
Lisette Allen
ISBN 0 352 33218 2

The year is 1073. The gentle convent-bred Elena, awakened to the joys of forbidden passion by the masterful knight Aimery le Sabrenn, has been forcibly separated from her lover by war. She is haunted by the memory of him. Then fate brings her to William the Conqueror's dark stronghold of Rouen, and a reunion with Aimery. Although he still captivates Elena with his powerful masculinity, Aimery is no longer hers. As the King's formidable knights prepare for war, Elena discovers that she must fight a desperate battle for him against her two rivals: the scheming sensual Isobel and a wanton young heiress called Henriette, who has set her heart on becoming Aimery's bride. The backdrop of war tightens around them and dangerous games of love and lust are played out amidst the increasing tension of a merciless siege.

Black Lace Booklist

Information is correct at time of printing. To avoid disappointment, check availability before ordering. Go to www.blacklace-books.co.uk. All books are priced £6.99 unless another price is given.

BLACK LACE BOOKS WITH A CONTEMPORARY SETTING

☐ ON THE EDGE Laura Hamilton	ISBN 0 352 33534 3	£5.99
☐ THE TRANSFORMATION Natasha Rostova	ISBN 0 352 33311 1	
☐ SIN.NET Helena Ravenscroft	ISBN 0 352 33598 X	
☐ TWO WEEKS IN TANGIER Annabel Lee	ISBN 0 352 33599 8	
☐ SYMPHONY X Jasmine Stone	ISBN 0 352 33629 3	
☐ A SECRET PLACE Ella Broussard	ISBN 0 352 33307 3	
☐ GOING TOO FAR Laura Hamilton	ISBN 0 352 33657 9	
☐ RELEASE ME Suki Cunningham	ISBN 0 352 33671 4	
☐ SLAVE TO SUCCESS Kimberley Raines	ISBN 0 352 33687 0	
☐ SHADOWPLAY Portia Da Costa	ISBN 0 352 33313 8	
☐ ARIA PASSIONATA Julie Hastings	ISBN 0 352 33056 2	
☐ A MULTITUDE OF SINS Kit Mason	ISBN 0 352 33737 0	
☐ COMING ROUND THE MOUNTAIN Tabitha Flyte	ISBN 0 352 33873 3	
☐ FEMININE WILES Karina Moore	ISBN 0 352 33235 2	
☐ MIXED SIGNALS Anna Clare	ISBN 0 352 33889 X	
☐ BLACK LIPSTICK KISSES Monica Belle	ISBN 0 352 33885 7	
☐ GOING DEEP Kimberly Dean	ISBN 0 352 33876 8	
☐ PACKING HEAT Karina Moore	ISBN 0 352 33356 1	
☐ MIXED DOUBLES Zoe le Verdier	ISBN 0 352 33312 X	
☐ UP TO NO GOOD Karen S. Smith	ISBN 0 352 33589 0	
☐ CLUB CRÈME Primula Bond	ISBN 0 352 33907 1	
☐ BONDED Fleur Reynolds	ISBN 0 352 33192 5	
☐ SWITCHING HANDS Alaine Hood	ISBN 0 352 33896 2	
☐ EDEN'S FLESH Robyn Russell	ISBN 0 352 33923 3	
☐ PEEP SHOW Mathilde Madden	ISBN 0 352 33924 1	£7.99
☐ RISKY BUSINESS Lisette Allen	ISBN 0 352 33280 8	£7.99
☐ CAMPAIGN HEAT Gabrielle Marcola	ISBN 0 352 33941 1	£7.99
☐ MS BEHAVIOUR Mini Lee	ISBN 0 352 33962 4	£7.99

To find out the latest information about Black Lace titles, check out the website: www.blacklace-books.co.uk or send for a booklist with complete synopses by writing to:

Black Lace Booklist, Virgin Books Ltd
Thames Wharf Studios
Rainville Road
London W6 9HA

Please include an SAE of decent size. Please note only British stamps are valid.

Our privacy policy
We will not disclose information you supply us to any other parties.
We will not disclose any information which identifies you personally to any person without your express consent.

From time to time we may send out information about Black Lace books and special offers. Please tick here if you do not wish to receive Black Lace information. ❑

Please send me the books I have ticked above.

Name ....

Address ....

....

....

....

Post Code ....

Send to: Virgin Books Cash Sales, Thames Wharf Studios, Rainville Road, London W6 9HA.

US customers: for prices and details of how to order books for delivery by mail, call 1-800-343-4499.

Please enclose a cheque or postal order, made payable to Virgin Books Ltd, to the value of the books you have ordered plus postage and packing costs as follows:

UK and BFPO – £1.00 for the first book, 50p for each subsequent book.

Overseas (including Republic of Ireland) – £2.00 for the first book, £1.00 for each subsequent book.

If you would prefer to pay by VISA, ACCESS/MASTERCARD, DINERS CLUB, AMEX or SWITCH, please write your card number and expiry date here:

....

Signature ....

Please allow up to 28 days for delivery.